PRAISE FOR AFTER STORY

'*After Story* is a powerful meditatio
and the lingering effects of trauma ;
novel … *After Story* is sprawling, ce
the brain, offers much-needed vica.
with hope that fraught relationships can be mended.' **Readings**

'This beautifully fashioned novel stands testament to the proposition that good fiction can cut to the chase of complex social problems in ways that might leave an entire library of self-help non-fiction found wanting in its wake.' *The Canberra Times*

'Della and Jasmine are both battling through their own trauma – their personal loss as well as the stolen land and lives which weigh on them – from different bases. In a novel where their stories converge so inevitably, and sweep so many other stories in their wake, Behrendt shows she is a writer of considerable, and increasing, power.' *The Australian*

'We might think we know what to expect from this whirlwind week of bookish sightseeing: family secrets, writerly anecdotes and a splash of tour-bus drama. These comfort-reading delights are certainly present in *After Story* but they're layered over something anguished, characterful and quietly consequential … with its glimmering seam of humour, Behrendt's novel offers a much-needed reminder that novels don't have to be relentlessly sombre to be serious.' *The Sydney Morning Herald*

'*After Story* delves into darkness to show that truth-telling can set us free … it's a pleasure to read and a wonderful opportunity to rethink what we have to offer the world around us.' *The Saturday Paper*

Larissa is the author of two novels: *Home*, which won the 2002 David Unaipon Award and the regional Commonwealth Writers' Prize for Best First Book; and *Legacy*, which won the 2010 Victorian Premier's Literary Award for Indigenous Writing. She has published numerous books on Indigenous legal issues; her most recent non-fiction book is *Finding Eliza: Power and Colonial Storytelling*. She was awarded the 2009 NAIDOC Person of the Year award and 2011 NSW Australian of the Year. Larissa wrote and directed the feature films, *After the Apology* and *Innocence Betrayed* and has written and produced several short films. In 2018 she won the Australian Directors' Guild Award for Best Direction in a Documentary Feature and in 2020 the AACTA for Best Direction in Nonfiction Television. She is the host of *Speaking Out* on ABC radio and is Distinguished Professor at the Jumbunna Institute at the University of Technology Sydney.

After Story has been shortlisted for the NSW Premier's Literary Awards, the Victorian Premier's Literary Awards and the ABA Booksellers' Choice Awards, and longlisted for the Indie Book Awards, the Australian Book Industry Awards and the Miles Franklin Literary Award.

Also by Larissa Behrendt

Home

Legacy

Finding Eliza: Power and Colonial Storytelling

LARISSA BEHRENDT
AFTER STORY

UQP

First published 2021 by University of Queensland Press
PO Box 6042, St Lucia, Queensland 4067 Australia
Reprinted 2021 (twice), 2022

This edition published 2022
Reprinted 2022 (twice), 2023, 2024

University of Queensland Press (UQP) acknowledges the Traditional Owners
and their custodianship of the lands on which UQP operates. We pay our respects
to their Ancestors and their descendants, who continue cultural and spiritual
connections to Country. We recognise their valuable contributions to Australian
and global society.

uqp.com.au
reception@uqp.com.au

Cover design by Christabella Designs / Christa Moffit
Cover image by Svetlana Kononova / Shutterstock
Author photograph by ABC
Typeset in Adobe Garamond Pro by Post Pre-press Group, Brisbane
Printed in Australia by McPherson's Printing Group

University of Queensland Press is assisted
by the Australian Government through
the Australia Council, its arts funding
and advisory body.

A catalogue record for this book is available from the National Library of Australia.

ISBN 978 0 7022 6580 8 (pbk)
ISBN 978 0 7022 6531 0 (epdf)
ISBN 978 0 7022 6532 7 (epub)
ISBN 978 0 7022 6533 4 (kindle)

University of Queensland Press uses papers that are natural, renewable and recyclable
products made from wood grown in well-managed forests and other controlled sources.
The logging and manufacturing processes conform to the environmental regulations of
the country of origin.

For Michael Lavarch

Thy firmness makes my circle just
And makes me end, where I began

—John Donne

But what after all is one night? A short space,
especially when the darkness dims so soon, and so soon a bird sings ...

—Virginia Woolf

DELLA AND JASMINE'S LITERARY TOUR

North Sea

Haworth ○ ○ Leeds

Eastwood ○

Stratford-upon-Avon ○ E N G L A N D ○ Cambridge

○ Oxford

London ○

○ Bath ○ Sevenoaks

Steventon ○ ○ Cranbrook
○ Chawton
Winchester ○

Southampton ○

○ Lewes

Dorchester ○

English Channel

ALL I CAN REMEMBER, *and this is what I told the police over and over again, is that there was a party at the house and I'd been drinking.*

I went to bed at midnight, one o'clock? The girls were in the bedroom with me. That's how it was back then, all of us in one bed – Brittany was seven, Leigh-Anne, five, and Jazzie only three. I slept right through to morning.

I was never much good at knowing what time it was or describing in measurements how far something was from something else. What I do know, is that when I did finally wake up sunlight was streaming through the holes in the sheet that covered the window, making rays of light in the floating dust. You'd have thought something so pretty was a good sign but luck was never much on my side.

I laid there for a while watching dust fairies dancing in the air. I felt groggy, like the alcohol I'd drunk the night before had affected me much more than it should've. I wasn't surprised that the girls were already up. They always did their own thing and there were plenty of people around to keep an eye on them. It's hard to imagine that now but back then you just never worried.

When I walked out of the bedroom, Jazzie was in front of the television playing with her cousin, plump little Kylie. My head was thick as stew so I made a cup of tea and took it out to the porch, more than ready for my first smoke of the day. We had some plastic chairs there so you could sit and watch the street, right down to the end where the town turned back to bush. From here I could see who was coming and going, see who was visiting who. It was the type of place where the neighbours would stop as they walked by to have a quick chat over the low rusty mesh fence.

The houses only ran down one side of the road; on the other side was bushland hiding a nearby creek. We called the part of town we lived in 'Frog Hollow' because it flooded first, although it was never called that on any map. The kids in our street didn't have much but never seemed bored because they made their own fun.

I could see Leigh-Anne riding a small pink bicycle that belonged to next door's girl – up and down their driveway she was pedalling, full of purpose. One side of the bike had streamers on the handlebars; on the other they'd all been ripped out. It's funny, the things you remember and the things you forget.

As I rested my head, tired and heavy from the night before, I scanned the street. 'You seen Brittany?' I yelled out to Leigh-Anne, so she'd know I was there, watching. She shook her head and kept concentrating on working the pink pedals with her little feet.

I wasn't concerned at first. Brittany's father, Jimmy, was living two doors down and she could just as easily have been there, or in any of the houses along our street. So, I can't tell you why, but as I sat in the slow-warming autumn morning I started to feel uneasy, like there was a fishing line in my stomach looking for something to hook.

I walked over to Jimmy's house and found him nursing his own savage hangover. Brittany wasn't there, so I went to Aunty Elaine's house, the last in our street. She rang my sister, Kiki, who lived two blocks over, close to a row of small family-run shops on the main road. By the time Kiki arrived, I was going from house to house knocking on doors. That deep, crawling feeling kept growing, spreading out like dark honey spilt over a tablecloth.

Together, Kiki and I tried every friend of Brittany's we could think of. No-one had seen her; no-one knew where she was. We searched down at the creek and in the surrounding bush, our voices echoing in the silence. And all the while, that darkness inside me kept growing.

By late afternoon, Kiki took me to the police station and we reported Brittany missing. Even then, I was hoping – against the howling blood in my veins – she'd walk through the door, oblivious to all the panic she'd caused.

But that's not what happened.

And life was never the same again.

PACKING

DELLA

I SHOULD'VE KNOWN that Kiki couldn't be happy for me when I told her I was going on a trip overseas. That woman has resented everything ever since we were kids. It's water off a duck's back to me now; that hard turn in her mouth, the lift of her eyebrow when she's none too impressed.

'I'm not looking after your pets,' she said.

'That's okay, I've made other arrangements,' I told her, even though we both knew I hadn't.

She couldn't dampen my mood this time. It's not every day you get to go on a holiday. Fact is, I've never been outside Australia before. I've been to Sydney and Brisbane on the train but mostly I've stayed here, in the town where I was born, where my parents and grandparents all lived, too. I'm just not one of those people who's always dreamed of going places. I'd rather stay at home with my memories and what I know. Pat at the salon goes somewhere every year, adding postcards to the wall of her shop when she returns. But I've never seen the need. I wouldn't know how to do all the organising, wouldn't know where to start.

To be honest, when Jazzie – or Jasmine as I'm supposed to call her now – rang and said she wanted to take me on a holiday to England, I said I'd think about it but I was really leaning towards 'no'.

It was Kiki who decided it for me when she said, 'Do you really think it's a good idea?' She used that same tone she always uses when she's criticising me. She's been using it on me since we were small and uses it mostly now when she has advice about my girls – and she always, always has an opinion about them.

Right then, when I heard her tone, I made up my mind to go. 'Jasmine picked it. It's a tour about books and writers. She thought it would be interesting.'

'What do you know about books and writers?' Kiki's always been one of those people who sees the world as half empty rather than half full, so when she asks a question I don't think she means it to sound as rude as it sometimes comes out.

'Jasmine says it doesn't matter. There'll be a guide to explain everything and it'll be all things I've never seen anyway. She just wants to spend some time with me.'

'Can't she do that by just coming back here?'

'Well, she wants to do it this way, away from everything.'

'Jimmy's passing's been very hard on the girls. Six months is nothing. It's all still very raw,' Kiki told me in her know-it-all voice, as if I didn't understand.

And here's what I wanted to say to her: I loved him, too. Loved him right through to the soft parts of me deep in my bones. Even though Jimmy and I never got back together after what happened with Brittany, we'd been close to it. But in the gloomy fog that followed, so many things were broken. And Jimmy and me, we were just one more thing. So, I'd lost him all those years ago but in my dreams he was always there and it was like I'd lived another life with him, even though it was one I'd only imagined. When you harbour a longing for all those years, well, it becomes a very big part of you. So losing him for real, losing the very being of him, was just as hard. There'd never be anything more between us.

These past six months I've asked my own questions of him.

His dying didn't stop my need to ask him things, it just stopped the chance of an answer. There's no consolation, no solace in his passing, but I know what he suffered in life so I feel a certainty in my guts that he's found his own peace now.

In the days after Brittany went missing I couldn't sleep. The world went on around me but time didn't count for anything. I could sit for hours, my eyes fixed as a raindrop on the rusty guttering would grow fat like a pregnant belly, weighed down by its own being, and then drop with a splat on the floor below, mixing with a pool of water and becoming part of something bigger, but lost to itself. Then I would stare as another made its way through the same cycle. How long did I keep doing that? Well, it could have been all the days I've ever known.

One night, during that half-life time, I went outside for a smoke. It was in the early hours where you can feel the promise of dawn. It was biting cold and I had a jumper on over my nightdress, but my feet were bare and I was suffering the numbing pain of the cold concrete porch. I remember savouring the hard hurt of it.

I shivered, drawing in warm, calming gulps of nicotine, and looked to the end of the street into the darkened bushland. Creeping down the road in a slow march was a thick mist. The whole world was still except for this swirling cloud and I can't tell you why but I felt a deep calm. I felt that whatever or whoever was caught in the mist, they were telling me that Brittany had found peace.

It was only after that night that I started to hear her voice, or would catch a glimpse of her from the corner of my eye. Aunty Elaine believed in spirits and I don't doubt her. Not one bit. Sometimes I can feel Brittany with me. Sometimes I hear her call out 'Mum'.

And that's what I wanted to say to Kiki but of course I didn't. She could twitch her mouth all she liked but I was going on that trip. I just needed to find someone to look after my pets.

JASMINE

THE ULYSSES BUTTERFLY lives for only eight months. It's not surprising that once they emerge from their chrysalis after two weeks of metamorphosis – from being something so sluggish, so earthbound, to something delicate and light – their first blind instinct is to fly, to escape, their fragile wings flapping for freedom.

Once, while Mum was going through one of her 'unwell' periods, Aunt Kiki took me and Leigh-Anne up to Cairns. What I remember most was the butterfly farm, a large netted cage filled with thousands of fluttering specks glinting ultramarine in the sky. It seemed so sad, so cruel that their natural migration had been stopped, even though they probably weren't even aware they were trapped, couldn't understand why they had the driving urge to go somewhere they'd never get to.

I grew up in a small country town – population 1200. There were just eight houses in my street. A highway bypass was eventually built and after that, businesses slowly closed, houses were abandoned, dairy farms sold, the tannery shut. In this stagnating place, I felt like a caterpillar – sluggish, squishy and earthbound. Everyone felt they knew everything about me, and what they knew most was that I was 'Brittany's little sister', defined by the ghost of someone I barely knew.

My years in the city, studying and post-university, should have been the time to spread my wings, become light and fly. But I'm starting to realise you can never escape what you hope to leave behind.

People often assume I chose to go to law school because of what happened to my sister. It's a good story but like all good stories it's not the whole truth. I've always liked to know what motivates people, why they do the things they do. That's what reading books is all about – writers attempt to reveal truths about human behaviour, about our inner workings, our flaws. I'd always thought if I understood the *why* of things, maybe I could help change them for the better.

As a child, I'd slip unnoticed into a room, enter silently, taking a smug pride in my secret power to become invisible. I'd listen, hidden, to other people's conversations, inquisitive to know what they'd let slip. I thought what I'd hear would make the world easier to understand, that I'd be able to solve mysteries by discovering the things I wasn't supposed to know. My mother would yell at me if she found me lurking. 'What's wrong with you?' she'd shout, as though curiosity was unnatural.

The only person who seemed to understand me was Aunty Elaine. She was my grandmother's cousin but like everyone else in town I called her 'Aunty'. I asked her once if she was the oldest person in the world, because I thought you'd have to live a long time to learn everything she seemed to know. 'No, Bub, bless you.' She giggled with delight and winked, 'I'm just the wisest.' She was always making predictions – who would leave, who was about to arrive, when the rain was coming, when the season was about to turn.

'But how do you know?' I'd ask her.

'Just a gut feeling,' she'd say, tapping her large belly. And then she'd laugh her deepest laugh, the one that made the lines around her eyes furrow.

People can be sceptical about talk of spirits, but when Aunty Elaine made a prediction it wouldn't be long before the weather would change, a cousin would come visiting, there'd be a funeral, someone's stomach would start to swell.

I'd go to her place after school to do my homework. I could never study at home, not at Mum's, Dad's or Aunt Kiki's – too many people, too many distractions. Without Aunty Elaine, I'd most likely have ended up like Leigh-Anne, dropping out of school and pretending that getting pregnant was what I really wanted to do.

I'd sit on Aunty Elaine's back porch in the oversized chair with the big cushions. Curled up there, I'd read. She was the only person on our street who had any books in their house. She'd come home on pension day with an already well-thumbed novel from the second-hand store. 'Look what I've found. I've been wanting this one for ages,' she'd say. It wasn't until years later that I realised she never read any of those books but I'd devoured every word on every page. *The Secret Seven*, *Anne of Green Gables*, Nancy Drew, *Little Women*, then Jane Austen, Charles Dickens, Thomas Hardy and the Brontë sisters. I could mark my journey through childhood with these stories, each one offering a world different from the one I was in, with mostly happy endings.

On Aunty Elaine's back porch, I could hide from the world – but I could also watch. Her house was slightly elevated, so I could see back down the street into everyone's backyard and to the pastures behind them. I could see the back of Dad's house and then two doors over was Mum's.

My parents living apart but so close might seem like a strange arrangement to anyone who didn't live in the Frog Hollow part of our town. Here, especially among the poor families like ours who never went anywhere, it was all one big interconnected web of kinship, with every degree of separation leading back to where it started with just two or three steps.

Aunty Elaine would say that if she told someone something on the phone and then walked down the street, by the time she passed the six houses in between hers and ours, my mother would already know the story even though what she'd say was mixed up with myth and the bare snippets of what people thought they knew. And these were the suffocating facts: we were 'Brittany's sisters'. Leigh-Anne was the 'loud one', me 'the quiet one' – like labels pinned to butterfly specimens, encased under glass.

Leigh-Anne is opinionated and vocal like Aunt Kiki. And like her, Leigh-Anne has striking blue eyes that flash, coffee-coloured skin and untameable curly black hair. When she arrives somewhere, anywhere, there's a noticeable change in the atmosphere, like a fire has begun to burn. Even without a word, she's loud of dress, of presence; when speaking, she's devoid of any subtlety. Chalk and cheese, my mother liked to say about the two of us.

'Huge mistake. Huge!' Leigh-Anne had thundered down the phone when I told her about our trip. 'Her behaviour at Dad's funeral was unforgivable. I'm so done with her. You're asking for a world of trouble.'

Leigh-Anne had said many times before in the heat of an argument that she was 'done' with Mum but always Aunt Kiki and Aunty Elaine had managed to bring her around. This was their longest rupture and it felt much deeper. I was sure if Aunty Elaine was still here, these bridges would already be mended.

'She's all we've got left,' I'd said, meekly.

'Not me. I've got my kids, remember? And we've always got Kiki. You know, Jazz, you can talk about all that stuff you read at your fancy university but I'm not going to say it's okay when it's not. I'm not making any more excuses for her. She's never going to change, you know. Even with all that study you've done, you're still not smart about people.'

The loud one; the quiet one.

You'd think that what happened to Brittany would engender nothing but sympathy for Mum and Dad, but as the years went by people thought it should become a thing of the past – 'you have to move on', 'time will heal', 'put it behind you'. The truth for my parents was that it never got easier, never stopped being a raw wound. Then the time came when people just didn't know what to say in the face of such entrenched, lingering grief. Mum and Dad made them feel awkward. They would look at Mum like she had a terminal illness, surprised she'd survived so long.

Dad, on the other hand, always had a gentle strength. He smelt of wood, stale alcohol and sweat, and while that might sound the antithesis of comforting, my visceral reaction to his scent was to feel soothed. Dad worked sporadically, first at the tannery until it closed, then at the local mechanic, fixing cars. He always preferred his own company, liked staying at home, drinking and watching television. I'd sit on the arm of his chair as he told me stories – about the time when he was a young boy and his old uncle warned him about the giant cod in the bend of the river. Swimming there one day he'd felt something brush up against his leg. He ran out of the water so fast, and never went back in there again. Or the time he went to a circus that was passing through town. He had no money, but the old Blackfella running the carousel let him on at the end of the night for free. I'd heard these few tales over and over, but each time I laughed as if it was the very first time.

And Dad could sing, a voice rich and heartfelt. He would, in the right mood, craft a song of disillusion, of disappointment, with his own complex interpretation. I'd be there right beside him but he always seemed to be talking or singing to someone else, like I was never enough. Even as a child, I could tell he was already beaten. When he passed away, sitting in his chair watching his football team, I felt like he'd left me a lifetime ago.

Aunty Elaine would say, 'They weren't always like this, not before.' I was only three when Brittany disappeared, so all I knew was the 'after'. I often wonder whether more could have been done to help Mum and Dad, to keep them with us. It was this that led me to a career where I could help people work out their problems – identify what was wrong and what they needed, so everything could be different.

Then the Fiona McCoy case crossed my path.

Fiona was sixteen years old when she was accused and then convicted of murdering a man by stabbing him thirty-six times with a pair of scissors. That's a lot of rage. The brutality of the attack attracted media attention. 'Monster Child', one of the newspapers called her, under a photo of her thick, hefty bulk and hunched-over frame, her face blurred.

Fresh out of university, new to Legal Aid, I had to assist in the preparation of her defence, pull together psychological assessments from experts and submit background information for the judge, particularly in anticipation of a guilty verdict and sentencing.

Law school teaches you about law, it doesn't teach you about people. It teaches you about the rules of evidence but it doesn't teach you about what it's like to be a victim of crime, to live with the impact of a brutal murder. It teaches you about the factors that can be used to mitigate responsibility for a crime or lessen a sentence, but doesn't teach you how to understand a client who has been accused of the worst kind of violence, who has killed someone in a fit of anger.

When we first interviewed Fiona, she sat in shackles, hands restrained. Her hair was cropped short, her wild darting eyes switching from fierce to frightened as quick as a twitch. I'd been trained to evaluate and assess a case but I couldn't disconnect from the emotion of it. I'd dream about Fiona covered in blood, breathing hard. I'd wake up tired, unsettled.

Even after she'd been sentenced, I worried I'd not done enough to put her case forward properly. Her circumstances were complex and the rules of evidence allowed some things in and kept other things out, so what did the court really know about her other than the facts of the terrible crime she committed? I'd felt out of my depth with too little experience to really do justice to her case. Even with a barrister briefed, I was never sure I was up for the task of preparing the evidence, of keeping a professional distance.

My first instinct was to ask Aunty Elaine about it. But she'd passed away – a fatal heart attack – during my first year at university. It had been disorienting, trying to navigate life without her in it, and I'd get that deep pang of loss that comes long after the death of someone you love. In the next instant I'd feel a primal need to have my mother comfort me, despite the long-surging resentment that would flow along with it. It seemed strange to still want her when she'd never really been there for me. Just like Dad, always absent.

I knew enough about loss to know that grief is a slow burn, an infinite void. After Dad's death, and on top of the case, I felt unnerved, unsteady. It was my friend Bex who came to the rescue. 'You need a holiday,' she pronounced. She'd been in my close group of friends from university and had studied communications. Her father and mother were both academics – Aboriginal professionals. I'd never met one of those before.

Bex was comfortable with having money in a way that was alien to me. She had confidence and ambition and shared her positivity with everyone around her. After university, she got a job as a junior producer at the national broadcaster and was toiling away, grabbing every opportunity she could.

She'd decided that she would do a series of travel articles, visiting different sites in England, and from there build her profile as a travel writer. Then perhaps try to get a spot on one of those travel shows. 'I think I'd be great at it,' she stated with enviable certainty. 'It would help give me a niche.'

I'll say this about Bex, if you looked at her from afar, you'd think she was a good-time girl who spent way too much time promoting herself on social media, but behind all of that she was a really hard worker and took very little for granted. She knew what barriers would stand in her way because she was an Aboriginal woman, so she worked four times as hard as anyone else around her.

I suggested the tour – I'd seen it on the internet one night and it was a dream for me. Bex liked the idea, too. 'That totally fits my plan,' she declared. 'They'll have a guide whose brains I can pick and you know all those books, you'll almost be like a research assistant.' She didn't say it unkindly, but to reassure me when she offered to pay half the price of my trip so I could afford to go.

Then, six weeks before we were due to head off, Bex rang to say she had bad news. Well, it was great news as well. She'd been asked to fill in for one of the newsreaders. 'If I don't take it, one of those other bitches will do it and who knows when I'll get the chance again.'

There was no point in asking about the travel writing and the travel show with the chance to now be on air. She needed to prepare and her first week was the same one as the tour. So, with the luxury of being able to throw money at the problem, she offered her ticket to someone else to go with me. I could have taken Annie or Margie, my other university friends. But something in my head, in Aunty Elaine's voice, said, 'Take your mother.'

It was more instinct than reason because she is the last person you would hold on to when you thought you were going to fall. I didn't have the same anger towards Mum's faults and failings that Leigh-Anne had. I could still distinguish her from the complications that surrounded her. I wanted to be closer to her but I didn't want to get caught up in the cycles of drama and routines of home.

Bex loved the idea when I said it out loud. And once she loved an idea, there was no backing away from it.

There was a part of me that was certain my mother would say no. She'd be pleased that I asked and then she'd decline. So, I was surprised when she said she'd spoken to Aunt Kiki and, whatever was said, she'd decided she wanted to go.

I took a deep breath, Leigh-Anne's words of warning still ringing in my ears.

DELLA

I CAN TELL you, I almost didn't make it. Jasmine sent some forms up for me to sign and send back. Kiki took me to the chemist to get a photo taken. We had to take several because I kept blinking at the flash. A passport – my first ever – arrived in the post. Those moments were all exciting, but packing just did my head in. Jasmine kept ringing and asking me about it and I'd just say, 'Yes, yes, it's coming along,' but I really didn't know where to start.

As the day to leave drew closer, I felt sick, it was all too much. I rang Jasmine and told her I couldn't go anywhere. I just wasn't well enough to travel. She pleaded and begged but I told her I just couldn't and there was nothing more to say on the subject.

Then Kiki turned up with a big suitcase. We sat down and made a list. I ticked things off as we put them into the case. She even drove me over to the next town where Leigh-Anne now lives and where they have a bigger supermarket. There we bought all the things I needed for my trip but didn't have, like lotions and shampoo in small bottles with plastic cases to put them in.

We packed everything in – clothes that didn't need ironing, travel-size toiletries, comfortable shoes for walking. I had to sit on the bag so we could close it, my bulky behind trying to squash everything down while Kiki, bigger than me, fumbled with the zip.

I don't remember the last time we laughed so hard together, both of us rolling on the floor.

And she agreed to mind my two cats and two dogs. So, there I was.

Last time I was in Sydney, Kiki and I stayed at a hotel in a tall building. I got dizzy going up, clinging to the handrail in the elevator. I had to go through the ordeal every time I wanted a smoke because Kiki wouldn't let me bend the rule that said you couldn't smoke in the room.

If you asked me, I'd have said I was afraid of heights but it turns out flying is different. It's cramped, I'll give you that, but I like how the food comes on little trays, all nicely laid out in little square containers or in little plastic wrappers, and I like how all the drinks come in tiny little bottles. I'm not used to being waited on, having someone fetch me what I want without it being any trouble at all. It's nice being where people judge you on what they see, not on things they think they know. I can see why Pat at the salon likes it so much. The hardest thing is not having a smoke for such a long time. I've been chewing that gum but it's really not the same.

I looked at Jazzie sitting next to me, my sweet, patient girl, her head always in a book. Her straight hair, light skin and big brown eyes are so like Jimmy it sometimes hurts to look at her. We used to call her Jazzie because we spelt her name Jazzmine, our special way we worked out on a piece of paper. But by the time she'd finished high school, she insisted we use her full name and even went to all the trouble to have the spelling legally changed to the way she preferred it, taking out all the zeds that made it special. That hurt me a little bit because I remember how much Jimmy and I loved the name but she was headstrong in her quiet, firm way. So, Jasmine she became.

Leigh-Anne, when she's not angry, is whip smart and always makes me laugh. I go red with shame sometimes when I see what she wears. I did tell her no-one will buy the milk when you get the cow for free. She tells me that's not the way the saying goes but it makes sense to me the way I say it.

It's hard not to compare, not to think about how Brittany would be if she were still here. Would she have gone to the city like Jazzie, or stayed close by like Leigh-Anne? Would she be sweet-tempered or always growling and rowing? Would she have gone to university or dropped out of school to have a baby like Leigh-Anne, and like I did?

I was only just sixteen when I had Brittany. Jimmy was the same age but ten months older than me. When I was pregnant, my stomach tight and bulging, I dreamt I was having a little girl. And I had one, all curly hair and smiles. I'd never known a moment when I was happier than when the nurse put her into my arms and I held her – of having someone to care for, someone who needed me, but also the promise of everything being different. They might have taken her off me because of my age and having no support from my parents but Jimmy's mum, who I called Mum Nancy, and Aunty Elaine – both as fierce as feral cats – had taken me in and helped. In time, my other two came along.

At Jimmy's funeral, after all these years, his sisters, Lynn and Jenny, still gave me the icy-cold shoulder treatment. You'd think you wouldn't get blamed for old mistakes, not if you never meant any of it to happen, not while you're mourning someone you love. And I thought to myself, well, you don't know everything that happened. No, you don't. People think they know all about it even though they don't see all those secret moments that pass between two people, binding them over a lifetime.

I'm thankful that the girls and Kiki were with me at the funeral because, whatever people think of me, Kiki frightens them and

Leigh-Anne is starting to frighten them in exactly the same way. Leigh-Anne seemed protective of me at first but afterwards, at the wake, we had a humdinger. I can't even remember all the details now – how it started, or what it was about – but I do remember the last thing she said, with her hand on her hip, chin pushed out. 'Kiki was more of a mother to me than you ever were.' That's what she said. Bold as that, in that same 'I-told-you-so' tone that Kiki loves to use.

'You watch too many movies,' I said back to her because of all her dramatics.

I forgive her for being mad at me, for saying such hurtful things, for taking it all out on me. We all have to grieve in our own ways. I know that better than anyone, but right now she's frosty cold and giving me the silent treatment. It's especially cruel because it means I don't get to see my grandkids. It's football season now and I would usually go to all of Zane's weekend games, but this year Leigh-Anne hasn't invited me along to any. And the girls, little Teaghan and Tamara, will be six next month and she hasn't let me know about any parties. I know I rub Leigh-Anne the wrong way sometimes so I just have to wait for her to get over it in her own time. She always does, always has in the past.

Many secrets died with Jimmy that are now buried deep in the dark earth with him. But I think back most to that time when we were both teenagers, when he was an escape before we became trapped again by what happened with Brittany, sharing our secrets into the night and having that feeling that a heart can be whole.

I thought of those times on the plane as I played the country music through the headphones. They played a song that Jimmy used to sing to me, back in the days when we were truly happy, the singer's voice all smooth as syrup like Jimmy's was. And the singer's name was Jimmy, too. *Telephone to glory, oh what joy divine. I can hear the current moving on the line.*

I pretended I was asleep as I listened and imagined Jimmy and me together once more – his gentle, unassuming nature, his tender lust when it was just him and me, skin against skin, hard to tell where one of us ended and the other began – and I had my own little cry.

JASMINE

'You're not going to get much of a holiday if your mother's there,' Aunt Kiki had warned me. I rang her after Mum said she'd changed her mind about coming. I would have lost the money for the flight and the tour but, worse, would have had to put up with a big self-satisfied 'I told you so' from Leigh-Anne.

When Mum got on the plane, you wouldn't have known that she'd been paralysed with doubt. She's not yet fifty, having had us all so young, but she took a child's delight in the free travel pack with its cheap socks, eye-mask and miniature comb. She's a beautiful woman by anyone's standards but the type who never thought about how she looked as a way to define herself. Her face may be aged with the frown lines of worry and the effects of her drinking but she still has soft, warm features, high cheekbones. The hostesses were charmed by her unassuming way and quaint turn of phrase. They didn't question her, jovial as she was, as she merrily asked for more vodka and lemonade, delighted by the tiny bottles.

In the final hours of our flight, I looked over at Mum. She's always been an amiable drunk – not angry or spiteful, mostly chatty and giggling, and occasionally melancholy. It took me a long time to realise that her drinking was a problem. I'd heard Grandma

Nancy say once, as I pretended to be asleep on her couch, that my grandfather – Mum's dad – was a violent alcoholic. In my child's mind, I thought it was the violence that was the thing that made drinking bad, and my mother and father were never that way. Drinking just seemed a normal part of life. Into my teens I began to realise that when Mum was 'unwell', when we'd be sent over to Aunt Kiki's, it was because she was on a serious drinking binge or recovering from the effects of one.

I asked Aunty Elaine once how you could tell if someone was an alcoholic. 'Goodness, Bub, what a question!' she exclaimed.

There were clinical answers: if you stopped drinking and had withdrawal symptoms; or if you drank, did something destructive but kept drinking again. Aunty Elaine responded, 'Some people have so much pain they know no other way to ease it.' It was the kind of answer she'd give that wouldn't seem like one until you really thought about it.

Now, looking at Mum's face, as she listened to music, her eyes closed, it suddenly hit me, the risk I was taking. I could hear Leigh-Anne's brassy voice – *big mistake*. But when you love someone, your most basic instinct is to want them to love you back. It's evolutionary.

Charles Darwin believed that who we are is determined by our biology, by our genes. It's in our DNA. Fate is out of our hands. The philosopher John Locke said we are a blank slate – a *tabula rasa* – on which our destiny can be written. The debate about whether our lives are determined by nature or nurture once deeply divided scientists but now it's accepted that both play a role in determining who we are and the new debates focus on where one stops and the other begins. We're all somewhere on a sliding scale. While one seems predetermined (nature) and the other is man-made (nurture) most people haven't got control over either, especially not while they're children.

Fiona McCoy had been on remand in a juvenile detention centre when, during an art class conducted by a volunteer, John Andrews, she took a pair of scissors and in front of the other horrified girls, repeatedly stabbed him. John was athletic in a sandy-blond surfer way, brushed by the sun. He worked as a furniture maker, hand-crafting wood, but on Sundays he taught a class to troubled teenagers. In hindsight, the department authorities conceded, Fiona shouldn't have been placed there – it was supposed to be only for non-violent inmates – and no scissors in workshops in future either. But that didn't diminish Fiona's culpability and was no consolation for John Andrews' family.

John's widow had turned up every day during Fiona's trial. Petite, raven-haired, she entered the courtroom surrounded by friends. Although they were physically very different, there was something about her that reminded me of Mum – that same bewildered, fragile look, like life was happening around her.

No-one from Fiona's family came to the trial. Her legal team were her only representatives in the court. On the second day of the trial, Fiona asked to speak to me. I leaned over so she could whisper in my ear as she sat handcuffed in the dock.

'Do you think they'd let me have a pet? Maybe a kitten?'

'In prison?' I asked.

She nodded, her eyes wide and expectant, hopeful.

'No,' I said. 'No, they won't.'

WELCOME DRINKS

DELLA

You WOULDN'T BELIEVE it but our tour guide, Lionel Cavendish, was on a television show. I can't wait to tell Pat at the salon as I don't think she's ever seen a celebrity on her travels or she'd have been sure to mention it.

'I might look familiar to those of you who watch the television show *Midsomer Murders*,' Lionel said in a voice that sounded like a telly commercial for something really expensive. 'I played the veterinarian Paul Greentree in an episode in series four. I was the key suspect in the murder – until the twist.'

Our tour group was meeting for drinks in a terrace house. Lionel threw his arms around the small foyer that was also a gift shop, almost knocking over some figurines with oversized wobbly heads in his enthusiasm. He certainly got the emotions up. My first reaction was to clap but no-one else did so I stopped.

Tall, a real gentleman type, with grey curling hair that looked like it had once been much thicker and eyes the colour of river stones, Lionel explained where we'd be going and what we'd be doing on our tour. He concluded, 'So here we are, beginning our adventure at 221B Baker Street, in the home of Sherlock Holmes.'

Lionel Cavendish. I always like it when people look like their names. There seems something up-front about it. 'That's a very theatrical name, isn't it?' I whispered to Jazzie.

'I doubt it's real,' she replied.

Jazzie has a way of dismissing things that always makes me feel a little sad for her. It's as if she's afraid you're trying to trick her. I don't think there's anything wrong if he did change his name. At least he picked a good one. Everyone probably wants to be a better, more interesting person, with dreams of being more than they are, so you can't really blame someone if they hope a change of name will help. Jazzie changed hers, after all. But I thought best not to mention it as sometimes people get annoyed when you tell them a truth.

I didn't know how anyone could be negative on a day like today when everything was, as Lionel called it, an adventure. That excitement of everything being so new does make the heart beat a little faster. London is bigger than any city I'd ever seen and everything – the streets, the houses – are so unlike the ones back home. In the black cab from the airport, just like in the movies with a little cabin, my eyes couldn't keep up. Everything looked so familiar from the telly but so different in real life at the same time. So, who could be glum?

As we huddled in the cramped foyer, overflowing with pamphlets, books and knick-knacks, Lionel introduced everyone in the group – all ten of us. The two eldest ladies, thin and all bones under their floral dresses, spoke first. When I looked at them, I thought of the word 'plumage' – more like a peacock than the kind of birds we have back home.

'Well, the first thing I guess we should say,' the one with the longer neck said, 'is that we are from Boston.'

'No, no, dear. The first thing we should say is that we are sisters.'

Through their squabbling, I didn't catch their names.

A bald man with round glasses said he was Professor Oscar Finn.

I thought he looked like a turtle. He talked about himself and some other things I didn't understand before he finally pointed to the woman next to him, who looked like a school teacher and smiled without warmth. I thought of the word 'matronly'.

'And this is my wife, Helen,' he said.

He's going to be trouble, I thought, giving him an eye-over. Sometimes you can just tell.

There were two women from Phoenix, Arizona. Sam, the talkative one had short, blonde hair and worked at a university in some kind of women's studies department. She had a jacket and pants on and one of those string ties you might see on a Texas oilman from the telly. She looked a lot older than her friend, Toni, who wore red lipstick and a leather jacket and had a kind of '60s hairdo, all swept up. Sam said that Toni was a poet.

There was an older Australian couple from Sydney – Cliff and Meredith, husband and wife, retired. They looked like they might be on *Neighbours*, living in a clean, tidy street in a nice, well-tended suburb.

Then it was our turn. My girl said, 'I'm Jasmine and this is my mother, Della. We're from a little town in New South Wales, Australia, four hours drive from Sydney, a little in from the coast. This is Mum's first time overseas.'

The ladies all cooed and I smiled at their gentle attention. I didn't say it but I was pleased that Jazzie said she was from our town. It feels like most of the time she's trying to get away from us. I kept my mouth shut about that, too – but I can tell you that it made me happy.

'Welcome,' said Mr Cavendish, so warmly it was hard not to think what a nice smile he had.

After the talking was done, we got to walk around. There were rooms crowded with magnifying glasses, leather bags, books and papers, as well as letters to Sherlock Holmes asking him to solve mysteries or offering to help him with his investigating.

In one of the poky rooms at the top of the stairs, a man sat at a desk. At first, I thought he was a wax figure but then he moved. It was a real person dressed as Sherlock Holmes, his funny hat and cape on, a pipe in his hand.

'Elementary, my dear Watson,' I said, as that's all I could remember about Sherlock Holmes.

The man looked startled and a little confused. Then he smiled and spoke to me in his posh English voice. 'Yes, indeed. Elementary. I just have to outwit the villains, my dear lady, by using logic.'

'Oh, I've never found much in life to be logical,' I told him. 'And that's the truth of it.'

'Well, maybe not in life *per se* – but it is essential in solving mysteries. You have to understand the clues, work out what they mean.'

'I'm not very good with puzzles,' I said. He had, for a fleeting moment, that look on his face that people get when they don't know what to say to me. I stood waiting to see what he would do next.

He shuffled himself, as if adjusting his clothes, and coughed softly to clear his throat. When he began speaking, he seemed more confident. 'You know,' he whispered, leaning towards me as if to tell me a secret, 'Conan Doyle tried to kill me off.'

'Really! What happened?'

'Well, apparently he didn't like me all that much and had me perish in 1893. He said of me: "*I have had such an overdose of him that I feel towards him as I do to pâté de foie gras, of which I once ate too much ...*"

'So, he had me struggle with my nemesis, the evil Professor Moriarty, on the cliffside of the Reichenbach Falls in Switzerland. I plunged to my death. But then he had to bring me back, you see. The public wanted it. They loved me. And he needed the money.'

He waved his hands around just like Lionel had, to emphasise his points. He was like watching a movie.

'But how did he bring you back after you'd died?' That's what I wanted to know.

'He had me fake my death to fool my enemies. Simple as that. And I was back.'

Afterwards, in our cosy little hotel room, barely large enough for two single beds and our suitcases, I thought about the idea that someone could return from the dead. I'd wish upon anything – stars, birthday candles, eyelashes, rainbows – and I'd beg the spirits to see Brittany again, to take me to an earlier time so that everything could be different. So, imagine if you could just write someone back into existence. What wonderful magic that would be.

I also thought about what the Sherlock Holmes man had said about clues. People thought they saw them everywhere. When Brittany disappeared, everyone had a theory. She ran away. Someone took her. It was me. It was Jimmy. It was my father. It was a stranger travelling through town. It was a drug dealer. It was this person or that person. Everyone thought this thing or that must be part of a clue, the snippet of information that would turn out to be significant.

The first people the police questioned were me and Jimmy. I was her mother and I was in the room; Jimmy, her father, was just two houses down. They asked me about what happened – what I did, who was at the party, what Brittany was wearing. They would get impatient if I couldn't remember things – when people came and went, what time I went to bed. The sorts of things you never think to take note of because you can't imagine that they could ever be important.

Kiki got angry with the policeman called Constable Summers – with his red beard and face the colour of fish flakes in a salmon tin. 'Stop harassing her,' she'd barked at him. And even

33

the nicer one, Constable Lawrence, younger and stringy thin, got a hard time from her. 'She doesn't need a cup of tea. She needs you to get off your lily-white arse, get out there and start trying to find her missing kid.'

They assured us that they had to discount parents and close relatives first, that all their questions were routine, just procedure. Just doing their jobs, they said, trying to sound sympathetic. And who was I to know any different? I told them that I'd spoken to Jimmy just before the party but he didn't come over to the house and I hadn't seen him all night. No-one at the party had seen him either, confirming my story.

'Could he have come in during the night and taken Brittany when no-one was looking?' Constable Summers had asked in a coaxing voice, as if it would be perfectly understandable if that had been what happened. 'If it were him, it would explain why you said you didn't see anything. You could be covering for him.' So that was his theory based on what no-one saw.

I was glad I hadn't told the police that when I saw Jimmy before the party he was already drunk. I didn't tell them we fought. I didn't tell them that the reason we argued was because I'd taken the girls over to Jimmy's house and asked if he'd mind them for the night. He refused, so I'd marched the girls back home. I kept all this to myself because I knew it would be used against him, twisted around so that it became something it wasn't. That was the thing about Jimmy and me. Our first instinct had always been to protect each other. So, all this was our secret, now buried in the ground.

JASMINE

As she gently snored in the bed next to me, I realised I hadn't slept in a room with my mother since I was a child. Her hand clutching her pillow, I thought of Mum earlier that evening, talking to the old actor pretending to be Sherlock Holmes, who'd seemed delighted with her. I doubt anyone had taken him seriously in years – or made him have to improvise his lines quite so much. My mother's ability to suspend disbelief and go along with someone else's fantasy was as much naivety as kindness. A glass half-full attitude, she would have said.

As Mum slept, I checked my work emails to make sure I hadn't missed anything about Fiona's case. Then I sent a few messages home. I started texting a message to Leigh-Anne, telling her about our day. Then I deleted the references to Mum, worried that it would just antagonise her. And then I decided to delete the whole message, fearing that whatever I said would only get criticised, and I wasn't in the mood for her put-downs.

Instead, I let Aunty Kiki know that Mum was doing fine and described the ladies from Boston with their squabbling. *Do you think all sisters bicker?* I asked her.

I looked at Bex's social media – she'd posted a picture of herself at brunch with Annie and Margie. I messaged that I wished I was there. There were other pictures – Bex with a country singer (*Look who just dropped by the studio!*) and a networking drinks where she was with other high-profile women (*Meeting some trailblazers*). I 'liked' them all. I hadn't posted anything since the day before I left Sydney. Bex can do it naturally but I find it intrusive. It feels like showing off. I don't understand why people want to share pictures of their food and every minute of their day rather than just living it. How often do people go back and look over all those photos? Bex will tell you she is building her brand, but it's not for me.

Lastly, I wrote to Annie. She studied history and is now doing her PhD on Aboriginal women in the cattle industry. I told her about the Professor of classic literature, with his turtle neck in a turtleneck, who had audibly spluttered when he realised he was on the same tour as a lecturer in gender studies; she'd rolled her eyes to her girlfriend as he talked. Annie was the one who'd most appreciate what happens when an old-school male immersed in the classics collides with a female seeking to challenge the curriculum.

Once in bed, I had trouble switching off my brain. I knew I shouldn't be on screens before sleep but that's the advice we all know and never take. It's comforting to think of a world where everything makes sense if you can work the clues out, where logic is all you need to solve a mystery. As I walked around The Sherlock Holmes Museum earlier that evening, I'd found myself more interested in the man who created him, Arthur Conan Doyle. His father, Charles, was an artist who came from an artistic family but suffered from feelings of inadequacy and low self-esteem – he had depression and became addicted to alcohol. As a result, he lost his job and was institutionalised. He spent the next twelve years, until his death in 1893, in asylums for the mentally ill. It was during this time that he created some of his best work – of elves, fairies and fantasy scenes, dreamy pictures of make-believe magical worlds. Charles would send these pictures to his family, including Arthur, the eldest of his ten children, to convince them of his sanity. Did Arthur as a child wonder why his father preferred alcohol to his family? Did he feel that his father was just out of reach, as though there was a wall created by grief and alcohol that couldn't be passed? Mum was also just like that. Even now, it was like she was here but I just couldn't reach her. Maybe on this trip, she'd really see me.

While Sherlock Holmes dealt with the world in logic and reason, Conan Doyle himself believed in mysticism, séances and fairies. He famously, very publicly, fell for the Cottingley Fairies hoax – a series of photographs doctored by two girls, cousins aged sixteen and nine, using cardboard cut-outs of fairies copied from a children's book. The photos purported to show real fairies in a garden, tendered by the girls as definitive proof of their existence. It's so easy to understand his desire to believe in the existence of the little creatures that were the subject of his father's best work. It reminded me of the way I'd hold on tightly to the fragments of a song or story that my father would share with me.

It's hard not to wonder what Sherlock Holmes would have made of the failure to consider what was logical, elementary, by his creator. Perhaps it's not surprising that Conan Doyle killed him off. He wrote of Sherlock Holmes falling off a cliff, presumably to his death, the same year his own alcoholic father died in a mental asylum. How painful to have to later bring his character back due to public demand and the pressures of his purse. He must have felt haunted by this ghost, unable to escape his creation who now seemed to have a life of his own.

Some things just won't let you run from them.

DAY 1

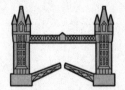

DELLA

LIONEL, LOOKING SMART in a grey suit and red tie, was waiting at the front of the hotel. He was with our minibus driver, a stocky man with sand-coloured hair who looked like he'd be good with gadgets and was introduced as Brett. We were all there ready to go except for the sisters from Boston. The Professor, sitting in the front row with his wife, was getting cranky about the delay and suggested we leave without them. His bad temper was making Lionel nervous. My father was like that, a foul temper so everyone was on eggshells. I never like to think of him so that was another black mark against Professor Finn.

Jasmine offered to go and ring the room of the Boston sisters. I'm proud she's so thoughtful, but just as she walked towards the front doors of the hotel, the two elderly women ambled out.

'I told you we had to be down here at eight, which is why I said we should have been at breakfast at seven.'

'You were the one who wasn't ready to leave until seven-thirty and I did remind you then that I thought you were going to make us late. I said as much.'

'I brought you along to keep an eye on those sorts of things. It's the least you could do.'

They took their seats without realising how annoyed they'd made

Professor Finn or the trouble they'd caused poor Lionel. You find those people in life who never see the damage they leave behind them.

I've seen city traffic before but you can imagine the difference between London and what I'm used to back home. As Brett weaved the minibus from one side of the city to the other, Lionel started telling us facts and figures about books and plays and writers. But all I could focus on were the waves of destruction – fires, plagues, wartime bombings – that had flattened the city at different times. I guess that by the time you're as old as London, you've survived a lot.

Our bus dropped us off near the white round theatre with the dark roof where people came to see Shakespeare's plays. Even with just a few tourists milling around it felt cosy inside. Lionel told us how three thousand people would flock to the theatre to see a show. They must have been as squished as I was on that plane.

I'm not sure where Jasmine got her book smarts from but it wasn't from me. I'd always been confused by Shakespeare with his 'thees' and 'thous'. His fancy words tie me in knots. The Professor and the Boston sisters – Celia and Nessa it turned out their names were – seemed to know them though. They talked excitedly about different stories; I smiled and nodded like I knew. You can get by with a fair bit of nodding along when people like the sound of their own voice.

Lionel said that the same year that Queen Elizabeth died – the one with the red hair and the lace collar – there was a plague that swept through London. Furious and fast, one in five people died. Rich people were able to leave the city but the poor had to stay locked up in their homes with a red cross painted on the door. Orders were issued with instructions on what to do – count the infected, collect the bodies and bury them. Some people are good at taking charge in a time of crisis. Kiki is like that. She'd think of all the things that a clear head would think of. She can get on my nerves but she's one of those people who you can rely on when things go wrong, when disaster strikes. You really want her around then.

When Lionel said that about the plague, I looked at the crowds swirling about the theatre and imagined one in five disappearing. You'd have known so many people – whole families – who were wiped out. Just think if you were at the club or the races and every fifth person dropped dead. How do you face so much grief, when just one person's death can rip your whole heart out?

Aunty Elaine once told me that when white people first arrived in Australia to build their colony and take over, disease was more lethal than bullets. Smallpox swept through the Aboriginal tribes that lived in Sydney and the country around it. 'Just imagine,' she'd say, 'the impact of that when you relied on each other to stay alive. And on our oral traditions, where knowledge is handed down from old to young.'

I wasn't very good at learning in school, always found it hard to concentrate, but I could listen to Aunty Elaine for hours because what she said made sense. I thought about what it must have been like for those Aboriginal people who watched the world around them change hard and fast when the colony was set up, who had to watch the destruction of the life they knew.

I'd said to Jasmine that I didn't know how I'd remember everything so she went to the gift shop and bought me a pretty notebook with a Romeo and Juliet on it – the girl on the balcony with a pink pointed hat, the boy looking up to her in green puffy sleeves and tight pants. She also got me a pen with a red London double-decker bus on it that moved up and down when you tipped it. I wrote in my spidery letters: *Plague, 1603. One in five people died.*

Lionel said it was an irony that no Shakespeare play dealt with plague since it would have preoccupied everyone in the audience, and been a big part of their own lived experience. I don't know anything about that but I do know that there's often silence about the thing that people are thinking about the most – the white elephant in the room, Aunty Elaine would call it. Or maybe Shakespeare knew that people didn't want to be reminded of it, that they came to see his plays so they could think about something else for a while. That would make sense, too.

'I don't know if that's right,' the Professor said. 'What about the famous phrase, "A pox on your house" from *Romeo and Juliet*? That's a clear reference to the plague.'

The Boston sisters raised their eyebrows in anticipation of a response.

'I meant it was never a main theme – or plot,' Lionel clarified.

The Professor looked reassured but it made me bristle, so I asked Lionel a question that I hoped might cheer him. 'Did you ever act in a Shakespeare play?'

His face lit up and I liked the way his eyes had soft lines around them. He rattled off some names, Richards and Henrys and some others that sounded Italian. I didn't know any but I nodded, impressed.

We walked around the streets and alleys next to the river as Lionel explained the things that happened here and there. At London Bridge, Lionel told us how it was once covered in shops and the heads of traitors were hung on it. It was hard to believe that such a thing ever happened here, on a sunny day like this, where parents pushed strollers and everyone was taking photographs. We passed the place where London Tower was and Ann Boleyn lost her head, then we arrived at a church that seemed to be away from the crowds. Lionel said there was a Roman road underneath but the stairs down to see it were too steep for me and I was pleased to finally sit down and take a load off my feet.

Afterwards, we walked around the streets that had names of the things that were once sold there – Fish, Milk and Poultry – like the aisles of a supermarket. Lionel took us to a park that was tucked away between the bustle and big buildings. You had to walk down a lane to get there and unless Lionel had shown us you'd never even have known it was there. Amongst all the trees and flowers were the ruins of a church that had been bombed in the war and its shell looked like the skeleton bones of a whale.

In this quiet moment I wondered at how, in between the skyscrapers, there were these pieces of history. Aunty Elaine had said that Aboriginal people had been in Australia for over sixty-five thousand years. So, when you think of it, even things from Shakespeare's day are all kind of new but it seemed that these old relics of London were scattered now amongst all the men and women in business suits hurrying on their way, moving the world forward.

Lionel then told us more about the Great Fire of London and took us to the bakery where it started during a dry, hot summer in 1666. The fire burned for four days and when it finally stopped, over thirteen thousand houses and eighty-seven churches were lost. It left over a hundred thousand people homeless but very few lives were lost. There was a monument to it standing 202 feet tall and 202 feet from the spot in Pudding Lane where it all began. Topped with a flaming copper urn, it had originally been the plan to put a statue of King Charles II on top of the column but he didn't like that idea because he didn't want anyone to get the impression that he was responsible for the fire.

I wrote in my book: *Great Fire 1666. Few lives lost.*

Aunty Elaine had talked about fire and burning. In the old days, before white people, our ancestors used fire to farm the bush to encourage the growth of certain plants and to keep others from overtaking the environment. They could read the land the way Jazzie reads a book. They would also use fire to create patches of grassland. In these cleared spots men would hunt, herding kangaroos and other animals. When the white people arrived, they didn't realise how sophisticated Aboriginal culture was. All they saw were patches of land that they could farm, that looked good for grazing. They didn't bother to ask what the traditional owners knew; they just wanted to replicate the same things they did in England, believing one country should be made the same as another and some people were better than others.

I remembered when Aunty Elaine told me all about it because it made me feel good to hear it. I was taught in school that Aboriginal people were primitive and inferior and stood in the way of progress. My father had a low opinion of Blacks even though my mother was one. They were dirty, they were lazy, they couldn't be trusted, they expected everything for free – these were the sorts of things he used to say. My mother would tell us that we would rise above it but we felt we were wearing something to be humiliated about. Mum Nancy used to say my mother 'acted white', even though in a town like ours everyone knew who you were and where you came from so you never could escape it.

I asked Lionel if the fire came before or after the plagues. He said there was a big plague the year before. But there were waves of plagues throughout the period and during the time of King James and Shakespeare, which came later. And I told him my theory that the fire might have burnt the city to cleanse it of the plague. Back home, I told him, the old people say that fire helps to regenerate.

Lionel looked interested and said he would add what I'd said to his notes. I felt real chuffed about that and looked around to see if the Professor had heard but he was off talking to Celia and Nessa, one on each side, fussing around him like chickens.

'Who's he?' I asked, looking at the marble bust of a figure the others were huddled around. The sign read 'Samuel Pepys', though Lionel said his surname as 'Peeps'. This fellow wrote a diary that was famous because it recorded the fire and things about his daily life.

'He suddenly stopped writing,' Lionel said, 'because his eyesight was starting to fail.'

The Professor, who'd heard Lionel talking to me, said to his captive audience, 'Pepys' eyes served him well for the rest of his life. He ceased his diaries due to a change in his circumstances, his going up in the world.'

I don't know. I didn't like that this Professor Finn was being disloyal, countering what Lionel had to say to make his own self look good. I didn't like it one bit. I wished that Kiki was here. She would have told the Professor to pull his turtle head in, which I thought but didn't say.

I'd intended to write more notes after dinner about what I'd seen and learnt during the day. I was sure that if I didn't write things down I'd forget everything because there was so much to see and so many snippets of facts and figures that I found interesting.

I thanked Lionel for a wonderful and interesting walk and said goodnight to everyone. I had a last smoke standing at the front of the hotel in the warm London twilight, watching all the English people pass by, rushing this way and that, each in their own little world. That's what I don't like about the city; you never pass anyone you know. No-one says hello. Back home, you're surrounded by people you know even if you don't like all of them.

I know smoking is bad for me. I'd love a dollar for everyone who's said, 'Don't you know that will kill you?' Then I'd be rich. I'd stop it if I could but once you get that craving, well, you just go crazy until you get it. I mean, like really crazy. Honestly, when people tell me to quit, I know they don't know what it's like. What it's like is having a sleeping beast inside you and you don't want to wake it up or provoke it by not giving it what it wants. And I suppose I shouldn't but I do like the quiet moments having a smoke sometimes gives me.

The truth is, I'm not used to so much walking around so when I got up to our room I just brushed my teeth and my hair and got into bed. I thought again about what Lionel had said about the plague and the fire. If there's one thing that I've learnt, you can only hope that after the worst thing you could think of happens, you can somehow get out of bed each day, keep going until your life has changed into a different shape.

When Brittany first went missing it was all frantic and hopeful. The longer we waited, the more life slowed down. I wanted time to stop, could barely stand to have more minutes slip away without Brittany back with us.

Aunty Elaine prepared meals I couldn't eat and told me to get some sleep. 'How can I sleep?' I snapped at her. 'How can anyone sleep?'

'Because Leigh-Anne and Jazzie still need their mother,' she said, as though I'd do well to remember it.

It helped in that moment, to think about what I still had, but Brittany going missing was a wave that would soon wash back and drown us all.

As I lay in bed I had a cry for Aunty Elaine, and for Jimmy, and most of all for Brittany when she was waiting for us to find her. And then I fell into one of those deep sleeps where your dreams are so thick you can't remember them when you wake up.

JASMINE

IN THE ANCIENT Chinese story of the Butterfly Lovers, a young woman, Zhu Yingtai, disguises herself as a boy so that she can get an education. At college, she falls in love with a boy, Liang Shanbo. He remains unaware that Zhu is a girl until she's forced to marry a rich man's son. Liang realises his mistake and dies, broken-hearted. When Zhu hears of his death, she takes her own life in despair. The gods take pity on them and unite them as butterflies. Some say this story inspired *Romeo and Juliet*, though Shakespeare certainly didn't give his characters a happy ending – no gods intervened for them. I never enjoyed reading Shakespeare but I liked it when I saw it performed, with the life breathed into it, the way it was intended.

The famous replica of the theatre that Shakespeare's company played in – the Globe – was rebuilt after the original burnt to the ground. In 1613 a cannon was fired during a performance of a play about Henry VIII and it set the thatched roof alight. I'd always thought it was called the Globe because of its round shape but something Lionel said made me realise that the concept of 'the globe' would have excited the imagination during Shakespeare's time. Sir Francis Drake had just navigated Earth, transforming the way people saw it. For the first time, the world – 'the globe' – became traversable, conquerable. It reminded me of the way I once thought the world existed just in my street; by the time I was in high school it had grown to the size of the town. When I left for the city, I lived in a world on campus, then Legal Aid and law courts. Now, travelling here, my world back home seemed so small, parochial.

Bex, Margie, Annie and I found each other at university. During orientation week I'd gone to all the sessions to understand the academic side of things but only one just for socialising. There was an event for Aboriginal students and I got as far as the door before I changed my mind and turned to leave. A girl arrived – long hair in big waves, dressed sleekly in black pants paired with a biker jacket and large framed sunglasses. 'Is it here?' she asked, nodding at the door. Before I'd answered she'd linked my arm with hers. 'Let's go meet some mob,' she said.

She was Bex. Short for Rebecca. Never Becky. 'I'm Jasmine,' I told her. Never Jazzie. She knew Margie already, who had enrolled in business majoring in finance. Margie had met Annie when they'd done a pre-university course. Bex and Margie both grew up in the city – Bex on the north shore, Margie in the southern suburbs. They'd both gone to private schools. Bex still had a group of friends from high school but she'd say of us, 'You're my tribe.' Annie, like me, had moved to the city from the country and gone to a public school. She most understood how dramatic the change was and how much the pressures from home threatened to drag you back. But there was no doubt Bex was our glue. For me, without this little group, I'm not sure I would have got through.

At first, I'd looked enviously at those students whose parents could pay their way – not just for their cars, clothes and all the free time they had, but also for their confidence at fitting in and feeling they belonged. It didn't take long to realise that this jealousy was a futile envy on my part and I soon gravitated to my new friends whose lives were more like mine. I worked as a research assistant for some of my lecturers and took some shifts at one of the university coffee shops, so I was on campus for much of the day. I was often in the library – not just to study for my courses but because it was quiet and if it wasn't sunny enough to be on the lawns, the library always had a nook where I could curl up and read. There I'd discovered the writers I hadn't known in high school – Toni Morrison and Alexis Wright, James Baldwin, Tony Birch, Anita Heiss and Chinua Achebe – and whole new worlds opened up to me.

As the tour made its way through the back lanes of Southwark we passed the Bear Gardens, where bear baiting pits had once flourished alongside theatres, brothels and churches. It was a reminder of how brutal life was not so very long ago, that things we would see as barbaric now were once not only normal but considered entertaining. Along the waterway, we passed a pub – The Anchor – where Samuel Pepys watched as the great fire burned the city. Lionel gave us a small lecture about him. Pepys was a success in his day, becoming a naval administrator and an influential figure with powerful connections. There were no newspapers when Pepys wrote his diaries as a young man – King Charles II's censorship laws were in place – so they are historically significant, providing an account of the cataclysmic 1665 plague and the Great Fire of London the following year. All this made them valuable but what was most remarkable for the time was what Pepys revealed of his own inner thoughts and private life.

Many diarists devote themselves to spiritual life and politics, to travel and sightseeing, to work and contracts, to theatre and other entertainments – writing of their external world and describing their external self. Not Pepys. He also recorded the minutiae of domestic life and its petty occurrences. He wrote of his turbulent relationship with his wife whom he treated cruelly, of his temper tantrums and flirtations with other women, of his anger, indignation and failures. He never self-censured and gave no explanation or justification for his bad deeds. He was confessional in a way that seems natural to us now – with Facebook, Snapchat, selfies, blogging and reality TV – but back in those days, before Freud, before psychoanalysis, before therapy, the idea of self-reflection was as alien as travel to the moon.

As our tour group walked along, I found myself drawn to Sam and Toni since they were the only others on the tour under forty. I've always found small talk awkward so I dawdled around the two of them as we made our way across London Bridge. I managed a few shy smiles and nods until Toni broke the ice and asked if I was enjoying the day and we fell into conversation.

I enjoyed watching Mum engage with her surroundings. I felt I was getting a glimpse of what she could have been like if she was born into, or had grown up in, different circumstances. Or maybe it was just being away from Aunt Kiki, who seemed to always take the lead. One hundred per cent nature; one hundred per cent nurture.

At school there had been taunts that Mum was involved with Brittany's disappearance, playground gossip from children who didn't understand how malicious they were being by repeating the words of the adults around them. I used to imagine sometimes that Aunty Elaine was my mother or that I was an orphan. Thinking of how I felt back then makes me ashamed now, even though I'd been a child and too immature to understand the social pressures I was trying to navigate.

We seemed to lose the packs of roaming tourists as we entered All Hallows by the Tower. Across the road there were queues waiting to see the Crown Jewels but here was a quiet, unassuming church built three hundred years before the tower with an underground crypt that held its own treasure trove, accessed by a tiny opening and a ladder-like stairway. In 1926 they found a portion of an excavated Roman road and remnants of the lives lived there two thousand years earlier.

History passes us and sometimes it just vanishes into the mists only to be rediscovered centuries later, things that you would never have thought could have been forgotten, like the Mayan pyramids. How do you forget they're there? If such big things can be forgotten, it's so easy for much smaller things to be lost.

Coming from a small town, it's hard to believe anything significant can fade from memory. There's a difference between forgetting about something and simply not talking about it, the things that lie just under the surface – those simmering secrets that never seem to fade. While some things turn to dust, others remain long after people can even remember why they're important. It's just one of the mysteries of life, as Aunty Elaine would say.

Aunty Elaine told us how when she was a girl there was one playground at the school for the white children and one for the Blacks. Only the white kids could use the swimming pool; the Blacks had to play in the river. It was only during sports that they would mix – as though that was the great equaliser. She had to go to the very back of the store to buy groceries and her parents weren't allowed to drink in the pub.

Over the years these forms of segregation broke down and were replaced by more subtle lines. Even now there was a delicately crafted 'us' and 'them'. No open hostility – the town would bristle at the word 'racism' – but there was still a sense that there were rules for who got jobs, who got the better houses, who was expected to succeed, who was expected to fail.

I'd have said out loud that I was no longer sensitive to these attitudes, accepting what Aunty Elaine did – that most people were motivated from a place of good even if they didn't have all the facts or couldn't see their own intolerances. And she'd say that with people like that, you work with them to help them through their prejudice. But you can say that, and try to truly believe it, while still carrying the wounds of past words, past snubs – of not being welcomed or considered good enough or capable enough, just because of the colour of your skin, or being judged by who your family is and what house you live in. I left the town for the city determined to leave it all behind but those hurts find a way to travel with you even when you constantly wish them away, no matter what kind of butterfly you turn into.

It was only later on, exhausted after the first demanding day of our tour, that I looked across at Mum as she slept in the bed beside me. I thought of St Dunstan in the East, the old church we saw during our walk that she said she had enjoyed the most. It had been destroyed by a bomb in the war and its ruins, amongst garden beds, were now covered with twisting vines.

DAY 2

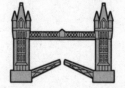

DELLA

I was pleased to see the two sisters from Boston already on the minibus when I got on the next morning. They nodded and said hello.

'I've got my pen and paper,' I told them. They should know that it's not that hard to be prepared.

Professor Finn seemed happy to see them, too, but bristled that they'd taken the front seat since he'd thought he'd claimed it for himself by sitting there yesterday.

Lionel was in his grey suit but with a pink tie today. Back home they'd still have things to say about men wearing pink. It's just that type of place. The way Lionel wore it though, it seemed very handsome, like a movie star. 'Elegant' was the word that came to mind.

'This morning we'll see some of the places that inspired Charles Dickens and discover where he lived and worked,' he announced.

I hadn't read any of his books but I knew the story about Oliver, who wanted more, from the musical. And I'd seen the one about the boy called Pip and the woman who grew old still in her wedding dress, on the telly.

One of the first places we visited was a tunnelled walkway in a street where once there was a rat-infested place – Warren's Blacking

Factory. It was here that a twelve-year-old Charles Dickens was sent to work when his family fell on hard times due to his father's debts.

I thought of a joke – that those colonists really would have wanted a whiting factory; a blacking one would have been their worst nightmare – but there was no-one to tell. Sometimes you just know people won't get where you're coming from.

'What's a blacking factory?' I asked Lionel instead.

'It's where they made boot polish. His job was to stick the labels on bottles.'

Meredith sidled up to me and whispered, 'I'm so glad you asked that. I didn't know either and was too shy to speak up.'

'Well, if you don't ask, you'll stay never knowing and die wondering,' I said, returning her smile. That's something Aunty Elaine used to say. I like it when I repeat her words. It keeps her close to me.

'Imagine how dirty he must have got with the shoe polish. Poor little urchin,' Meredith said.

Dirty. Poor. Aunty Elaine said when she was a girl many white people considered Blacks to be dirty. My father was one of them and my mother made sure we were always tidy – clothes pressed, not a hair out of place, nails clean and trimmed. She'd inspect Kiki and me and if we didn't meet her standards, we'd get a whack on the back of the legs with a hairbrush. There was no arguing with that.

Sometimes people do things we can't understand because we can't see inside their dark hearts. I never could work out why my father married my mother if he disliked Black people so much – dark and lovely featured, quiet and meek, she was obviously Aboriginal, not one of us who could 'pass'. If he'd ever loved her that would be one thing but I never did see any evidence of it. He fancied himself better than not just the Blacks but most of the whites as well. By his measure he had a larger house, more expensive clothes and a shiny new car. He chose to stay in a place he thought he was too good for and stew over his hatred, punishing her and us, too. That's the kind of mean person he was.

Lionel told us how Dickens had felt betrayed by his parents, couldn't understand why they pulled him out of school to work in a factory alongside a bunch of ragtag kids in a job he found demeaning.

I smiled and nodded at Lionel to let him know what he said was helpful even though I couldn't really write down everything. He just spoke too fast and I wrote too slow. I wrote in my notebook: *Charles Dickens – 12 years old. Blacking = shoe polish.*

Lionel went on to say that Dickens' father got out of prison because his grandmother died and left enough money to pay off the debts. Young Dickens thought he'd be able to stop working in the factory but his parents kept him there. His nightmare only ended after his father had a fight with the factory owner. Even then his mother was keen for the misunderstanding to be patched up and for her son to keep pasting labels on bottles. Lucky for him, his father wanted him to return to school but he had to leave once more when his parents got into debt again. By this time, he was fifteen years old and ready to go out into the world on his own. A relative noticed his potential and got him a job as a law clerk.

I guess you could say the smart ones always get out. Like Jazzie. But sometimes life just works against you. Jimmy was good at school, every bit as good as Jazzie, but when we were young, we weren't really encouraged to have dreams. I'd always thought if I could do something, I'd like to work with animals – like be a vet or work in a zoo – though I'd never tell anyone that for fear they'd laugh at me.

Kiki had potential too and there was one teacher who talked about her going to Sydney to study to become a nurse but nothing ever came of that. It's luck as much as smarts and talent where you end up I reckon. That's the tragedy of it all.

I thought about little Charles Dickens, left alone in a factory, abandoned like an orphan. 'Do you ever notice how it's always, in fairy stories, the orphans who turn out to be special? Like Cinderella or Harry Potter?' I asked Lionel as we walked from one place to another.

'That's true. I hadn't thought of that,' Lionel replied in his beautiful accent. 'You could see in Dickens' writing that his experiences as a child affected him profoundly and he was always very concerned about the poor in London, particularly children.' He paused, thoughtful. 'He must have been deeply scarred by it all, as he only talked about working in the Blacking Factory later in his life – and then only briefly. Other than that, he kept that part of his life a secret.'

Dickens seemed to know that what happened to him as a child made him who he was as an adult. That's the truth of it for everyone, I'd guess, for better or for worse. Lionel said that Dickens supported his mother for the rest of his life even though she would have kept him doing menial, soul-sucking work in the factory if she'd had her way. He must have been very forgiving. Not like me. Whatever happened in my house growing up could stay there and rot as far as I was concerned. I never wanted to go back. My parents broke with me when I left there for good. Fairy tales often make us believe that the worst horrors are outside our homes but some truths are just too unspeakable for stories.

We came to an odd dark-wooded hotel, Ye Olde Cheshire Cheese public house. I wrote that down in my notebook because you don't see names like that every day. There was a pub built on the spot in 1538 and when it burnt down in the Great Fire, this one replaced it. My notes from yesterday said *Great Fire – 1666*. See, that's why you write stuff down. Then you can join the dots and see how everything's connected.

Lionel said Charles Dickens would come here and I could see

why if you were writing about orphans and being left at the altar and other sad things. It was gloomy – no windows and light. People must have been very short back then because the roofs were low and the doorways lower and there were stairs winding further and further down. I was almost overcome in the cramped stairway and I lost sight of Jasmine. I found a quiet spot, a little table in the corner where I could catch my breath. Meredith came and sat with me.

'A bit much for us older girls,' she said, and I smiled even though I reckoned she had a good fifteen years on me and I don't like considering myself old. Her husband went to get us both something to drink.

She asked where I was from and I told her. She said she was from Mosman and she chatted about an art exhibition she'd been to see by some Aboriginal artists about a fellow in the early days of the colony who saw the dramatic changes unfold.

'Have you heard about him?' she asked me.

'Jasmine might. She's the one who knows all those things. Can you spell it for me and I'll write it down?'

It was Bungaree. I looked at the name of a person I'd not known before.

'It's like yesterday with the basement in the church,' I told her. 'I didn't go down there but it was all hidden underneath. I was sitting in the pew and thought, there's a Roman road under me. Like, history is sometimes right under our feet.'

After this stop we made our way down some more streets and then we came to the Dickens Museum. Lionel said that Dickens, his wife, his sister-in-law and first child moved into this house. Two more kids came along while they were here. Lionel said that this house would have suited a man whose fortunes were on the rise and after two and a half years, they moved to somewhere bigger and had more children.

'It would have been so cramped,' exclaimed Celia.

'Living on top of one another,' said Nessa.

'I thought he was rich,' her sister replied.

'Seems not,' sniffed Nessa.

Well I had to laugh at that. Once I moved to the Frog Hollow part of town and into Mum Nancy's house with Jimmy, everyone was on top of one another – Jimmy's two sisters, a cousin and his wife and Jimmy's grandmother. At least we had a flushing toilet and a washing machine. It was just how it was then when you didn't have a lot of money but there were lots of people in your family. Imagine what my parents must have thought when I ended up there, sixteen and pregnant, with all the other Black families. I'll be honest, the thought of their reaction gives me a little smile.

Of course, all this was used against us when we lost Brittany. They made out that living the way we did was like a form of child abuse or neglect even though we loved all our girls and never hit or hurt them. The way we lived, everyone looked after everyone else. And here's the thing – I'd lived in a large house with my parents growing up, not only did we all have our own room, there were even spare ones though no-one ever came to visit us – not once did anyone care what happened there.

The largest room in the museum was the study where Dickens would write. In one of the glass cabinets, there was a portrait of a woman with large eyes and bow-like lips. There was another drawing of the same face, in a bonnet and with ringlets, but with the thickness of age erasing the pretty features and replacing them with more solid ones. Age. I asked Lionel who it was and he said that it was Catherine, Mrs Dickens. There was a gold ring beside the pictures with blue stones in it. *Turquoise*, the little card beside it explained.

She'd been the daughter of the editor of a paper Dickens worked for, was described as 'sweet natured and kind' and Dickens wrote many letters to her. But when he left her in later life, long after he was famous, most of his children and his sister-in-law stayed with him, leaving Catherine almost on her own. She was heartbroken and moved to a separate house but stayed loyal to Dickens the rest of her life. His letters were amongst her most treasured possessions until one afternoon, in her final years, she gave them to one of her daughters so they could be given to a museum 'so that the world may know he loved me once'. And I felt for her, loving a man who she could no longer be with.

I'm sure all of that leaving-your-wife business was scandalous once upon a time but not if you live in a town like ours where the plumber's wife ran off and left overnight with the young man from the bakery, leaving the plumber to raise his four children alone. Or there's Belinda at the craft store whose husband left her for her sister and they are now living one town away. Even Kiki's husband now was the cousin of her first one, who left her when he got one of the teachers at the school pregnant after telling Kiki for years that he didn't want any children.

In the back garden, there was a little stone bench and although it was cold and hard to sit on, I had another rest. I thought about what Lionel said about Mrs Dickens and her loyalty to her husband. It reminded me of Jimmy and the way we were, even though we weren't ones for letters. Some things link two people forever no matter what happens.

After the Dickens Museum, we walked four blocks and across a large green lawn and came to a big red-brick building, The Foundling Museum. I'd never heard of a foundling before, but Lionel explained that it was a name for an abandoned child and that once upon a time this was a place that took in unwanted children.

Lionel said the Foundling Hospital had been set up in 1741 by a Captain Thomas Coram, a small feisty man with a big personality. Like Dickens, but a century before, he would walk through London and every day would come across the bodies of dead and dying babies who'd been 'dropped' onto the streets by their parents and left to die. Mothers who killed their children were executed but just leaving a child on the pavement – 'dropping' – was not a crime so that's what lots of people did. Can you imagine such a cruel thing?

When it first opened, Lionel told us, so many people brought their children to the hospital they had to set up a lottery system to deal with them all. Each desperate mother reached into a cloth bag and pulled out a coloured ball. Black meant she and her baby had to leave; white meant the baby was accepted provided it passed a health examination; red meant the baby was put on a waiting list. During the first five years of the lottery system, 2500 mothers drew a ball from the bag and 763 of them left their babies at the hospital. It would have been as awful for the ones who had to part with their children as it was for the ones who could not afford to provide for those they had to keep.

As Lionel told it, later the government agreed to help, but required that all infants brought to the hospital be admitted. Mothers could then ring a bell and a porter would come and take their baby. On the first night 117 babies were left there; by the end of the month, 425 new babies had arrived. During the four years of the open admission policy it received fifteen thousand babies. That's a lot of unwanted little ones. Even though a few mothers tried to reclaim their children, most were denied by the governors who felt that they could do a better job of raising children. And that sounded like all those people who thought they could do a better job at bringing up Aboriginal children than their own parents.

All these ways of punishing people who were poor. All those children told they weren't wanted. It seemed to me that many of those children probably were wanted and loved but their parents couldn't afford to keep them. That's a big difference. And sometimes, like I know, you can love them and want to keep them and they're just taken from you.

Each mother was required to leave a 'token' in the event that she wanted to one day reclaim her child. Some of those trinkets were displayed under a glass case in the museum. There was a silk purse, a tiny fish carved of ivory, buttons, lockets, coins and ribbons. All these things to give a child you can't keep. I thought of the rainbow jumper and pink unicorn that Brittany used to love.

'Gosh, what a thing,' Meredith said, who'd been standing next to me. 'We might complain about all those single mothers rorting the system but it's better than all this.'

I nodded, but it was the first time I found myself included in the 'we' who might complain rather than the 'those' who are being complained about. I didn't know what to say about that. I'd been a single mother and lived in the Aboriginal Housing with my pension and part-time job at the school canteen. Sure, Jimmy lived a few houses away but not with us. That all just gets too confusing for other people so I kept it to myself.

Lionel said it was time for lunch but I wanted to sit outside. I wasn't hungry, not after that all-you-can-eat buffet breakfast we'd eaten in the morning. I encouraged Jazzie to join the others so I could be with my thoughts, plus I needed a smoke. I could see the cafe they were going to from the bench in the park where I wanted to sit. I reassured her that I knew where they were. 'I'll catch you up,' I told her.

To be honest, I could have easily packed it up then and there, headed back to the hotel and spent the afternoon in the bar. Who would have thought that being so far away from home would bring up so many bad memories?

Luckily, I still had two small bottles of vodka from the plane in my handbag. They were just nips but they did the trick. The clear liquid shot through me. I sat back and watched an elderly couple walking through the park, two teenaged girls basking in the sun and a group of children playing with a soccer ball watched over by a woman who seemed to be paying more attention to her mobile phone.

Despite Kiki getting angry with the police who were supposed to be looking for Brittany, we learnt later that they weren't homicide detectives, those ones that first came to interview me, but were from the child welfare branch. They were thinking of taking my other two girls. Not only had they thought that Jimmy and me were somehow involved with what happened to our missing daughter, they were looking to see whether we were able to look after Leigh-Anne and Jazzie, too.

Aunty Elaine, Mum Nancy and Kiki gave the wrath of God to those nosy social workers with their forms and checklists. They threatened to go to the papers and the radio and say the government was taking children off the parents of a missing child and how would that look? Aunty Elaine told them that back when she was growing up, welfare would take Aboriginal kids whenever they liked, no questions asked, but all of that had to stop now.

The worst thing in the whole horrible ordeal, apart from actually losing Brittany because that was the worst part of all, was that people thought that I could have done something to harm her. What can be more shocking than a mother hurting her own child? Than beating them with a hairbrush, or standing silent while someone else beats them with a belt, or always having a headache so she can't see what's happening in her own house, or doesn't care? That was my mother and I was nothing like her but before I could think any more about all of that, Jazzie came to join me.

'You missed a feisty lunch,' she said, handing me a chicken sandwich. She's thoughtful like that, my Jazzie, and in those moments she reminds me of Aunty Elaine, seeing the things people need that no-one else notices. 'Are you okay to go on?'

'I've had my little rest now,' I said.

'Well, think of how much weight we're going to lose,' she replied.

'They should take those overweight people on the telly who are trying to get skinny out on a day like this,' I added.

'They could call it *Fat and Fiction*.' Jazzie laughed and I love how her face changes from when she is more serious. With a pang I realised how little I'd seen her really laugh.

We walked to a big library and I wasn't much keen on seeing books so I said I'd wait in the courtyard out the front and eat my lunch. I had another cigarette and put the sandwich in a bin. I thought of Jimmy and how he'd close his eyes when he sang a song or how he'd always come over and fix things for me. If I got someone else to do it, he'd get a bit hurt and would always complain about the job they did, finding some fault to prove they hadn't done it properly and how the way he would have done it would have been much better.

I decided I'd go in and I asked a friendly looking older woman at the information desk if I could see the letters that Mrs Dickens had given over.

'Mrs Charles Dickens?' she asked.

'That one. The ones she sent over so everyone knew that he loved her.'

She looked on her computer. 'You'll have to make a request for them as they're not on display. But, you can go online and find them. Would you like me to show you?'

'That's alright,' I told her. 'I'll get my daughter to show me. She's good with computers and all that.'

She gave me a pamphlet and I thanked her, then I went back outside to enjoy the sun until Jazzie and the others came out.

The next part of the walk was through some quiet, neat squares where some writers used to live. This London, with its clean streets and white buildings, seemed totally different from the one Lionel had described in the morning – full of slums and pollution. It's always different for rich and poor – even back home, the side of town where I grew up and where I ended up were like chalk and cheese, and it wouldn't take you more than an hour to walk from one end of town to the other.

Lionel talked about this person and that, but this time I didn't take any notes. I was just happy to be in the sunshine and listening to Jasmine. She was chatty as all get-up as we walked around looking at this door and that house. I sometimes felt like she was a strange creature who I didn't understand even though I'd made her, but at that moment in the sunny squares it felt so easy to float along with her and to see the world as she sees it.

Leigh-Anne is so like me and although we fight – and boy do we have some fights – I always know how to talk to her. The truth is, it's harder with a child smart the way Jazzie is. I've never been a reader and I didn't finish high school so it's difficult to know what Jasmine needs from me. She's always got so much going on in her head and is a real thinker, whereas I'm all gut reaction and find it hard to say what I mean. Jimmy was book smart at school but that didn't lead anywhere for him as life had different things in store and our town had views about what Blacks could and couldn't do when we were young, though that's all changed a lot now. I guess I always felt that Leigh-Anne was more like me, and Jazzie more like Jimmy. And Brittany, well, she sort of hangs, trapped in the air, hard to define but linking us all together. It was enough on this afternoon to be close to my quiet girl, my little mouse. I squeezed her arm affectionately and she looked at me with surprise.

'Is everything okay?' she asked.

'Yes, my girl,' I replied, but I felt a little wounded that my show of affection was treated suspiciously.

What I wanted to say to her was that she was like a miracle to me when she was born, like seeing an angel or a fairy appear. You're fascinated by their specialness. You want to touch them, to hold them, to show them you love them but you're afraid you'll crush them. You don't know what to say, whether they even speak the same language. But that doesn't mean you don't love them. Because you do, with all of your heart. But of course, I didn't say any of that. We don't have that kind of relationship where you can say what you really feel. Just realising that made me sad, like it was one more thing I'd failed at.

Finally, we came to the last stop on our walk. The British Museum. Jasmine told me that they had the remains of Aboriginal people there – that white people in the early days of the colony had taken bones and skulls from Australia back home to England to study. Imagine those poor people, not buried and put to rest, treated like a bug in a glass. It makes me suspicious, all this studying of us. Seems to me from what I've seen they only do that to make us out to be inferior. My father had books in our house – not that I ever saw him read one – that he said were written by experts who had all those theories about our head sizes and our natural tendencies and they all sounded like hooey to me but there was no point in saying anything. That sort of talking back would have only got me into trouble.

'There was a great warrior, Pemulwuy, who led a resistance in the Sydney basin when the colony was being established,' Jasmine told me. 'When the colonists eventually shot him, they brought his head back here.'

'I think I know about that one,' I said, as I looked into my notebook.

Bungaree, it said. Jasmine looked at it. 'No, that's a different person,' she said.

'How many of them were there?' I asked.

'Lots. There were over five hundred Aboriginal tribes across a really large continent.'

'Well can't we bring this one home? To his own country? It's not right he's sitting over here as a specimen.'

'People have been trying to do that, Mum. The Brits deny that they have him now. They say things were moved during the war and his remains have been lost. Kind of convenient.'

I liked this side of her. Fiery and connecting to our culture and more than any other time I could see Aunty Elaine in her. And I liked knowing there were lots of warriors and more to learn about it all.

As we walked into the imposing white building there was a big glass bowl with money in it and a sign asking for donations.

'We already gave,' I said to the guard who was standing next to it.

He smiled and nodded at me.

Jasmine wanted to see the Greek things and said we were going to see some marbles. I thought they'd be like round stones that children used to play with but it turned out they were part of a big building on the top of a hill in Greece.

There was a lot of stuff in that museum that the British had taken – large statues, urns and gold necklaces and there was even a whole temple. And I thought, you've got to be pretty cheeky to take a whole temple. It's not like you can just shove that up your shirt or slip it into your handbag. No wonder they never thought twice about our poor warrior's head.

I went to the gift shop while Jazzie finished looking around. There was a boy there, around nine like Zane, with a football jumper on. He was begging his father for a model of the solar system that you stick on the roof and all the planets spin around it by remote control. I don't know if Zane likes the solar system but I thought since this boy, who looked about the same age and also liked football, thought it was worth having, maybe Zane would like it, too. For Teaghan and Tamara I found pink backpacks that were filled with things about fairies, including wings you could put on your dress. They like pink – and who doesn't like fairies?

The rest of the day was 'at leisure' and I told Jasmine that I'd like mine back at the hotel. Between the walking and the foundlings, I was ready for a drink.

Later on, as I was getting into bed, Jasmine was watching telly and a newsflash came on. A five-year-old girl had disappeared from a place called Hampstead Heath. Police were looking for her and asking the public if they'd seen her. Shona Lindsay was her name. They had a photo of her – blonde wispy hair and big blue eyes. Maybe it was the knitted cardigan that reminded me of Brittany. I felt that all too familiar panicked feeling in my guts.

I wrote one more thing in my journal. *Shona Lindsay*. As I fell asleep I thought of the blue heart pyjamas Brittany was wearing when she went missing, the pink hairclip she loved putting in her hair and the way she would carry that unicorn with her wherever she went. When I realised she had left her unicorn behind, I knew right then – right through my bones – that something was very wrong.

JASMINE

WE'D ONLY BEEN in London two days and the small hotel room was a mess. All my clothes were hung up or still packed neatly in my bag. Mum had tossed hers all over the place, her personal items scattered throughout the bathroom and across the tiny desk. She never was a housekeeper, her home always strewn with toys when we were younger, Leigh-Anne's make-up when we were older (there was no room for it all in the bathroom), and always baskets of unfolded washing and things bought in bulk because they were cheaper. None of this was helped by three people living in a small two-bedroom house, four if you count my cousin Kylie who was there more times than not.

Aunty Elaine's house was full of sentimental knick-knacks, porcelain figures of angels and saints, pictures of our family and little inspirational messages – *Be the change you want to see* – but it was always clean, not a spot of dust or a cobweb anywhere. In my tiny one-bedroom apartment, I like everything spotless – white walls, few decorations, no clutter, no food left out, no dust. One thing about my childhood I refused to take with me was the mess and I suppressed my irritation at Mum who'd brought it all back to me.

Mum changed clothes three times that morning – should she wear pants or a skirt? A dress? This cardigan? That jacket? Her rejected items were strewn across the bed. I knew there was no use getting annoyed about it because she's always been oblivious to how irritating her indecision is but I could feel my agitation rising. I took a deep breath and counted – *one, two, three* – in my head.

That I finally got her downstairs to breakfast with enough time for her to make three trips back to the buffet – 'trying to get our money's worth' she said, 'waste not, want not' – was the first miracle of the morning; getting her onto the minibus was the second.

We started our tour at Rudyard Kipling's house and by the time we'd reached the site of the factory where Charles Dickens had worked as a child, I'd calmed down and lost my prickles.

Of all Dickens' books, *David Copperfield* was the most autobiographical. Dickens, like Copperfield, had the experience of a fairly happy, easy-going early childhood. He'd been raised to believe that the lower classes didn't deserve any better so he was horrified to have to do manual labour next to working-class boys, to find himself one of them.

Copperfield goes to stay with the family of Wilkins Micawber, a gregarious man who lives well beyond his means. In the end, Micawber overcomes all obstacles and shows those who doubted him that he'd been underestimated. He uses his charms – his gift for talking, his grand ambitions, his excitement at the world around him – to his advantage when he starts a new life in Australia. Being so close a portrait of his own father, perhaps Dickens couldn't resist giving Micawber a noble, victorious role in the story, making more of him in fiction than his father made of himself in real life.

It's the best kind of fantasy, the most irresistible – to create a world, one that other people visit, that is shaped the way you want it to be. Don't we all have an imaginary place we escape off to as we fall asleep or drift off into daydream, a place where life is better, people are kinder and we are a better version of ourselves? In mine, Aunty Elaine is still alive, so is Dad, and Brittany never went missing.

At the time Dickens worked in the factory, one-quarter of the British workforce were children. From as young as five, they toiled twelve to sixteen hours a day, six days a week. In the mines, they had to wriggle into narrow shafts deep underground. In the mills, they had to crawl under machinery to retrieve bobbins or other items that were dropped. In match factories, they spent long days dipping tiny sticks into phosphorus, the chemicals causing teeth to rot and ruining lungs. There were no laws or other protections from exploitation, no assistance if injury or illness occurred. There was no time to play and no opportunity to learn, so no chance to climb out of poverty through a better education.

We walked through the grassy and leafy Inns of Court where Dickens observed a legal and penal system that offered little redress to those who found life already so stacked against them. We walked through the streets where he would have seen the taverns and gin palaces where people drank themselves into early graves, where he saw the victims of violence and those who died of starvation or disease, the thin children, undernourished and neglected.

When he became a journalist, Dickens wrote about the underbelly of the city, about prisons and public hangings, about old people with broken spirits and ragged children pleading for a penny. He attacked the Poor Laws that established the brutal, impersonal workhouse regime where the destitute lived in misery, in which families were often separated.

At the Dickens Museum I stood in front of the desk where Dickens sat and penned his thoughts on all he saw in the streets we'd just walked. It would have been so easy for Dickens to conclude that the problems he saw were so entrenched, so overwhelming, that he could do nothing to change them. Or he could have tried to tell himself that the circumstances in which the poor found themselves were their own fault – if they wanted things to change, they had to help themselves. But instead, through his writing, he found a way to facilitate profound social change.

He started to sketch a story, one so compelling that people would read it, would not be able to look away. Through the adventures of a young orphan caught in the system – and by the people debased by it – Dickens made his most eloquent argument against the laws he so despised. In *Oliver Twist*, he persuaded his readers more with a fictional character than the real poor people they passed every day in the streets could.

Dickens knew what it was like to have someone else controlling your life, to be impoverished, miserable and hungry, to have your dreams and aspirations thwarted. He came to understand that you had to accept that good and bad are *'inextricably linked in remembrance'*, that you cannot choose *'the enjoyment of recollecting only the good. To have all the best of it you must remember the worst also.'*

I caught up to Mum as she peered over the sketches under a glass-topped cabinet. I thought about how mad she made me that morning with her usual carry-on, but how when I glimpse the sides of her I barely know, this curious person looking into someone else's life, I feel the possibility that there's still a way she might get me.

'What's caught your eye, Mum?'

'Look how she's aged,' she said. 'It still looks like her though.'

While Mum continued to look at the portraits of Catherine Dickens, I wandered off to look in other rooms. I thought of Dora in *David Copperfield*, the pretty, kind-hearted girl Copperfield marries who doesn't prove to be his intellectual equal. He struggles in the marriage and eventually Dora dies, neatly packed away to make room for Agnes, the real love of his life. It seemed another case of writing what you wished for. Whatever the magic formula to a happy domestic life, Dickens, with all his insights into the human character and condition, had trouble finding it.

My parents had an odd relationship where they were devoted to each other in their own way, never were with anyone else, yet couldn't be together. Instead, they held a strange, stubborn vigil for each other. I never saw them fight, never heard either one say a bad word about the other. They were soul mates who couldn't quite complete the circle to make a whole. If Dad got angry or frustrated with Mum, he'd just withdraw back to his house until his mood passed. When he did lose his temper, it was usually with his sisters when they tried to badmouth Mum. It's family legend now, the day Dad was fixing Mum's sink and through the open kitchen window overheard my cousin Kylie, my Aunt Jenny's daughter, telling me that her mother had said mine had left the door open to a murderer. I remember Dad yelling out through the window, telling Kylie to get the hell out of our yard.

'But I didn't say it,' she pleaded in her own defence.

'You repeating it is you saying it,' he'd thundered. 'Now get out of here and don't come back.'

'But this isn't your home,' she'd countered meekly.

As Dad moved from the window towards the back door, Kylie decided to cut her losses and leave before he reached her, only managing a slow jog with her substantial frame. She did come back to our house but for a very long time stayed out of Dad's way, leaving through the back door as he was coming in through the front.

When I finally reached the gift shop I could see Mum out of the window, sitting on a stone bench in the small backyard. I couldn't decipher if the look on her face was one of boredom or peace. The glass in the window was thick and distorted her image, removing all nuance, making it impossible to read her.

I had a heightened anxiety about Mum as we approached the Foundling Museum. It was dark, grim and sobering, just as you'd expect of a monument to mothers who'd given their babies up and to the children abandoned there, the kind of place that could remind her of Brittany. I hovered nearby but Meredith seemed to keep engaging her in conversation and I couldn't help smiling at the idea of my mother and a North Shore housewife hitting it off.

It was clear that the people who ran the Foundling Museum thought that poverty made people bad parents and that children in those circumstances were better off here than with their families. But when choices are limited, what does consent really mean? And what limits choice more than poverty?

I'd done an assignment at university about the government practice of removing Aboriginal children from their families. I'd focused on a legal case where people who had been removed under the policy as children sought redress for what had happened to them. There was a document that purported to show that one of the mothers had given her consent to have her child removed. There was an 'x' where the signature was to go. The mother claimed she didn't know what she was agreeing to. Historians gave evidence about the circumstances in which Aboriginal people lived at the time and how little they could challenge or question government officials who had so much power over them. What sort of consent could be given in that context? But the court looked at the cross on the page, the two strokes, and read the marks as proof of a 'yes'. Nothing outside of that piece of paper mattered to them. Aboriginal children could be taken and the fact that none of the things the state promised them when they took them – to keep them safe, educate them, give them a better life – ever happened was of no consequence, even though it very much mattered to those children who endured it. All that mattered, the court decided, was the cross on the page.

Others argued that if the children had stayed, they would have been worse off, neglected or abused. The removal was 'for their own good'. You can only speculate about what might have been. What you do know is where children were put 'for their own good' and how they're treated there is what you are responsible for, and you can't rely on a fictitious 'might-have-been' to lessen that responsibility. Abuse happened so often in most places where children were – church-based orphanages, reform schools, boarding schools – paedophiles will always go to the places where they can access vulnerable children. So why go to such effort to discredit the children who suffered? It just seemed mean-spirited, cruel.

In this place, as I was worried about my mother's thoughts straying towards Brittany, mine turned towards Fiona McCoy. Her time in State care, from the age of two, had been plagued with a series of foster homes where the neglect or abuse in one led to increasing behavioural problems in the next, all culminating in a deeply troubled young woman whose own violent acts had now caused deep grief and left her labelled a monster.

And not far away from these thoughts about Fiona is knowing that once there was a possibility that this could have been me. After Brittany's trial, I had overheard Aunty Elaine talking with Aunt Kiki about how the welfare had been around, seeing whether there was any evidence that Leigh-Anne and I were in danger. My 'home' was between four places – Aunty Elaine's, Dad's, Mum's and Aunt Kiki's. To an outsider it might have looked like I was running wild but everyone around me knew where I was.

When I was young, I'd often imagined that I was adopted, that my real family was educated, worldly. But with what I know now, I was lucky to have stayed where I was, where there was no doubt I was loved, with Aunt Kiki watchful in the background and with Aunty Elaine to really look after me. If Fiona had been given these simple things, how different would her life be now?

As we took a break for lunch, Mum wanted to stay in the park. I didn't want to leave my new friends and get caught next to the Professor or the Boston sisters so I wrote our hotel address on a page from my notebook in case she walked off and got lost. She wouldn't learn to use a mobile phone. I bought her one and she never turned it on.

I joined the others at the cafe across the street and nabbed the seat next to Toni.

'So, how did you two meet?' I asked.

'Sam did her PhD on androgyny in Virginia Woolf's writing. I'd written an article about how her concept of stream of consciousness writing had influenced me as a poet. It was published in a small literary journal. I was surprised that anyone saw it. But Sam did and she contacted me on Facebook.'

'So, it was a kind of romance via literature,' I observed.

'Sort of. Turns out she really just liked my picture,' Toni said, giving Sam an affectionate squeeze, 'and she wasn't averse to a little bit of cougaring.'

'You must be looking forward to this afternoon,' I said to her. 'So much Virginia Woolf ahead of us.'

'Oh, the mad genius,' Professor Finn interrupted, overhearing me. 'I've often wondered why anyone would read Virginia Woolf unless they were being punished. I tried once and it rambled on and on like a hippie on hallucinogen mushrooms.' He was now directing his comments to the Boston sisters, no doubt intuiting that he'd found his natural audience. 'It seems to me that it's a certain type of snob who says you can only write with £500 and a room of your own.'

'Her point was,' said Sam, with a bite in her voice, 'that she didn't have time to write seriously until she received a stipend from her aunt and had a quiet place to write. She saw what a difference it made to her.'

Toni put her hand into Sam's under the table for support.

'Well, lucky for her that she had an aunt with that kind of money,' he retorted.

'I wonder how many of his wonderful books Mr Dickens would have written if he'd never got out of the Blacking Factory?' Meredith said to no-one in particular.

We had been together for just two days and had already divided into tribes, into an 'us' and 'them'.

To break the tension, Lionel cleared his throat and told us about the afternoon walk ahead of us, ignoring the glowering between Sam and Professor Finn.

'Bloomsbury was once an ancient village surrounded by lush fields. In the seventeenth century, large residences started to appear in the area with both the British Museum and University of London being founded at that time,' Lionel read from his notes. 'The area soon became extremely popular with the wealthy and it was well known for its public gardens, including Bedford Square, which is the only intact Georgian garden that still exists today.'

'So basically, once it was fields, and then some things were built, and then some more things were built,' Professor Finn mocked, stifling a yawn.

'Do you know in what year the British Museum was built, Professor?' asked Celia.

'Yes,' added Nessa. 'Or the university, since it was the same time?'

Lionel rummaged through his notes. Professor Finn took a sip of his wine.

'Why don't you google it?' suggested Toni, and within a flash her thumbs were dancing across her phone. 'It says that the British Museum was established in 1753, largely based on the collections of the physician and scientist Sir Hans Sloane. The museum first opened to the public on 15 January 1759.'

Any sense of triumph Toni felt over Professor Finn seemed to be quickly extinguished by the dejected look on Lionel's face.

Luckily for everyone, the food arrived.

Mum was sitting in the park exactly where I'd left her. It took me a moment but I could smell that familiar scent on her, that vinegary, acrid smell that meant she had consumed alcohol. I looked around and all I could see were a few pigeons picking in the grass. Over the years, you stop wondering how an addict manages to get their fix.

I asked her if she wanted to go back to the hotel but she seemed happy to stay on the tour. I walked beside her on the way to The British Library, keeping her in conversation so the others wouldn't realise she'd been drinking.

'Is your mother alright?' Lionel asked, as we arrived at the expansive red-brick building. Mum had wanted to sit outside and eat her sandwich and I thought the food would do her some good, so I told her to sit tight and that I wouldn't be long.

'She's just feeling a little tired from the walk,' I replied, used to covering for her.

Lionel looked over in her direction, seemingly worried.

'She'll be fine,' I reassured him quickly, annoyed that I looked like the bad daughter. 'I just want to see the Magna Carta and the illuminated manuscripts and I'll get right back to her.'

Once upon a time, a book was a work of art. Manuscripts were drawn and illustrated by hand; texts were sacred, rare and expensive. Then along came the Gutenberg's printing press and looking down at its first pressing, a copy of the Bible, it was hard to quantify how much that invention changed the world. Reading was suddenly democratised, no longer something that was just a sign of wealth, a privilege of the elite. Stories became something you could hold in your hand and carry with you, read on your travels or curl up in bed with. Even a young girl in a small country town, surrounded by chaos, could find refuge in them. They could ensure oral histories were recorded, that folklore and epic poems were kept and treasured. A feeling of gratitude swept over me as I walked among the cabinets that displayed rare copies of *Beowulf*, *The Canterbury Tales*, *Le Morte d'Arthur*.

I entered a side room dedicated to the Magna Carta. In mediaeval language in mediaeval script, it looked plain after the colour and artistry of the illuminated works. Intended only to apply to aristocrats, not the poor, women or the people in the parts of the world left to be colonised, eventually the ideas – life, liberty and protection of property, security – would trickle down, become universal, allowing us all to think differently about the protections we're entitled to now. If Dickens reminded us that the system is not fair, here was the hope, the ancient promise, that it might be. Aunty Elaine's generation had advocated for changes that made opportunities in my life different from those for Mum and Dad. It's not just the words on the page but the people who push the ideas at the heart of them who really alter the world.

Mum was sitting in the sun when I rejoined her. Her head was tilted back to feel the rays on her face, her eyes closed. She looked serene, protected from the breeze by the walls of the courtyard, the air around her warm and still.

'How are you going?' I asked, taking a seat beside her.

She handed me a pamphlet that explained how to search the online library catalogue. 'You can show me how to do that later,' she said. She took the pamphlet out of my hands and tucked it carefully into her notebook for safekeeping, as though I'd lose it, even though I knew like everything else she started, she'd most likely never look at it again.

When the tour resumed, we walked to Tavistock Square and stood outside of the building where, in 1924, Virginia Woolf and her husband, Leonard, had moved the offices of Hogarth Press after starting it as a hobby in 1917. Along with their own books, they published works by Sigmund Freud, Katherine Mansfield, Gertrude Stein, Vita Sackville-West, T.S. Eliot, E.M. Forster and Maxim Gorky. *A Room with a View*, *Howards End*, *Orlando* and *Mrs Dalloway* were all old friends to me but I knew the significance would be lost on Mum, the tour for her more about visiting new places than familiar references and embraced ideas.

'So, Mum, Virginia Woolf was a famous writer and her sister Vanessa was a well-known painter and interior designer. They had a large circle of friends who were also famous writers and painters and, because they lived and met here, they became known as the Bloomsbury Group. They were smart, had strong views about what artistic and intellectual freedom meant, and they challenged the strict Victorian social rules of the previous generation.'

'Sounds like they were just rebelling against their parents?' Mum said, causing me to smile.

'I suppose they were.'

We walked past a corner where a plaque noted another former residence of Dickens and came to 46 Gordon Square. Mum gave the appearance of listening to Lionel's short talk, though knowing her as I do, I could tell her thoughts were floating elsewhere.

'It was here,' Lionel began, 'after the death of their father in 1904, Vanessa, Virginia and their two brothers, Thoby and Adrian, resided. After their mother died in 1895, their step-sister Stella took over the running of the house. When she died in 1897, the role fell to Vanessa, then just eighteen. Her father was a difficult man who had violent displays of temper and no-one could blame her for feeling a sense of liberation upon his death. Virginia herself admitted later that if her father hadn't died, she wouldn't have been able to become a writer. The siblings began their 'at homes', inviting Thoby's friends from Cambridge, including Lytton Strachey, Leonard Woolf, Duncan Grant, Saxon Sydney-Turner, Clive Bell and John Maynard

Keynes. They'd talk about how they should live and what philosophy could be found to support and justify the good life.'

To escape the small world of my home town, I'd read the novels of E.M. Forster and Virginia Woolf and read about the lives of the Bloomsbury Group. I imagined an intellectual life of soirees with people who felt like me, where I was part of a like-minded group. I dreamed of a sister who was warm and shared my ideas and ideals, who was a friend and confidante, a Vanessa to my Virginia. I bought Leigh-Anne some paints one Christmas in the naïve hope she'd find a creative side and we'd form a greater connection. But she sniffed when she saw them, tossed them in a cupboard and they weren't seen again until Kylie eventually claimed them.

We crossed Russell Square and the corner of the block where the publishers Faber & Faber had their offices, and where T.S. Eliot worked for forty years. We then passed the imposing monolith of London University's Senate House that housed the Ministry of Information during World War II. Evelyn Waugh and George Orwell both worked there and there can be no doubt that the latter based his Ministry of Truth in *1984* on the building.

'You'll like the British Museum,' I tried to assure Mum, aware this part of the day may have seemed tedious to her. I told her about a connection to home – the Aboriginal remains that were rumoured to still be there. She'd not heard of Pemulwuy and her curiosity about this man who'd led the resistance to the first colony surprised me. As did the name written in her notebook – *Bungaree* – another figure who'd had to navigate the cataclysmic changes after the First Fleet of convicts and their overseers sailed through the heads of Sydney Harbour in 1788; he later sailed around Australia with the navigator Matthew Flinders.

Aunt Elaine had often told me stories from our culture but I'd never known Mum to be interested in those sorts of things before.

Was it that I didn't know her or just that away from home she could be so different?

Inside the white marble of the British Museum, it was easy to be in awe of the antiquities, a sign of the dominating power as the British spread their Empire and collected colonies.

Leaving Mum in the gift shop, I entered the large white-walled space that had once been the famous Reading Room. It was here Virginia Woolf had come to research her lectures that would become her essay, *A Room of One's Own*. She sat amongst the tomes penned by men and pondered what they'd written about women and why women hadn't written more about themselves.

When men did write about women, they did so '*in the red light of emotion rather than the white light of truth*'. Men had power, money and influence; women often had few options but marriage. So, why were men so concerned about the weaknesses of women? Woolf concluded that men were emphatic about the inferiority of women because they were really concerned about protecting their own superiority. Take away the looking glass, she wrote, and '*man may die, like the drug fiend deprived of his cocaine*'.

While Virginia Woolf spoke for most women of her time, and many before and after, these realisations turned into a profound personal liberation for her. By rejecting what men had written about women and embracing the fact that women can write as well as men if given the chance – even if they write about things that men might not value – she was encouraged to explore new, unconventional and innovative ways of novel writing and took radical literary risks. The results were novels like *Orlando*, *To the Lighthouse* and *Mrs Dalloway*.

She showed that if you deconstructed the power structures, understood where bias and prejudice hid, the very articulation gives you the freedom and the power to create a new way of thinking, a new way of going forward. She proved to me that once you understand the 'why', you can start changing the world around you.

As we drove back to the hotel, I checked Bex's social media and 'liked' all her posts, looked at what Annie and Margie were up to and then scrolled through Leigh-Anne's feed. Her and the kids were sitting around the table eating takeaway fried chicken: '*When you can't be bothered cooking…*'. I looked at the family photo, my family, and I felt the chasm between our lives and how different we were. I 'liked' the post, just so she'd know I'd been there.

I was pleased to see the notebook and pen by Mum's bedside table as she settled down for the night. Despite her surreptitious drink at lunchtime, there were moments in the day when I'd felt closer to her than I had for a long time – the walk through Bloomsbury, our talk about Aboriginal warriors, her note-taking. They felt like strands that we could tie together, that could be bound into something tangible.

Then a banner passed across the TV screen catching both her eye and mine. *News Flash: Four-year-old girl abducted from Hampstead Heath. Police looking for white van.*

I looked across at Mum as an image of Shona Lindsay, a cherub-faced girl with blonde hair in a ponytail, filled the screen.

'She's a cutie,' Mum said, but I could see her mood change, could tell where her thoughts were going and Brittany was back between us.

DAY 3

DELLA

THIS MORNING WE set out to visit the country. It was an effort to get everything in our room packed and I had to keep calming Jazzie down as she's a worry wart. But we got to the minibus on time, just as I knew we would.

I enjoyed driving out of London through what seemed like endless suburbs. The house types were different to what we have at home, more cottage-like, as if they're used to squeezing more people into smaller spaces. And their bricks are different from ours, too, darker brown in some places and different reds. I guess that's because their soil is different from ours so the colour of the bricks reminds you that you're on someone else's country.

As the city fell away, we drove along highways surrounded by fields, then those gave way to roads lined with deep-green leafy trees that formed thick coverings overhead. When you drive between our town and Leigh-Anne's there are trees everywhere but they're silvery, not a lush emerald green like the ones here.

All up, the drive didn't take too long and Lionel gave us a talk about the place we were about to visit because it was one of the largest houses in England. We approached it through a park that looked more like a forest to me. It was full of deer and we could see a herd stop eating to look up as we passed by.

'Are they allowed to hunt deer?' asked Celia.

'This is a National Trust property now, so I doubt it,' Lionel replied.

'Good, because I don't believe in hunting,' she said, with the firmness of a mind made up.

'It's very cruel,' concurred Nessa.

'It's okay so long as you show respect,' I said, because I didn't agree with them.

Celia turned to look at me as if she hadn't seen me before, even though I'd been here since the beginning of the trip. 'How do you show respect for something when you have just killed it? I've never heard of anything more ridiculous.'

She turned back before I could answer.

'There, there,' I heard Nessa say, 'don't get upset about the ignorance of others.' They kept talking but in a whisper so I couldn't hear anymore.

Sometimes people like to jump on you quickly if they think they know more than you do and can make you look stupid. It seems to make them feel better about themselves.

'Don't worry about it, Mum,' Jazzie said to me in a tone that didn't have much sympathy. I could always tell when she felt embarrassed by me and that can twist your heart up, so I couldn't explain to any of them what I was trying to say. It was about what Aunty Elaine had said about the way our people treated animals in the past and what she said one night when Brittany was still a toddler and Leigh-Anne was growing in my stomach, and she'd cooked rabbit for dinner.

'Bunnies are so cute,' I'd said to her. 'I don't want to eat one.'

Well, Aunty Elaine was cross about that and told me that it was wrong to waste a living creature. Back in the old days, you didn't throw away any of the rabbit. You'd eat all of the meat; you'd use the fur. You'd even use the bones, the teeth, the guts and the claws. Rabbits only came when the white people arrived but once upon a time we felt that way about all animals. That's what she said.

'Now that you buy things in supermarkets,' she told me, 'you don't even think about where they come from. You forget that what you're eating was actually alive. You forget you're linked to everything else, forget you need it. That's why we aren't good to the environment anymore, why the world's such a mess. In the old days, we had our totems,' she explained, 'to remind us.'

'Do I have one?' I'd asked, because that sort of thing was never discussed in my house growing up even though I would have been interested in knowing all about it.

'Of course, you do. They come through your mother. And you're an emu woman, like her, and like your grandmother, and like all your female ancestors before you.'

One of the things this would have meant was that we weren't allowed to eat emus because they're like our relatives. It would have always reminded us that we had to look after them, keep the environment healthy for them and make sure they weren't overhunted.

That's what I really wanted to say but nobody gave me the chance so I just kept it to myself, though I thought I might tell Lionel about it later as he seemed to like my stories from home.

When Lionel said the house was big he wasn't kidding. It was an enormous mansion, greyish, the same colour as his eyes. Lionel said it was a calendar house because it had three hundred and sixty-five rooms, twelve staircases and seven courtyards, so I wrote that down because that's really something.

I also wrote down *1456* because that was the year the Archbishop of Canterbury bought the estate and started building. Henry VIII, the one with all the wives, took it away from the church and made it bigger. Then it ended up in the hands of a Thomas Sackville who was related to Queen Elizabeth I on the Anne Boleyn side and it's stayed in that man's family ever since.

Lionel told us that some people said the house was a gift from the Queen but it wasn't. That first Thomas Sackville was like a treasurer and he sold the estate – which he'd been leasing from her – to a third party and then bought it off them in 1603. The Queen preferred to give her big houses to the people in her court so they had to pay the money needed to keep them going and they'd also have to cover the costs when she came to stay with them during the summer, bringing the rest of the court along with her – so she was a bit like Pat at the salon, watching every cent.

According to what Lionel said, this Thomas Sackville was sent by the Queen to get a marriage proposal for her from the French king's younger brother. Nothing came of that but years later he was asked to break the news to Mary Queen of Scots that she'd been sentenced to death. Sounds like he got all the worst jobs so I guess he deserved the big house if that's what he wanted.

We got to walk around inside and it was all very impressive with long halls, dark wood and stone walls but it wasn't very welcoming. Even in the parts where all the pictures were and there was furniture, it looked like a lonely place.

I could see that Celia and Nessa were impressed. 'It's very much to my taste,' I heard one of them say, but since they had their backs to me I couldn't tell which one.

I don't think that big houses are all they're cracked up to be. I grew up in one of the biggest in town and it was nothing to envy. It was just more space for coldness and for the things that happened there to be kept quiet. Imagine how many secrets this big pile of bricks must hold since a place consists of everything that's happened there; it's a pool of memories, good and bad, all held in.

I asked Lionel if he knew if there were any ghosts floating around because it looked like a place where they would like to be.

'Some say Richard Sackville, the Third Earl, also known as the Black Knight, has been seen roaming the house whenever trouble is about to arise, but when things are going smoothly he can be seen riding out among the trees.'

Lionel showed me that man's picture in the large gallery – and there he was, from head to toe in black and white and you could tell that even though his clothes weren't what we'd expect these days, he was well dressed and handsome, like an old-time movie star.

'He was a gambler,' Lionel continued, 'had many mistresses and bankrupted the estate, so not surprisingly his long-suffering wife is also said to haunt one of the groves.'

Lionel said there was a coffee shop downstairs if I'd like to have 'a refreshment' before we got back on the minibus. Meredith and Cliff were keen and since Jazzie was off with the other two younger ones, I thought a cup of tea would do me nicely. I asked Mrs Finn if she'd like to join us when I saw her lingering at the other end of the hall. She hesitated then said thank you very much, but she had to keep an eye on her husband. I'd seen enough of him to understand why.

We were sipping the drinks and enjoying the slices of cake that Cliff had bought us when Meredith asked Lionel about the famous legal cases that had happened over this house. My ears pricked up at that because I'm always interested in what happens in court.

Lionel explained that one of the Sackvilles, who was also called Lionel, had a long affair with a gypsy dancer and they'd had five children. One of them was a daughter, Victoria, and Lionel had her come and live with him here at Knole. She ran the house and was resourceful, investing on the stock market when money was short and at one stage opening a shop to make extra cash. As fate would have it, Victoria fell in love with her cousin, *also* called Lionel, who was the male heir set to inherit the property. When old Lionel died,

Victoria's oldest brother, Henry, claimed the estate saying that he wasn't illegitimate. He eventually lost the case, unable to prove his parents were married, but he fought to the end, even trying to forge church documents.

'So that was the first one,' concluded Lionel just as Mrs Finn came and sat down, joining our circle, her husband nowhere in sight.

'Victoria was genuinely in love with her cousin Lionel,' he continued, 'and was deeply hurt when he took a series of lovers. She took up with a Sir John Murray Scott or "Seery" as she called him. He was very rich and contributed significantly to the costs of running this place. He left her a substantial legacy in his will – £150,000 in cash and the contents of his house in Paris, estimated to be worth around £350,000 and that was a fortune in those days.'

It was no small cheese today and more money than I'll ever see, I wanted to say, but I didn't want to interrupt.

'Seery loved his time in Knole and thought Victoria would appreciate the antiques and they'd be a fitting addition to this house. Although the rest of his family were well provided for, they sued her. Victoria charmed the judge and the court; they probably could see exactly why Seery preferred her to his dour family. She won, but rather than keeping the antiques for Knole as Seery had wanted, she quickly sold them. She left Knole forever when Lionel's relationship with one of his mistresses became serious and she went to Brighton with an architect and lived the rest of her days there with him.'

'She was quite a character,' concluded Meredith, 'and, frankly, seemed to have done as much for this place as any of the men did.'

'It's hard to believe in this day and age,' Lionel responded, 'that women back then couldn't inherit and own property. And in the case of this house, despite what some of the guidebooks say, it wasn't always passed from father to son but more often to nephews or brothers; one heir even changed his name from West to Sackville-West in order to keep the connections to the first Thomas Sackville.'

I looked back at my notes and saw that he'd got the place for himself in 1603. That wasn't really that long ago – four hundred and something years – even if the house stayed in the same family all that time. Aunty Elaine told me once that we were the world's oldest living culture so ours is a pretty impressive inheritance. What she said about the emu totems going down the line through the women, not the men, meant that we could trace our ancestry back, unbroken, for tens of thousands of years.

Lionel said that there was one Sackville-West woman who couldn't inherit so she bought another place and Lionel told us we were going to look at that next.

Sissinghurst had once been a large country mansion but when the lady who'd been disinherited bought it, there were only ruins, no electricity, no running water. The buildings were gradually restored and it wasn't one dwelling but scattered parts of a house. The parents slept in the South Cottage and the husband had his study there. The sons slept in the Priest's House, but the wife's sitting room and study was in the tower. It kind of reminded me of how our family – Aunty Elaine, Jimmy, Kiki and me – all lived in separate houses but were at each other's places all the time.

'Not much consolation,' said Celia as we walked in.

'Even with the charming garden, it would hardly have made up for it,' agreed Nessa.

I know the house we'd just been at was much bigger but I liked this one better, especially the garden. No-one had a garden in our street, except for Aunty Elaine, and since she'd passed away most of her plants seemed to have died, as the people who moved in didn't care to keep them going.

'Do you like to garden?' Meredith asked.

'I've never tried but I like the idea of helping something grow. My yard is just grass and I haven't even been able to keep on top of that since Jasmine's father died about six months ago.'

'Oh, I'm so sorry,' she said and gently put her hand on my arm. I knew that I'd made her think the situation was different from what it was but her sympathy matched what I felt and I was grateful for it. I was also glad Jazzie was climbing the stairs in the tower and wasn't here to correct misunderstandings.

I wandered over to an older man who had a wheelbarrow near one of the flowerbeds.

'Is it difficult?' I asked him.

'Pardon, Madam?' he asked, looking at me with his gentle eyes.

'Gardening. Is it hard if you want to start?'

'Well, you need to know what type of soil you have and where the sun shines and where there's shade. And you need to work out what plants grow best in the climate. A good gardening centre or nursery can give you advice and maybe a book is also a good place to start. The main thing is, the more you do it, the better you get.'

I thanked him. Just as we finished talking, a woman came up and it turned out that she was his wife and that he was just another tourist, not working in the garden like I'd thought, so it was nice he chatted and gave me advice when he didn't have to.

I wished I'd taken the time to ask Aunty Elaine about growing things when she was alive. She'd often talk about this flower or that coming out but I never paid much attention and I'm sorry for that now.

As we looked around, Lionel told us that the man who lived there, Harold, had designed the garden and the woman, Vita was her name, had overseen the planting. Meredith said that she had all the ideas about their garden and Cliff was the one who dug things up and put things in. She seemed to have it all sorted out over all their years together, working out how they fitted best. It made me feel envious, I can tell you that.

I walked into the gift shop and looked at the books. The one about gardens that looked the easiest also came with a pot and some seeds. I could try that first and take it from there.

As I approached the counter to pay, Jazzie came in.

'What have you got there?' she asked.

'A book to help me start a garden.'

'Mum, it's a children's book.'

'I have to start somewhere. It won't take up much room.'

'You can't take that back into Australia. They'll take the seeds off you at Customs.'

I put the book back on the shelf and, when Jazzie went back outside, I asked the girl behind the counter what a good book for starters would be and bought the one she said was best. I put it into my handbag so Jazzie wouldn't see.

The Boston sisters were late back on the bus and Lionel said that because of the delay we'd only have forty-five minutes at the next place. This turn of events made Jazzie's two friends sulky. They'd been looking forward to it most and grumbled from their seats behind us.

I could see how it would have been easy to lose track of time in the garden but I didn't feel like saying that aloud since I thought those two sisters had been mean to me the last time I tried to express an opinion, so I kept this one to myself. Besides, they were thoughtless about Lionel and everyone else by making us all wait and seemed not to have cared much about how that affected others.

Compared to the mansions we'd been in first that morning, the next house was like a shed but still it was bigger than the one I lived in back home. It also had a pretty garden, all rambling and wild, and a room out in the backyard where the lady who'd lived here, Virginia Woolf, wrote her books. If there was one thing I was learning today it wasn't about books but about how lovely a garden could be. I wondered that I never thought about it until now but I guess that's what seeing the world is all about – opening your eyes to things you haven't seen before.

Lionel said that one day Virginia Woolf took her walking stick and crossed the fields to the river. She left her stick on the bank, put a large stone in her pocket and walked into the water, letting it carry her away. Her body wasn't found for three weeks.

I asked Lionel if he knew why she'd killed herself.

'She'd suffered from mental illness since she was a teenager,' he told me, 'and she felt another bout of it coming on. That's what she'd written in a letter to her sister. There was also speculation that, since it was 1941, the constant fear of the Nazis invading – Leonard, her husband, was Jewish – pressed on her mind and added to her stress. They were right to be fearful; both their names were on a list the Germans had compiled of people they intended to round up if an invasion did indeed succeed.'

I nodded my head as he spoke. It's not easy living under a threat, a constant shadow. Don't I know.

Lionel did well to get us all back onto the bus on time and to the town where we were staying that night. He said 'Lewis' but it was spelt Lewes. There was another castle that was going to close in an hour so Lionel said Brett would drop everyone off there while he took our bags to the hotel. I wanted to go to the hotel, too – I felt tired, I told them. I didn't doubt that the old castle would be interesting but the thought of more steps put me off. Jazzie decided to come with me, which I was pleased about because apart from sitting on the bus I hadn't really seen her much during the day.

Our room was pretty with yellow-flowered fabrics and a view out to the backyard of the hotel that was a lawn with chairs, surrounded by a hedge. Beyond that it was a patchwork quilt of fields that spread out into the distance.

I rested on the bed and Jazzie turned the telly on. They mentioned Shona Lindsay again and I wanted to listen to every word but Jazzie skipped the channel, fast enough for me to know she hadn't wanted to watch it, and picked one of those game shows where you need to know trivia questions to win. When I lay down, I felt all the steps I'd taken that day all at once. I took my gardening book out of my purse but all I could think of was Shona.

My book said that first I should wait to see what I had already growing in my garden but I think that was more for people who had a new place rather than people like me who'd been in their house for years and years. There'd be nothing sprouting up I didn't expect. But what about Aunty Elaine's place? I wondered. Maybe some of her flowers had survived, especially those roses at the front, and since the people in her house now didn't care for them, maybe they wouldn't mind if I took them. I made a note in the back of my notebook – *Aunty Elaine's flowers?* – to follow up when I got home.

Then the book talked about a thing called a 'site survey' that was just looking at what else was there. I can tell you, there was a broken concrete path in the middle of my backyard that went from the back door up to the clothesline and, frankly, that was the main feature. The front had a path from the porch to the footpath and another to the carport. On either side of the yard were houses just like mine and behind the back fence were paddocks. So, concrete and grass was pretty much what I had to start with.

The book said I also needed to know where the 'house services' were, because if there were water mains and cables in the yard I needed to make sure I didn't damage them when I was digging around. About that, I wouldn't have the first idea. It would have been the sort of thing Jimmy would have loved to work out – in fact, he probably knew where all those things were since he'd been the one fixing them over the years. But without him, I wouldn't know where to start.

When Jazzie said it was time to go downstairs to meet for the evening walking tour of the town I told her I was too tired and I'd rather stay and read my book. As soon as she left I turned the telly back on to see the news. Shona's family had been having a picnic when they'd realised she wasn't there. At first they thought she'd just wandered off. When they couldn't find her, the police were called. They were still searching through Hampstead Heath, which looked like a big park, inspecting the ponds, talking to people who were there at the time and asking about a man seen lurking around. There was also a picture of the white van like the one seen near where Shona had disappeared.

Once the news started to repeat, I switched it off, grabbed my cigarettes and went downstairs. I asked the waiter where I could smoke and he pointed me to the back lawn, then handed me a menu and asked if I'd like a drink.

'That would be nice,' I told him.

When he returned with a second one, the waiter asked if I'd like to eat something and as soon as he said it I realised how hungry I was, and that fish and chips were just what I felt like. I decided right then to miss the tour dinner that night as I wasn't really feeling like company, especially not Professor Finn or those sisters, even though Meredith was nice and I liked her husband, too.

It was tranquil sitting on the lawn as the sun was slowly heading down the sky. The gardening book said you could create your own haven and that's the word that came to mind in that moment. Haven. It felt good to find a place to relax after a day of being on the bus and lots of walking, of the thoughts of Aunty Elaine and Jimmy, of Brittany and that terrible time when we were going through what Shona's parents now were – waiting for news, hoping for life.

I know that unless that little girl comes home, it's only the beginning, and they'll have to do what we tried to do – what we're still trying to do – build something else with what's left and accept, despite every last thing you'd do different if you could do it again, that what's done is done.

After Brittany went missing, the police sorted through the clues – looking at who saw what at the party and what other people had seen that night, following up stories of cars going places at different times and looking into who was in our house, who might be the sort of person who'd do something so unspeakable – I couldn't sleep and cried all the time. Not the type of crying where your body heaves but the kind where your eyes are always weepy. I couldn't remember things, found it hard to do the small things I used do every day without even thinking.

Kiki eventually took me to the doctor to get the medicine that stops your feelings from becoming too deep. I didn't really like how it numbed me to the things around me but I knew I needed something. Those thoughts of how everything was my fault, that I was no good, how everyone would be better off without me. The feeling that the evil in life was so much greater than the good would flood over me and I thought I'd drown in it.

I knew how easy it could be to decide to put a walking stick down, find a heavy rock, step into cold, clear water and let it take you away from all your troubles. But as Aunty Elaine often said, 'What's done is done and there's no changing it.'

'What's done is done,' I said to the waiter as he placed another drink down for me.

He smiled as though I had thanked him.

I was just about to head back to the room when Jazzie came out.

'I thought you were tired,' she said, in a way that showed she was mightily annoyed.

'Why are people surprised to find the smoker outside?' I replied.

But I knew the empty plate in front of me and the half-finished vodka gave me away. I asked her to join me but she wanted to keep being angry, and I didn't help by calling her Jazzie so she found an extra reason to be cross.

I watched her stomp back inside. Sometimes I think she likes to play the victim, likes to work herself into a little brooding huff, but she gets over it soon enough and tomorrow is another day.

'What's done is done,' I said to myself as she disappeared inside.

JASMINE

By the end of the day Mum had once again made me feel those prickles that only she and Leigh-Anne can make so sharp. It was a stupid idea to bring her on the trip, to think that she'd be any different just because she wasn't at home. Why did I think things would change now? Deep breaths – *one, two, three.*

That morning we'd had to repack to meet the minibus as our tour was leaving London. Mum was failing at the job, just placing one thing on top of another, making an enormous, bulky pile. She didn't know how to fold things to keep them compact, how to make the most of the limited space.

'How'd you get everything in when you packed it at home?' I asked, reaching over to rescue a jumper that had fallen out of her suitcase.

'Kiki helped.'

'Too bad she's not here now.'

'Don't worry, we'll get there.' Mum sat on the bed watching my efforts, as I started organising her clothes.

'It's not helped by all this extra stuff you've bought,' I told her. 'Can't you just buy presents when we get back to London – and an extra suitcase if we need it?'

'It wasn't that much,' she said, sulkily.

'Why don't you go downstairs and get something to eat? There's no point us both missing out on breakfast.' The only way I'd get the job done was by putting some of her things into my bag.

'There was,' Professor Finn told the Boston sisters, 'a Charles Sackville who won a poetry competition judged by John Dryden – I assume you're both familiar with the poet – with an entry that stated: *I promise to pay Mr John Dryden, or order on demand, five hundred pounds.*' Encouraged by their laughter, he added, 'That seems to me to be about the most significant literary reference to this house.'

'Some of the Sackvilles were great patrons of writers,' Lionel replied defensively, as we drove to their impressive ancestral family home in Kent – Knole House. 'And it was the childhood home of the novelist Vita Sackville-West.'

'You have to admit that she's hardly a significant literary figure today. It's arguable whether she was one in her own time,' the Professor scoffed.

'Everyone's heard of Virginia Woolf,' interjected Sam, 'and her novel *Orlando*, and how Vita's family inspired it, so it's worth a visit just for that.'

'That woman again,' muttered Professor Finn, not making it clear whether he was referring to Sam or Virginia Woolf.

From the seat behind us I heard Toni mutter, 'He would have known what the tour was about when he booked it. If he didn't like the sound of it, why'd he come?'

Mum was looking out the window, lost in her own world as we entered the estate. One of the Boston sisters made a comment about the cruelty of hunting and though I didn't hear it properly, I was mortified when Mum piped up to support the practice. 'I think it's okay,' she'd said.

I don't know where she gets her ideas from or why she only joins the conversation when she has something embarrassing to say. Remembering that Toni and Sam were vegetarians, I was worried about Mum offending them, too.

Vita Sackville-West had been born in the great Tudor home with its slate-grey towers and glinting windows in 1892. The only child of Lord and Lady Sackville, she was thirty and already a published novelist when she met the formidable Virginia Woolf. Vita's first impression of her new friend was that '*at first you think she is plain; then a sort of spiritual beauty imposes itself on you, and you find a fascination in watching her*'.

Their relationship became intense over the next few years and Virginia was a great source of comfort to Vita in the months following her father's death in 1928, an event that not only meant the loss of a much-loved parent but also the loss of her family home. Knole passed instead to a male cousin who wasn't particularly interested in it.

Virginia consoled Vita in the form of a novel. Using the Sackville family history, she created a biographical story, beginning in the year 1500 and continuing to the date of publication, with a hero who transforms into a heroine. Orlando is favoured by Queen Elizabeth I, has his heart broken by a Russian princess, converses with poets and becomes an ambassador. Then he falls into a deep sleep and awakes as a woman. She lives with gypsies, rejects a marriage offer from an archduke, then takes a sea captain, Shelmerdine, as her husband. She also wins the battle for her ancestral property and publishes a book. The story is steeped in a playfulness, where four decades stretch over centuries and moments are far more important than years. Through *Orlando*, Virginia linked Vita forever to the house she loved, the home she'd lost. She gave the original manuscript to Vita, who in turn gave it to the estate.

And here it was.

Toni, Sam and I crowded around this treasure locked under glass, looking at the fluid, curling handwriting in purpled ink that had been shaped by Virginia Woolf's pen. We could see her second guesses, her afterthoughts, words altered on the page, a line drawn through them, an amendment added.

Virginia illustrated the novel using photographs taken of Vita in various costumes and outfits and using portraits taken from the gallery in Knole. I loved the unconventional boldness of the book – it broke all the rules, the way only a woman as privileged and irreverent as she was, could.

Toni had invented a competition for us, to see who could find the manuscript of *Orlando* (her), the portrait of Edward Sackville used for 'Orlando as a Boy' (Sam), the portrait of Mary Sackville 4th Countess of Dorset used as Archduchess Harriet (Toni again) and the portrait of Lionel Sackville as 'Orlando as Ambassador' (me).

Toni concluded, 'Sam gets one free drink; Jasmine, one; I get two.'

'How does that work?' asked Sam. 'If I buy you a drink and Jasmine buys you a drink, you get two. If you buy Jasmine a drink she gets a free one. Who buys me one?'

'I'm a poet, not a mathematician.'

'Had Vita Sackville-West been a man she would have inherited. But if she had, we would not have Sissinghurst,' declared Lionel as our minibus pulled up in the parking lot. 'Built not as a fortress but as a country estate, it does not have a literary history, per se,' Lionel directed his gaze at Professor Finn, 'but it was restored by Vita and her writer and diplomat husband, Harold Nicolson, in 1930 after they moved in.'

Sam, Toni and I walked up the small spiral staircase of the tower to find a room that housed a printing press. Surprisingly small, it was the first one used by Virginia and Leonard Woolf for the Hogarth

Press, later given as a gift to Vita. Another room was a study. It was here that, after Vita's death, her son Nigel Nicolson found a leather bag. Inside was a manuscript of a story about Vita's love affair with Violet Trefusis, the daughter of Alice Keppel, mistress of Edward VII. The affair between Vita and Violet had begun in 1918, lasted three years, and included a plan to elope. Nigel Nicolson wrote *Portrait of a Marriage*, a biography that contained both Vita's unearthed manuscript and his own understandings of the events she described, derived from various sources. It was a meditation between mother and son about the effects of a relationship that had impacted the whole family. He believed his mother to be unconcerned about how her affair affected him and his brother when they'd been small boys – especially her long periods overseas – but admitted that, until he found the manuscript, he'd never realised that she could love so deeply, be so tempted, so rebellious, so weak.

What consolation was there, I wondered, in finding such capability of his mother's feelings for her lover while also confirming a lack of self-reflection about the impact of her behaviour on him, her child? I know how hard it was on Mum to have lost Brittany, but knowing that never compensated for feeling I was always competing with her grief.

Vita married Harold when she was twenty-one. They shared interests in writing, gardening and literature – and they both had same-sex affairs even though they loved each other. Vita's affair with Violet was her most passionate. At its height, Harold wrote: '*I know that when you fall into V[iolet]'s hands your will becomes like a jellyfish addicted to cocaine.*' But the affair never shook Harold's devotion to her. He who wrote to her every day, who never left her. Over time, she must have realised that he loved her for who she was, would always forgive her, would be constant and offered her a stable foundation; Sissinghurst was the tribute to choosing a life with him.

When I saw Mum enter the gift shop I thought I'd better check that she wasn't indulging in more impulse buying. Apart from the lack of luggage space, I was aware that she didn't have a lot of money and we weren't even halfway through our trip. I reached her just in time.

'You really can't be left alone for a minute,' I told her, unable to hide my testiness. I told Mum to put the book back and went to join Toni and Sam outside.

When I looked back through the window, I could see Mum back at the counter. I took a deep breath – *one, two, three*.

'She's so annoying. And I'm sorry about what she said earlier,' I apologised. Toni and Sam looked at me blankly. 'You know, my mother. About hunting.'

'I liked the way she stood up to those two old ducks,' said Sam, smiling.

'You could tell they're not used to having anyone challenge their opinion,' Toni added with a laugh.

As Professor Finn boarded the minibus, he offered a magnanimous observation. 'Well, I do concede that she was a greater gardener than she was a writer.'

We had all taken our seats by the allotted time – all except the two sisters from Boston. Lionel and Brett disembarked to look for them.

We sat and waited for thirty minutes on the bus until Lionel finally returned with the missing women. They'd taken themselves to the teashop where they had been sitting comfortably having afternoon tea, oblivious of the time and to the fact that Lionel had been searching up the tower and around the gardens for them.

Toni, Sam and I had been looking forward to the next stop the most, and now we were running late.

Nestled at the bottom of a winding lane, Monk's House was purchased in 1919 by Virginia and Leonard Woolf. With a large garden and views over an orchard and a churchyard, the ramshackle cottage had no running water, no central heating and on cold days the wind would whistle through holes in the wooden walls.

'If one seeks a parallel to Vita and Harold's relationship, it was Virginia and Leonard,' Toni mused.

'Except that Leonard wasn't gay,' replied Sam.

'But they allowed each other freedom – their love for each other, their shared intellects, the savouring of life, the challenging of conventions,' argued Toni.

'You're such a romantic,' said Sam, with more dryness than affection.

We walked straight to the pavilion, a single structure at the back of the yard, because it was where Virginia would write from ten in the morning until one in the afternoon, using the rest of the day to ponder and mull, walk and work in the garden. In this space, detached from the house, she wrote her books including *Orlando*, *Mrs Dalloway* and *To the Lighthouse*.

When the shadow of the Second World War fell on them, Leonard suggested to Virginia that they gas themselves if it came to that. She kept a supply of poison on hand for that purpose. She'd seen parts of London destroyed by bombs and had lost long-time friends in the conflict. The spectre of death hung closely around her – either from a German bomb or by her own hand in the event of invasion.

Virginia's walk into the river had been preceded by several suicide attempts during her lifetime. Her first bout of mental illness occurred in 1895, the year her mother died. She once described having '*waves of very strong emotion – rage sometimes; how often I was enraged by my father then!*'. After her father's death, Virginia focused her anger on her sister, Vanessa. Then, after she married Leonard in 1912, she focused it on him, testing both her sister's and her husband's love for her even though their devotion was unquestionable.

We walked to the place in the garden where once two trees had stood, one called Virginia, the other Leonard. It was here that their ashes had been buried. Virginia's marker was lost in a storm; Leonard's still stood firm.

'There's little doubt she suffered from depression, but depression isn't another word for madness,' I said. 'And that's the thing, isn't it? Who gets to define what "madness" is? It defines behaviour that doesn't conform to expectations, behaviour that is contrary to what is considered "normal". It's a construct. Subjective.'

'And men have usually decided what that means,' added Sam. 'Ironically, she was treated by a doctor who believed that energy was being sapped out of the Empire by a "new breed of intellectual women" who wanted to do work like writing. He believed a woman's sole purpose was to have as many children as possible and anything that took her away from that – particularly intellectual activity – moved her from sanity to madness.'

'It's hard to imagine anyone more ideologically opposite to Virginia Woolf than that,' I concluded.

'She had a lot to carry – the grief of losing her mother while still a teenager, her violent-tempered father, and she revealed she'd been sexually abused by her step-brother,' Sam reflected.

'If it's still difficult today for women to admit they've been abused, it must have been impossible for women during her time,' Toni said.

'Funny how there's this theory that it was the threat of the Nazis,' said Sam. 'And I don't doubt the stress of living through a war and the toll it must have taken, but it does seem that it's easier to talk about Nazi invasions than childhood trauma caused by a family member.'

'People don't like to see what's right in front of them,' I added.

The first time I spoke with Fiona McCoy I was shocked by her appearance. When she came into the interview room, she was in shackles, her hands cuffed and linked with a thick chain. This wasn't usual and I'd interviewed violent offenders, more dangerous than Fiona. The handcuffs weren't to protect me; they were to protect her from herself. She used a plastic fork to slash the skin on her wrist when she was first taken into custody. As the wounds were healing, she opened them with a paint brush. And then, later, did the same with a pen. She'd been warned that if she continued, the damage might result in the need to have her hand amputated.

Fiona sat in the room, across the table from me, sedated and slumped over, her head lowered. She didn't look up, never looked me in the eye, answered only some of my questions and then mostly with a shrug, a nod or an almost imperceptible shake of the head.

'Do you understand why you're here?' I'd asked her.

She nodded.

'And why is that?'

'Because I killed him.' She shrugged. 'I didn't mean to.'

'You stabbed him thirty-six times.'

She shrugged again.

I needed to assess whether, at the very moment she committed the crime, she had the capability to form the intent to commit it. If so, even if she had other mental illnesses, she had the *mens rea* and was guilty. The prosecution said she did. The psychiatric reports all said she did, and she was pretty much saying the same thing to me as she sat in front of me. So now for factors in mitigation – things that could be put before the court to help them work out an appropriate sentence. It was clear that she had an extreme personality disorder – evidenced by her suicidal behaviour and her violent outbursts towards others. But from what I observed, from what I could glean from Fiona, her suicidal behaviour, her compulsion for self-harm, came from deep self-loathing, a desire to destroy herself and not because she was sorry for what she had done to John Andrews and his family. There were underlying issues that had caused her to become psychologically damaged well before she crossed his path. As I came to know what had caused her behavioural problems, she and her memories began to haunt me, too. Some things, once you see them, you can't unsee.

As we reluctantly boarded the minibus, I mentioned to Lionel that less than an hour at Monk's House wasn't enough.

'I've already been getting criticism from Professor Finn because we didn't include Lamb House in our itinerary today,' he said defensively. 'He's made it quite clear that it's an oversight not to have included Henry James and we've spent too much time on Vita Sackville-West. You really can't please anyone.'

I immediately regretted making him feel bad, and instead let him know how much Mum and I were enjoying the tour. In saying that to him, I became aware that I'd abandoned Mum for most of the day. I'd been caught up in the excitement of discovering Virginia Woolf with Toni and Sam who knew and appreciated her, like I did, and in a way that Mum simply couldn't. So, I didn't mind missing the stop at Lewes Castle and making sure Mum would be rested enough to do the walk around town that was scheduled for later in the evening.

All hotel rooms quickly start to look the same. When we got to our room Mum laid down on the bed as I turned on the television. I skipped over the news about the little girl who was still missing, mindful of Mum, and quickly changed the channel. I checked my social media and 'liked' one of Bex's posts where she was in the news studio: *Big day tomorrow! Getting prepped!* I looked on Leigh-Anne's Facebook page, scrolling through pictures of Teaghan and Tamara dressed for ballet practice and Zane in his football gear. I 'liked' the images but didn't leave any comments. As I started checking my emails, I heard the rustle of a paper bag from behind me as Mum took a newly purchased book from her bag.

'What have you got there?' I asked.

'A book about gardening. It doesn't have any seeds in it so it's okay to take home.'

I turned and looked at her, intent on calling her out, but something about seeing the book in her hand softened me. This, I thought, was why we were on this trip, so she could see inside my world. Leigh-Anne always says that I just want things on my own terms and that I want others to be like me or I think they're inferior, but that's not true. I just want the people I love to experience what I have a passion for in the hope that they'll love it, too.

'It's almost time to meet downstairs for the walking tour,' I reminded her.

'Do you mind if I stay here?' she replied. 'I'm a bit tired.'

It was hard to argue with that, even though it was more time on the trip that we wouldn't be spending together, so I breathed through my disappointment and left to join the others.

The evening air was warm. The sun set so much later here, the light was like late afternoon back home. We walked back past Lewes Castle, to the sandy-stoned, red-roofed Southover Grange, and on through its picturesque garden, passing the half-timbered Tudor house that was part of Anne of Cleves' divorce settlement after Henry VIII sent her packing. Then we went to the ruins of The Priory of St Pancras Lewes that was destroyed by Thomas Cromwell in 1538 and walked amongst the skeletons of the stone buildings that marked its long-lost magnificence.

'What was your thesis about?' I asked Sam, to make conversation and take my mind off Mum.

'Oh God, her favourite subject,' jested Toni, with an exaggerated roll of her eyes.

'I'm really interested,' I said.

'I was fascinated by Woolf's concept of gender fluidity. She believed that everyone had two "powers" – one male, one female –

and in the man's brain the male prevails over the female, and in the woman's brain the female predominates. A mind that is purely masculine can't create any more than a mind that's purely feminine can. What is needed is balance – androgyny.'

By now we were walking back to the hotel but Sam was on a roll, and I thought of Annie and the way she would get excited by ideas and critique.

'Woolf explored the idea of the male and female being in a kind of balance when Orlando meets Shelmerdine,' Sam continued. 'Remember, he asks her: "*Are you positive you aren't a man?*" And she asks if he's sure he's not a woman. They're surprised at the other's empathy – surprised that a woman could be as free-spoken as a man and a man as subtle as a woman. Their perfect love was the result of two equal parts coming together in harmony.'

Toni took Sam's hand. And for some reason my thoughts turned back to Virginia Woolf and what seemed like her pathological need to push people away. It's an instinctive thing to do. Who wants rejection, to feel the humiliation of not being deemed good enough?

An image of Felicity Fletcher popped into my mind. I'd never been one for lots of friends at school, didn't need company my own age while I had Aunty Elaine as my confidante. I didn't have sworn enemies either, and no-one picked on me or bullied me after Leigh-Anne had terrorised the playground.

Waif-like with flyaway hair, Felicity had liked reading and for a while she was my only friend. I felt close enough to her that on her birthday – were we eight, nine? – I wanted to give her a gift. I had no money – there was no such thing as pocket money in our house – but I had a notebook that Aunty Elaine had given me with a rainbow on it. It was so pretty that I never felt I had anything important enough to put in it, so it had remained in plastic. I wrapped it up carefully in paper that was really a page from a newspaper magazine advertising perfume that was pink and had flowers. I carried the little package over to Felicity's house. Her mother opened the door and I could hear the noise and activity inside.

'I guess you can come in,' Mrs Fletcher said with a sigh, nodding down the hall towards the party.

'I can't stay,' I said, handing over the present and walking straight back to Frog Hollow. Instead, I spent the afternoon taunting Kylie with card games I could always outwit her at.

'Are you mad at me?' Felicity had asked me the next day at school.

'No,' I lied. I didn't know how to put the burn in my chest into words.

'Good,' she said, 'I would've let you come if it was just up to me.'

But it was never the same between us. Even as a child you know when you're being excluded.

Although the history books speak of segregation finishing in the 1960s and '70s, there's a vast difference between what's on the law books and what takes place in real life when it comes to prejudice and age-old biases about imagined racial superiority. A lot of people say they don't care, but Leigh-Anne is the only person I know who says that and truly means it.

When I got back to the hotel, I found our room empty. Through the window I spied Mum out on the lawn. There was an empty dinner plate in front of her and she was sipping a glass of clear liquid that I knew wasn't water. I felt the old anger boil up in me and stomped down the stairs and out into the garden to confront her.

'I thought you were too tired to join us?' I demanded. I could tell by the way she looked at me that this was far from her first drink. There's a slight shift in her face when she's trying to act sober.

'I just came down for a smoke before I turn in for an early night. Come, join me.' She patted the seat beside her.

Breathe – *one, two, three*. 'Looks to me like you'd much rather be alone.'

'Don't be like that, Jazzie'

'It's Jasmine, Mum. I'm Jasmine.'

'If there's chicken, I want the chicken,' Celia said to Nessa as we sat down to eat in the wood-panelled hotel dining room.

When the food arrived, Celia took one look at her chicken and wanted to swap it for her sister's fish and waited for Nessa to swap the plates.

'How does one reach the elevated status of professor?' Nessa fluttered at Professor Finn.

'Well, it's not as easy as it might sound – and it doesn't sound that easy, does it?' he warmed to his subject. 'You have to be recognised as doing something significant in your area. In my case, it was my deep understanding and extensively cited publications on Hesiod's poems.'

'Hesiod? Would I know anything he's written?'

'He was a Greek poet, writing around the same time as Homer. My work has primarily concentrated on his poem – *Works and Days* – that has as its basic thesis that a man who is willing to work will always get by in life.'

'I cannot say that I'm familiar with it,' said Celia.

'Sadly,' he added bitterly, 'there is not much interest in the classics anymore.'

Professor Finn's wife gave him a sympathetic look.

'I'm going to need those drinks,' muttered Sam.

After dinner, out in the garden bar where I'd discovered Mum earlier, we found a way around Toni's mathematical problem. Four rounds, with the bill for each round split between the two people who didn't find the treasure. We drank to Mary Sackville, Vita

Sackville-West, Virginia Woolf and, finally, to the manuscript of *Orlando*.

'I think it's great you've come on this trip with your mum,' Toni said, as we were waiting for the bill.

'Brave,' added Sam. 'I couldn't do it.'

'Brave is the most overrated virtue,' I told them. 'It's often just taking action when you haven't thought through all the facts.'

Perhaps because of the alcohol with Sam and Toni, perhaps because I was still brooding about Mum drinking and not wanting to spend time with me, as I lay in bed with my mother making noises of half-sleep from her side of the room, I summonsed the courage to ask, 'Mum, why did you and Dad never get back together?'

'What's done is done,' she replied.

And I remembered why I never bothered asking her anything.

DAY 4

DELLA

We lost the sunny weather of yesterday. Today it's drizzling rain. Lionel says it's not all bad because we don't have much walking planned. I don't mind as you don't get to see the real side of things if it's always sunny – it's like only seeing someone's pretend face.

When you go into the Payne's store back home, the one that sells all the kids' toys and colourful clothes and lots of other things that catch your eye, Shelley who runs it always has a happy face on for the people she likes or the strangers in town who she thinks are the right kind of people. Once she had these dancing sunflowers made of bright plastic that moved as music played. They were so cheerful looking and I thought Kiki would like one. I asked Shelley how much they were. She shook her head firmly. 'Not for sale,' she said, her mouth stretched tight, even though they were right there in the window and that woman would do anything to squeeze a dollar out. I could tell by her look and the tone of her voice that it was just me she wasn't selling to. And I thought, well, that's who you really are then, isn't it? Aunty Elaine used to say when someone shows you who they really are you should believe them. There's a lot of truth in that, I always think.

'I'm beginning to know how a sardine might feel,' Jazzie said cheekily as we got back on the minibus. Even though everything was grey outside, at least the cloud between us from last night seemed gone.

I like that about Jasmine. She's like Jimmy in that she doesn't hold a grudge for long – unlike that other daughter of mine. I wonder whether Brittany would have grown to be the sort of person who holds a grudge or not? I think not. She had that thing people call a 'sunny disposition'. A half-full person. All those half-empty people need the half-full people around so the world can balance itself out.

Today we were driving to a place where another famous writer had been born. This one I knew because her books had been on the television and she was also one of Jasmine's favourites. One Christmas, Aunty Elaine had given her a set of Jane Austen books. They had brown leather and inside were drawings along with the stories. Jasmine was so happy with them that I got that little jealous pain you get when your child seems to like someone else more than you.

When we arrived at the little church where Jane Austen's father had been in charge the rain was like a mist, not like the heavy raindrops back home. It wasn't enough to deter me and I walked through the graveyard while the others went inside the church.

Lionel had said the difference between a cemetery and a graveyard is that a graveyard is attached to a church and a cemetery isn't. Jimmy and Brittany are in a cemetery I realised, because I'd never known the difference before, and I liked knowing a small something-more about them.

I looked at the old headstones, some cracked apart by centuries, others leaning over, weighed down by the passing of time. The graves of some Austens were in one corner of the churchyard but I couldn't help thinking about all the children buried close by, their little lives long lost, no-one left now to tend their graves.

If Brittany could see over where we'd laid her to rest, she'd see how we all kept visiting her. In the years after she'd left us, we would leave plastic toy animals, balloons, little bits of beads and glass, and other trinkets a little girl would like. As more years passed, we left flowers and the occasional little china or glass angel, as if she'd outgrown the other kinds of gifts. However much we all fought amongst ourselves, we all kept our own vigils where we buried her.

Outside the churchyard was a large tree and Lionel said it was a yew tree and thought to be about nine hundred years old. 'It would have seen Jane Austen,' I said to him. And I thought, well, at least the tree has watched over the graves and tended to them in its own way. I asked him if the tree was named like the letter 'u' or like the word 'you' as in 'you and me' but he told me the proper way so I could write it down right.

'I like all your little facts and things. It brings everything to life,' I told him. I could tell by his smile that he was chuffed and I got that warm-sunshine feeling inside when you've made someone else happy.

It's funny how so many words in English never sound like they look, which must make it hard for people to learn it all. When Aunty Elaine explained a word in our old language it always read like it sounded – 'yaama' for hello, 'dinewan' for emu, 'biggibilla' for echidna. Our old language wasn't written down so maybe there was no correct spelling. And if people only wrote it after white people came then maybe they just spelled it the way they heard it. That's the sort of thing I'd have liked to ask Aunty Elaine more about if she were still around.

Hearing about the yew tree made me want to know more about plants and what their proper names were and how you grow them. Maybe that might distract me from my sad moods. When things had gotten really bad and I had to speak to another doctor about what was going on in my head, they'd sometimes suggest that I take up a hobby but I could never think of anything I wanted to do. But as they say, 'you're never too old to learn'.

We were soon back in the bus and on our way to another village where Jane Austen had lived. As the others continued their talk I had that anxious thought about where I'd be buried. Jimmy had been laid to rest beside Brittany and that's where I'd like to be but I couldn't see how Lynn and Jenny would let that happen while they were still taking a breath – and would probably work to stop it even if they were stone cold dead in their own graves.

I don't know what happens when you die but Aunty Elaine said that you'd be reunited with the spirits, with your ancestors and loved ones. I worried that if I was buried too far away from those I loved I wouldn't find them or they wouldn't find me. If Aunty Elaine did turn out to be wrong about all that and we just turned into dust, it would be nice to think that mine would be close enough to Jimmy and the girls that we might somehow mix together in some way and all be back together.

Then the bus arrived at our next stop so I didn't have any more time to think about those sorts of things.

This next house was made of red bricks and had two levels. There was a garden you had to walk through before you got to the front door. Inside, there was a sitting room – Lionel called it a dining parlour – and it was here that Jane Austen would write her stories. Lionel said that her sister, Cassandra, was head of the house, looking after the money and the housekeeping. Jane would make the breakfast – tea and toast – and then she'd sit down to work and she'd write but would hide her pages if anyone entered the room. She knew someone was coming because the door squeaked when it opened. Lionel said the door still creaks today.

Jane's sister made me think of mine and all those things Kiki does that make life easier for everyone else. She just gets on with it and does what needs to be done and I can tell you, I've never once heard her complain. It's one of those things you think about someone from time to time but never say to them.

'I read somewhere that they would spend the evening reading aloud,' said Meredith, looking around the room at ghosts of the past. 'You can just imagine Jane here reading her work to her family.'

'You can see why she was limited as a writer,' said Professor Finn to whoever was listening. 'She never moved in literary circles. Never mixed with other writers. Never got to exchange views with people who understood the wider world, so she couldn't develop her craft.'

'Yes,' replied Meredith. 'I'm sure she'd have been enriched by the patronising views of the men of her day.'

'All I'm saying,' said Professor Finn with pretend generosity, 'is that it's hard to imagine anything in this insular country village that would sharpen the mind. She just didn't have the opportunity to develop whatever talent she may have had by interaction with those whose gifts bettered hers.'

When we moved into another room I asked Lionel why Jane Austen never mixed with other writers. 'Well, she published her novels anonymously, so for a long time no-one even knew who authored her books,' Lionel explained. 'And her sister urged her to keep her anonymity even though her identity was eventually discovered.'

On the upper floor was the bedroom that Jane and Cassandra shared. There was only one single bed in the sisters' room now and you could see that two wouldn't leave much space.

'That's very cosy,' said Meredith, in a tone where you could tell she thought it was a bad thing.

'At least you could still talk to each other at the end of the day,' I replied.

'They shared a bedroom their whole lives. It must have been suffocating.'

'I don't know, it's easier to spend time crowded up with family than with strangers.'

'Not my family!' Meredith laughed. 'Besides, you heard Lionel say that it was Cassandra who'd wanted Jane to remain anonymous. Doesn't that seem like a sign of jealousy, a little simmering resentment?'

'Maybe she was just afraid of losing her. Afraid's not the same as jealous.'

'What about this then?' she handed me a tourist booklet about Jane Austen that had a sketch on the cover – a woman in a bonnet with largish eyes, a roundish face and a slightly crooked nose. She looked bookish and, while not quite mousy, she wasn't what you'd call beautiful either. I wasn't sure what Meredith's point was. I looked at her waiting for her to explain.

'Well it's not very flattering, is it? And by other accounts, Jane was handsome, described as a beauty, with a slightness of figure, liveliness of movements and quickness of step. So why make her look so unattractive?'

'Maybe her sister just wasn't very good at drawing. Or maybe, if you like her stories like you do, you just imagine the person who wrote them as more beautiful than they might have really been because you like their mind and spirit.'

'True,' smiled Meredith.

'Besides,' I continued, 'Lionel said downstairs that the sister destroyed the letters she thought made Jane look bad. She wouldn't have done that unless she was looking out for her.'

'We only have Cassandra's word that the letters did that. We don't know, really, do we?'

'You're a very suspicious type of person,' I told her in a way that she knew I was teasing.

'Don't you think she might have been a little bit jealous of her clever sister?' Meredith asked, half-joking.

'Well, you have to look at her actions. They speak louder than words.' That's what Aunty Elaine would say.

On the minibus heading to the next place I kept thinking about the two sisters sharing the bedroom. I thought about how I'd sometimes crawl into bed with Kiki when we were little until one night my father found me there. He told me to get back to my own room and for the rest of the night I swam in the fear of what would happen the next morning. Nothing was ever left unpunished in our house. Sure enough, it fell to my mother to give us both a hiding, even though I explained that it wasn't Kiki's fault. I never did it again but that didn't mean I didn't crave the comfort anymore because I did.

There were those years I shared a bed with Jimmy and when the girls came along we all slept in the bed as a family. Even when Jimmy no longer joined us I still slept in the bed with the girls from time to time if they wanted to. It always made me feel safe and I thought it must have done the same for them. At least I hoped it did. And I did love it – those moments when my whole world seemed made up of just the people with me on the mattress like it was a lifeboat in the ocean. I'd get a flush of a feeling that I could only describe as a clean, pure happiness. I thought it was just a natural thing – everyone sleeping together – until that night changed everything. Until the trial.

When I had to tell the court what happened, what I remembered, the lawyer twisted things around. He asked why we'd all sleep in the same bed and I didn't know how to explain that feeling of happiness so I told him that it was just what we did – and that wasn't an untruth. When I said that, he'd made a face as if to say it wasn't normal, like I was a bad mother who'd done something seriously wrong.

And then he went on: Why was I drinking? Why would I let my children be at a party where adults were drinking? How could I remember things if I was drunk? Was this something that was a regular thing? There were other questions worse than that, which don't bear remembering, but you can see why I began to feel that it was all my fault.

When we finally had a break in the court I was shaking. I felt like all the breath and blood had been sucked out of me. Kiki was fuming and stormed up to the lawyer who was bringing the case, the prosecutor. 'Why did you let him do that to her?' she demanded. 'Why didn't you stop it?'

'Calm down,' he told her, dismissing her rage. 'It's usual. It won't affect the outcome.'

No, it didn't affect the outcome but it sure deepened the scars.

'She's suffered enough,' Kiki replied, leaning close to his face. She then grabbed my arm and took me out for a smoke before we had to begin again. That was Kiki through and through. For all the things she'd say to me about what she thought I'd done wrong or should do differently, she was the first one to get in there if someone else came after me. Then she'd come out fighting. You could tell more by her actions than by her words, if you see what I mean.

I had a sudden urge to talk to her. Then I realised we hadn't gone this long without talking since I could ever remember. Even when I was unwell and Kiki would take the girls away on a trip she'd call me on the phone at least every second night to check up on me.

While I thought of all that on the bus, everyone was still taking issue with what someone else or other had said about Jane Austen. Lionel was sitting in front of me. 'She sure causes lots of conversations,' I said to him.

'Not bad for someone whose brother said of her that she didn't have an eventful life.'

'I don't know much about it,' I said, 'but I'd think that there's not really anyone who can say that they have a life like that, you know, where nothing happens.'

'I suppose so,' Lionel said thoughtfully

'Like Pat at the salon. You'd think she was just a hairdresser but she's travelled all over the world. And didn't you say Jane Austen had lots of nieces and nephews?'

'Twenty-four.'

'There you go. That's a handful right there.'

'I think her brother meant she didn't do much outside the family.'

'If that's his attitude, no wonder he said what he said. He's just judging by what he thinks is important. It's like what the woman yesterday who died in the river said.'

'Virginia Woolf,' Lionel said.

'That's her. She'd said that thing about men thinking wars and politics and the like are important and so they dismiss women if they talk about other things. Besides, I reckon everyone must have some sort of story.'

'What about you?' he asked.

'What do you mean?'

'Well, what makes your life eventful?'

'I couldn't tell you what's special about me,' I replied.

'You were just telling me that everyone has something,' his voice sounded teasing. He had me there.

I just shrugged my shoulders because, really, the thing that had shaped my life was a can of worms best to keep the lid on. I'd felt looks of pity so often about it all and knew I'd find it hard to bear if I got one from Lionel.

'Well, this tour's given me lots of new things to think about,' I said, pleased I'd come up with an answer that had a fact in it.

The next town we went to was the last for the day and was called Winchester. I liked how it was old. Lionel said it was 'mediaeval'. He said that Winchester Cathedral was the longest in England and was nine hundred years old. That was the same age as the yew tree we'd seen earlier. People are always impressed when a church is hundreds of years old but they never stop to think how impressive the trees are.

As we walked into the large cathedral, I thought it was like being in a big stone cave and the word I thought of was 'magisterial'. It's not a word I usually use but then I don't usually come to places like this. Even if you don't believe in a god, you can't deny there's a sacred feeling in a church, that same feeling you can get when you're out in the bush and everything feels like it's all in harmony and you're just another part of it and a peace washes over you.

We walked across the large stones on the floor that were the colour of honey, all written with who was buried underneath them. Halfway up the left aisle, between what Lionel said was the choir and the west entrance, was the one that marked where Jane Austen was buried. The words carved into the stone said things like 'benevolence of heart', 'sweetness of temper' and 'extraordinary endowments of her mind'.

I looked at that last one. Whatever Professor Finn was saying he thought of her talent, in stone it said she was clever. Those words would be there long after he would turn into nothing more than dust.

I was going to ask Jasmine more about her books but when I looked around she was off with her friends. Perhaps Kiki was right and it was stupid of me to go on a trip about things I knew nothing about, and probably all I'd managed to do was remind Jasmine of how unalike we are. The distance between us felt as big as the cathedral.

I sat on a pew and wrote in my notebook. *Winchester – very old. Cathedral. 900 years like yew tree.*

When I looked up, I could see Meredith and Cliff slowly walking around, hand in hand, with the easy affection that I reckon you could get only through many long years together. I thought of Jimmy. And then that if I didn't get some fresh air I'd be sure to start crying.

When I got outside, I walked down the length of the cathedral and, not expecting to, I came upon a little garden, hidden away. The sign said 'Dean Garnier Garden' but it wasn't locked and when I peeked in the gate there were other people there including a young couple underneath the drooping leaves of a tree. I wondered who Dean Garnier was that he got to have such a nice garden. There were a few Deans back home – Dean Barrett ran a lawn mowing business and he was always pleasant and would say hello; Dean Pitt was a cook at the club, a surly man who always seemed red from sweat – but neither of them would inspire a garden.

I went in through the gate, walked amongst the neatly framed flowerbeds and found a stone bench to sit on. From somewhere I could hear a choir and I thought again about what it said in my gardening book about how you can create a haven. I made a mental note to myself that I'd read more about it later that night and shouldn't be put off.

Kiki often tells me that I can't stick to things. I've never been one with grand plans or big ambitions. I think you just have to try to be happy with what you've got. I decided that when I was back in the hotel room, I would look in my gardening book to see what it said the easiest thing to grow was. I wrote in my notebook, but in the list at the back because I didn't want to put it in with all my notes on the tour and mix everything up: *Easy to grow?*

Suddenly, Lionel appeared. He seemed as surprised by me as I was by him.

'You've found the most beautiful part of Winchester without my help,' he said. As he took a seat on the bench beside me I noticed a look of tiredness as he gave himself a moment to relax.

'It must be hard work, doing these tours, away from home,' I said to him.

'People can be stressful,' he replied, with a deep sigh.

I thought of what Aunty Elaine might have said at a time like this, when she saw a face like the one he had now. 'You can't worry too much about the things you can't change. Sometimes people just like an argument.' I was thinking of Jimmy's sister Lynn.

'I've never met anyone like you before.' Lionel smiled.

'Maybe you just haven't travelled that much before. There's plenty like me back home,' I told him.

He laughed at that and I was reminded of how much I liked his smile. I was going to ask him about who this Dean Garnier was but I got the sense that he wanted a moment of peace and quiet. I must have been right because the silence between us was calm – I thought of the word 'serene' – not awkward. It was a few minutes before he spoke again.

'Sorry, I overheard you telling Meredith that your husband died only six months ago. My condolences.'

'We'd been together since high school,' I found myself saying. That was a truth amongst everything else.

'That must be hard on you. It's still so very soon.'

I nodded.

We looked over the flowerbeds and tried not to look at the two young people who were getting ever more romantic with each other.

Then Lionel gave another sigh. 'Well, I'd better go face the enemy.' He stood and offered me his hand to help me get up from the bench.

When everyone had come out of the cathedral, Lionel took us all on a walk around Winchester that included the house where Jane Austen had died. I liked this walk better than the ones through London, even though I liked them too, but maybe I'm just a person who likes a town better than a city. Jazzie stayed close and that made me happy and towards the end of the walk, when we were in a Great Hall where King Arthur was supposed to have been, Jasmine took my hand. It was a turn of events because we just aren't a family that does that. That's a sad fact, too.

We finished the walk at the little inn we were staying in that night. Each of the rooms was named after a famous writer and Jasmine and I were in the Keats Room. As Lionel handed me the key, Professor Finn said, '*Season of mists and mellow fruitfulness, Close bosom-friend of the maturing sun.*'

I didn't know what he meant or why he was talking about bosoms but the Boston sisters were impressed. 'Oh, Professor,' they tittered, like sparrows hovering around a biscuit.

In the room, I lay on my bed and thought about gravestones and how what you write on them tried to explain a whole life. I thought about the church and the stones that marked where people were laid to rest and how hard it is to say what's most important about a person on a simple piece of rock. How do you explain everything that happens in that little line between the date that says when you were born and the one that tells when you died?

Jasmine put the telly on with the sound down.

'Turn it up,' I said.

'I thought you were asleep,' she replied.

If you thought I was asleep, why'd you turn it on? I wanted to say, but held my tongue in my mouth because why make trouble you don't need especially when things between Jazzie and me were on the mend. 'Want something?' I asked, as I got up to search through the minibar.

A news report came on about Shona. Jasmine quickly changed the channel.

'I was listening to that,' I told her.

She clicked it back on.

The police had released a sketch of a man they wanted to speak to – dark face, large eyes and a hoodie. Jasmine and I both looked at the screen to see what the face of evil might look like.

Nothing prepares you for death and that's a fact. People say, 'time will heal' but I can tell you the longer it goes, the worse it gets. At first there's numbness. Police investigations, coronial inquests, people coming through the house. But when they go and the house is empty, well, that's almost the worst time. That's when it's just you and your thoughts and nothing else.

Loss pulls you down slowly. With Jimmy, when something funny happens my first instinct is to tell him about it. When the roof needs fixing or it's time to work out money matters – I never was good at numbers – that's when the reality seeps in that he's not there. That's when there's true emptiness, when you can't deny you're really all alone.

One thing that reminds you of the person you've lost is their smell. With Brittany it was the strawberry shampoo she loved and the raspberry iceblocks that made her mouth as red as berries. I could smell her in her clothes until years had passed. Even now when I smell a fake strawberry scent an image of her rushes into my mind and I have to catch my breath.

With Jimmy, it was the smell of his skin – woody citrus. I could smell it on his clothes. When we were together, I'd wear his shirts just to feel his smell all over me, and one of my darkest secrets was that when he moved to another house, I still kept a pillowcase of his. Later, when the smell on that faded, I would occasionally take a piece of his clothing when no-one was looking – a T-shirt here, a shirt there – and keep it until the smell faded again. That might sound strange but a scent can keep a person very close to you, especially if it's one that reminds you of being curled up with them.

Maybe that's part of why I did what I did at Jimmy's funeral. And why his sister Lynn confronted me. 'You put him in that coffin. You might as well have just sliced a knife through his heart,' she'd said. And that just made me so angry, like a ball of fire had risen up in me. I could see what she thought she knew but didn't. Before I could think, I took a swipe at her. I wanted to knock the hate right off her face.

She ducked. I missed her, lost my balance and fell to the floor.

'Drunk!' she spat at me. 'Just like your father.'

I know what I did even though I pretend to the others that I've forgotten. Honestly, it's not the sort of thing that is easily pushed out of your mind. And I know it was wrong. I just didn't think that Leigh-Anne would get so mad about it. Or stay mad for so long.

'It's almost dinner time,' Jasmine announced. 'You coming?'

She put out her hand and pulled me off the bed.

I didn't talk much at dinner because most of what people were talking about were things I didn't know. When the food came, they got my order wrong and although they said they would fix it, I didn't want to trouble anyone or waste anything so I was stuck with chicken when I wanted roast beef, which isn't the world's biggest problem but is the kind of thing that can turn you sour.

Jazzie was sitting next to me with Celia sitting on my other side but her attention was on Professor Finn who was sitting opposite her. I was sitting opposite his wife, Helen, and she didn't say any more than I did. I wondered if she'd be interested in the yew tree and how it was as old as a cathedral but then thought not.

Celia kept talking loudly, keeping Professor Finn's attention. He seemed to say things in a cranky voice that made her laugh. She hadn't spoken to me since I said that thing about respecting nature when you eat it. I noticed there was a piece of lamb on the plate in front of her. Did she think it grew on a tree? I wanted to ask her. Another thing that started to get under my skin as they kept up conversation about this and that was Shona Lindsay, missing, waiting to be found.

Professor Finn was talking about how we didn't have enough Keats during our walk that day and that it was a chance to explore a really great writer rather than so many average ones. He was like someone just picking away at a scab – pick, pick, pick. Couldn't leave it alone. Poor Lionel sat mutely next to him. I don't like know-it-alls so I guess that got under my skin, too.

'You are such a tease, Professor,' Celia said with mock shock.

'Yes. Outrageous man,' echoed Nessa.

Celia needed more water and asked her sister to pour it for her even though the jug was right in front of her. She's as bossy as Lynn, expecting she can give orders and everyone do as she says. That got my goat.

I looked at the Professor's wife. She was still quietly eating her dinner. And I thought about how some people just get overlooked. Like the way the woman who drowned herself in the river had said happened to so many women. And I thought about how often we're afraid to say anything. Like I was often afraid to say things to Lynn, to stand up to her. I was too afraid to put my foot down about what I wanted even when it came to the father of my own children.

I thought about how tired Lionel looked in the garden and how he thought of the tour as 'the enemy' and how glum he looked down at the end of the table, and then about how Professor Finn had made snide comments all day – just like Lynn – and how people judge a book by its cover and think they know all about it even though they've never bothered to read it. Helen Finn would know all about that, I bet. She'd understand if I told her about how Lynn made me feel.

'Some people think they're more important than everyone else,' I said to her, but she was looking down at her meal. She mustn't have heard me or just thought that, as usual, everyone was ignoring her, so I said it again louder. She looked at me, confused, so I continued on about how badly Lynn treated me at the funeral and added, 'I just mean people like your husband and those two.' I nodded in the direction of the sisters. 'They just don't realise that other people have feelings. They're rude and think that everything they say is what other people should do.'

The Professor, Celia and Nessa stopped eating and looked at me.

'Mum,' Jasmine whispered sharply, 'do you want me to take you up to bed?'

'No,' I told her in a tone that I hoped showed she'd hurt my feelings. 'I haven't even had my dessert yet.'

I needed a smoke but when I got outside into the still, light evening, I felt dizzy. Why would Jasmine bring me here if she was going to ignore me and make me feel ashamed for saying things? My rage pushed a tear from my right eye, and then one from my left.

'I've just come to see if you're okay,' Jasmine said, stepping out of the shadows.

'I'm fine,' I lied, wiping my face quickly so she wouldn't see.

JASMINE

'I THINK ONE of the reasons so many women love Jane Austen,' I mused to Sam and Toni, 'is that all her great heroines are readers. She believes reading is good for you, especially if you're a woman. Willoughby endears himself to the Dashwoods in *Sense and Sensibility* through reading. Lucy Steele's lack of literacy shows how unsuited she is to Edward but Elinor shares his passion for it. In *Emma*, when the heroine determines to better herself, she takes to reading. Fanny in *Mansfield Park* is always reading a book while the Bertram sisters never go near one.'

Jane Austen read from her father's library of five hundred books, a large number for a country rector. She studied the globe of the world he owned and enjoyed the culture of learning created by her parents, who ran a small school for boys within their home. Her father had been a classical scholar and a Fellow at St Johns College at Oxford; her mother was known for her sharp wit. This was a household that valued intelligence in both men and women.

Jane enjoyed writing from an early age and shared her work openly with her family who listened and applauded. In this environment she penned first drafts of *Sense and Sensibility*, *Pride and Prejudice* and *Northanger Abbey*.

I envied her that – a culture of learning in her household; a father whose faith in her wasn't drained by his own disappointments in life. Dad would warn me not to aspire – 'Don't get your hopes up,' he'd say, reflecting his experiences with life. I know he just didn't want me to get hurt but of course it just made me feel let down by him.

On the tour today we would be going to the house where Jane Austen drafted her first three novels, and then to the one where she wrote her last three.

'Virginia Woolf said,' Sam observed as the minibus trundled along, 'that without Jane Austen, the Brontës and George Eliot, she could no more have written than Shakespeare could have written without Marlowe or Marlowe without Chaucer.'

'Your Virginia Woolf also said that it was difficult to catch your Miss Austen in an act of greatness,' Professor Finn responded provocatively.

'What she meant,' Sam replied, 'was that it was impossible to take a single scene or paragraph as the epitome of her greatness. But rather it was her ingenuity with her style and her characters.'

'Henry James also thought that Miss Austen had not known what she was doing, technically speaking,' Professor Finn challenged.

'Henry James was very conscious of his own writing methods. Jane Austen left no record of hers but that doesn't mean she didn't have any. We just don't know what they were. And our absence of knowledge about her has given rise to a long tradition of condescension towards her,' Sam replied tartly.

'Mostly by men,' mumbled Meredith.

'Professor Finn, I marvel that you have so little regard for her,' Celia said in a style of flirting that felt from a different era.

'One of my problems with Miss Austen,' Professor Finn replied firmly, 'is she took no interest in the dramatic changes to the world around her. And if a writer is not a commentator on life, what are they?'

'So, you think a novel should be a chronology of current events, do you?' asked Toni.

Professor Finn made a noise that sounded like a cross between a cough and a grunt.

'I'm not a scholar,' Meredith piped up, 'but I remember the Napoleonic Wars were a backdrop in *Persuasion*. And there were tensions between new wealth and old. She seemed to have a bit to say about that.'

'*Mansfield Park* is also about the friction between old money and standards and new money and morals,' added Sam.

'It also touched on the immorality of the slave trade, which Jane Austen was against,' I added.

'And,' chimed in Toni, 'in her day, there was no harsher critic of the church than Austen.'

'This is all just clutching at straws,' Professor Finn retorted with a flippant flick of his hand.

'Oh Professor, you can't be so dismissive,' Celia gently chided.

I could have sworn I saw Professor Finn smirk with satisfaction and I was reminded of something that Aunty Elaine used to say when she thought I should show more self-belief: 'Hold yourself with the confidence of a mediocre white man.'

I thought about the young version of myself, grateful to hide in books on Aunty Elaine's back porch from the humiliation of rejection. And that made me think of Joshua Payne. We were often the only two in the small high-school library at lunchtime and always at the top of our class. We both loved reading, were competitive but friendly, well matched in intellect, temperament and introverted nature, all leading to a teenage infatuation. Jane Austen would have thought us a perfect match.

When the junior school formal was approaching, shyly he'd

asked if I'd go with him. I rushed, dizzy with expectation and promise, to Aunty Elaine's house and begged her to make a copy of a red dress I'd seen in one of Leigh-Anne's magazines.

'Yes, yes,' she'd finally agreed, even though we both knew the cost of the fabric was an extravagance.

The following day, Joshua didn't turn up in the library and was distant during class. After three days of this, I waited at the front gate after school, and not until it would have been thought deserted did Joshua come out of the science room.

'What's going on?' I asked him.

'My mum. She doesn't want me to … Not because of you. Just … you know.' He was looking at his shoes.

'No. I don't know.'

'She thinks your family's a bad influence.' He was mumbling a word that sounded like 'sorry'.

Aunty Elaine sewed the red dress. I stood patiently as she fitted the red satin on me, not able to confess what had happened.

I spent the evening of the formal with Dad, watching game shows and then the football. When Aunty Elaine asked me later how the dance was, I said okay. If she was aware that I didn't go (it was a small town and everyone knew everything) she allowed me to keep up the pretext.

The playful friendship with Joshua evaporated after that and we went through the next two years living with the awkwardness in our different ways – him not wanting to challenge his mother's prejudices; me seeking to prove them wrong.

I kept that red dress at the back of my wardrobe, a galvanising push for my determination to get away from my family, especially my sister and parents. The afternoon I sat my final school exam, I caught the first train out of town, my early enrolment offer to law school printed out and tucked in my bag. I once wore the red dress to a law school function, grateful for the only elegant thing I owned.

Jane Austen was thirty-three when she moved to the ample, squarish red-brick house at Chawton. The building came into the Knight family in 1769. They'd adopted Jane's brother Edward and raised him to be the heir of Godmersham Park and their other large estates. These he inherited in 1809 and soon after offered his mother and sisters Chawton Cottage. Edward's elevation in society gave Jane the chance to see inside his world. A sensible, practical man, a good landlord and a caring father, he became Jane's idea of a true gentleman, models for Mr Knightley and Mr Darcy; Godmersham Park inspired Mr Darcy's Pemberley.

We entered the parlour where Jane's genius once again flourished and where she wrote *Mansfield Park*, *Emma*, then *Persuasion*. At the time she moved here, a London publisher, Crosby, was holding the manuscript for *Northanger Abbey*. He'd acquired it for £10 back in 1803 and although he undertook to bring it out without delay he'd sat on it for years. As Jane's other books were published and became bestsellers, Crosby was never aware that he was holding a work by a new, successful novelist because Jane had published under a pseudonym – 'A Lady'. Her brother Henry helped her buy the book back in 1816 for the original £10 before Crosby realised his mistake. The novel was not published until after Jane's death in 1818.

Looking in their tiny bedroom, it was easy to see how closely entwined Jane's and Cassandra's lives would have been.

'No wonder sisters are so close in her books. Elizabeth and Jane, Kitty and Lydia, Elinor and Marianne, even Lucy and Anne Steele,' observed Toni.

'But notice how in her later novels,' replied Sam, looking around the cramped space, 'the ones written while she was living in this room, the sisters are not so close. Emma has a sister but is basically an only child. Anne Elliot's sisters treat her as little more than a doormat.'

Following Leigh-Anne into a room was just one way to be eclipsed by her. Following her in school, teachers assumed I'd be the same disruptive, argumentative force. By people in my town, I was always judged by her behaviour and felt I had to work to prove otherwise, to show I wasn't a bad influence.

Once, when playground gossip was swirling around about Brittany and our mother, Leigh-Anne stormed up to Brian Bolger, the usual ringleader, and punched him in the stomach. She grabbed one girl by the hair and slapped another in the face. Unashamed and unapologetic, she cemented her way into school legend.

But she was no Cassandra to my Jane. To her, 'bookworm' was an insult, aspiration to university a 'wank' and any attempt to talk about an idea was met with a rolled eye. There seemed many more things that pulled us apart than knitted us together.

As we entered Winchester, I wondered what Jane Austen thought as she arrived here. Tired, her nights feverish, she took to lying down after dinner. She must have had an intimation of her early death, knew her symptoms portended no good, especially when she was so capable of making fun of hypochondriacs in her novels, like Mr Woodhouse and his fear of colds and Mrs Bennet and her nerves.

Winchester Cathedral was an imposing monolith. It was hard not to be impressed by its daunting architectural beauty.

'Even though her father was a clergyman – and her brother was one, too – she created characters like Mr Collins and Mr Elton,' observed Toni, 'I wonder what that says?'

'Edmund Bertram and Edward Ferrars both became clergymen and are honourable characters,' countered Sam.

'Maybe she did value the church and that's why she was so critical of them,' I mused.

'Gave them some tough love,' replied Toni. Today she was wearing a red and white polka dot '60s style dress with matching bandana and a biker jacket. She held hands with Sam, who was in her usual cowboy style shirt and jeans, as we walked.

I looked around to find Mum but couldn't see her. Meredith and Cliff were wandering down near the side chapels at the apse and Lionel was talking to the two sisters from Boston at the memorial stone for Jane Austen. Mum must have been outside having a smoke.

There's a scene in *Mansfield Park* where Edmund and Julia arrive back from the Crawfords. Maria is sulky, pretending to read, Lady Bertram is comatose, Mrs Norris is cross and uncommunicative. Edmund asks where Fanny is. Mrs Norris says she doesn't know but then Fanny is heard from the other end of the room. She's been there all evening but no-one noticed. I'd felt that way through long moments of my childhood and into my adult life.

I just didn't know how to be noticed like Leigh-Anne. The loud one, the quiet one. My love of sneaking into places unnoticed started as a test to see how long it would take for my parents, especially my mother, to notice me. Sometimes I'd give up and leave. There was no breaking into Dad's distracted thoughts and Mum's distant wistfulness.

When I used to ask Mum about Brittany, she said that she really loved her sisters, especially me. She dressed me like I was her doll and put ribbons in my hair and polish on my nails. I have a memory of it but as I was only three years old when she disappeared, I suspect it's a false one created from visualising other people's recollections.

But just because I don't remember her, doesn't mean that I don't feel her. I've often wondered how different life would have been if my parents hadn't been distracted by grief and if I'd had a sister who was perhaps more like me or could have mediated the behaviour of a strong-willed girl like Leigh-Anne. And maybe Leigh-Anne would have been different too, if she'd grown up as a middle child rather than the eldest; if she, like me, but in her own way, wasn't always trying to attract the attention of distracted parents. People think shared loss will bring you closer together but it can sometimes create gulfs that can't be crossed. It was just another thing that was taken from us when Brittany was taken from us. You can waste a lot of time thinking about the 'what-ifs'.

We know that what happens to us in our childhood shapes the person we will be in later life. When we are born, we are connected with our mothers and our first task is to distinguish what our separate entity, our 'self' is. When I first began working on Fiona McCoy's case, I studied her file and read up on how childhood shapes adulthood, on how memories are repressed. She'd come into the care of the child protection agency at the age of two. She wouldn't communicate with other people, was anti-social, her development behind that of her peers. She also had a venereal disease. What chance, I wondered, did she ever have?

As our group started to assemble in the large forecourt of Winchester Cathedral, Mum suddenly reappeared. I couldn't smell anything on her breath except stale cigarette but I watched her carefully as we went for the walk around town. We ended at Winchester Castle, a place with its own King Arthur legend. A large wooden 'round table' hung on the wall and Mum tried to work out what its symbols meant.

'They don't even know if there was a King Arthur,' I said, 'but there is so much mythology he might as well have been real. Stories just got handed down.'

'That's like our way in the old days. Sitting around the campfire, handing down our stories,' she replied. 'I sometimes wonder how much we lost because they weren't written down,' she said.

'Think how much we have lost just with Aunty Elaine,' I said, a thought I'd pondered many times in many ways. 'Even after all this time I still miss her.'

She nodded. 'Me too, Bub. Me too.'

I slipped my hand into hers.

While Mum watched television, I checked Bex's social media. There was a clip she'd posted of her reading the news. She was confident, poised, warm, engaged. All the things she actually was in real life but magnified on the screen. *So proud of you*, I wrote, but since it was amongst hundreds of comments I didn't think she'd see it so I texted her as well.

I sent an email to Aunt Kiki assuring her Mum was doing alright, that she seemed to be enjoying the trip and had made some friends. I added that I'd pass on to Mum the news that her cats and dogs were doing just fine. Kiki loved a house frantic with creatures needing to be saved, and that often included Leigh-Anne, Mum and me.

I hoped to see an update on Fiona but there was silence on my work email. No news is good news, I consoled myself. Finally, I looked on Facebook to see what Leigh-Anne was up to. She'd been out drinking with her friends and Kylie at the local Workers Club, not far from where we'd grown up. Her friends now were the same ones she'd had right through school. I didn't have a single tie and that made me feel both triumphant and melancholy. I started to type a message but once again struggled with what to say. She always thought I was mocking her, wilfully misunderstanding me.

Dad's passing had brought out the cracks we had papered over. In preparing for his funeral, Leigh-Anne and I made most of the decisions. We agreed on the music and the readings, Leigh-Anne kept Aunt Lynn and Aunt Jenny at bay and I wrote the eulogy. We had worked together but at the times I felt that I wanted to hug her it never felt as if she'd welcome it. If we weren't close in those moments, would we ever be?

Dinner was classic English pub food. It reminded me of the uncomplicated meals we used to get back home at Aunty Elaine's or Aunt Kiki's. I was deep in my conversation with Sam, Toni and Meredith about our favourite moments of the day when I felt an anxious grip pull tight inside me.

'Some people think they're more important than everyone else,' my mother said loudly. I know how she speaks a little higher and starts to slur her words when she's losing control.

'People like your husband and those two,' she shouted, her voice dominating the whole table now, her slurring more audible.

'Mum,' I grabbed her arm. 'Shall I take you up to bed?'

She shook me off, stumbling as she got up and knocking her glass of red wine across the table. The mortification of her behaviour was nothing new to me, though it burned with each new audience.

The fuss of everyone cleaning up after her was a distraction.

'I'm so sorry,' I said, as people resumed their seats.

The Boston sisters seemed unmoved. Professor Finn was faking an attempt to brush the incident off.

'My father died recently and Mum's aunt, who was like a mother to her, not long before that. She's still taking it hard, still processing it,' I added, building on the lie. I could feel, the more I covered for her, the mood of our small group shift from shock to sympathy. 'I thought this trip would help her but maybe the stress is too much,' I added.

'There's no easy way with such things,' Meredith agreed.

'I should go and see how she's doing,' I said, receiving nods of encouragement.

I went outside but hung back, watching Mum sway as she exhaled plumes of smoke. When she was almost finished her cigarette, I emerged from the shadow of the doorframe.

'Are you okay?' I asked. She didn't answer, keeping her back to me. 'I told them you weren't well. They understand.'

'You don't need to apologise for me,' she said, putting her cigarette out with her heel before walking past me and heading back inside.

Oh but I do, I wanted to tell her. And I have been for most of my life.

I followed her back to our table where she was greeted with sympathetic nods. She ordered two more drinks but drank them quietly. Only when Lionel came down from the other end of the table to wish us goodnight did she speak once more.

In the darkness, I listened to Mum's heavy breathing in the bed beside mine. Alcohol can be a crutch to get through trauma and it has been so for both my parents. But the deeper questions, the blurry lines, are when does someone like me move from being a support to being an enabler? As a child, you can't understand, but as an adult now, I'm not sure I'm any clearer about the best way to help. It's been such a part of our life for so long now, all this drinking to deal with grief, it's taken too long to realise we shouldn't have allowed it to become so normal.

DAY 5

DELLA

I started packing as soon as I woke up. I can tell you I was still hurt that Jasmine can feel ashamed of me, especially in front of the others. It cuts deep when it's your own child even if you know they love you in their own way. Love and pride are two very different things. I know I'm not clever like people who finished school or went to university but I don't think I'm a stupid person.

Without Kiki sitting on my bag it just wouldn't close. I still didn't know the trick that means you get everything in.

'I'll help you,' Jasmine said, emerging from the bathroom, already dressed, brushing her wet hair.

'I can do it myself,' I told her.

'I'll show you a trick.' She put the brush down and opened my case and took out some clothes.

'Try this,' she said as she folded a pair of trousers in half lengthwise and rolled them up tightly. It worked to create more room and even though it was a tight fit, everything got in.

While Jasmine packed her own bag, I turned on the telly to see what news there was of Shona. It was doubtful that anything much had changed overnight but you never know. Eventually they showed the picture of her in her pink cardigan and the sketch of the dark man in the hoodie. The search, they said, was ongoing, hope still hanging on.

When I flicked off the telly, Jasmine asked me about breakfast. To be honest, I never eat it at home unless you count a cup of tea and a smoke. It's just hard to say no when it's free and you can have all you can eat. But this morning I really had no appetite.

When I got on the minibus, Meredith and Lionel both asked if I was feeling better. I said I was, thank you, even though I hadn't been sick.

We drove to a place called Southampton and Lionel said it was where Richard the Lion-Hearted left for his crusades and the *Mayflower* set sail from. I don't know about any of that but Lionel said Southampton had a double tide that meant it was a high tide for an unusually long time so big ships could use it. He said the *Titanic* had left from there and I definitely knew about that because it's Kiki's favourite movie. She watches it over and over and makes a fuss whenever it's on the telly even though she's got it on DVD. I tell her it's a silly film because you know the ship's going to sink but I really like it, too.

I wrote in my diary: *Southampton – Titanic – double tide – deep**. I put a star beside it so I'd remember to tell Kiki all about it.

I liked the bit when we walked along the sea wall and Lionel said there'd once been towers there. I looked over the harbour and thought of all the people on the *Titanic* who were so excited to be leaving on their adventure, not knowing that many of them were sailing to their deaths.

I often wondered if Aunty Elaine saw her own death. She predicted so many other things – a bird would mean this, a flower would mean that, a dream would mean something else. She saw meanings everywhere, like reading a book. It's the sort of thing that if she did know something was coming, saw a sign that meant no good, I reckon she'd have kept it to herself because it seems the people who carry everyone else's burdens never want to be a burden themselves.

We stopped for cups of coffee before getting back on the minibus. Cliff got ones for me and Meredith, which I said was very thoughtful of him.

'He's a keeper, isn't he?' Meredith said of him proudly, as she watched him place the order. It made me think of the times Jimmy wrapped his arms tight around me. My head would fit perfectly into the curve of his neck and I could smell that skin, that wood and citrus.

The bus pulled up at a red-brick house called Max Gate on the outskirts of Dorchester. Lionel said it was where Thomas Hardy had lived.

'Who was Max Gate?' I asked him.

'It wasn't a person. It was the name of a toll-gate once located here. The house is built on a Neolithic religious ground that has been dated back to 2000 BC. It was later a Roman burial site.'

'There'd be a lot of old ghosts around here then,' I said.

Lionel said Thomas Hardy treasured his privacy, 'but a lot of famous people visited him here – Virginia Woolf, Rudyard Kipling, Robert Louis Stevenson, W.B. Yeats, James Barrie, Robert Graves and T.E. Lawrence, who was the real Lawrence of Arabia. Even the Prince of Wales came for tea.'

Lionel showed us around the house and then we went upstairs to the third-floor attic where, he said, Mrs Emma Hardy had lived.

'It seems more fitting for a servant than mistress of a house,' Celia observed.

'Very odd,' her sister agreed.

'What was going on there?' I asked Lionel as we walked downstairs again.

'I think they were very much in love early on but as time went by they grew apart. Emma died in 1912 and Hardy married his secretary, Florence, two years later, though there's always been much speculation about exactly when his relationship with her started.'

'Malarky,' I agreed. Everything gets complicated when feelings start to come into it.

'It was rumoured that when the maid came to tell Hardy Emma was dying,' Lionel said, 'he simply told her to straighten her uniform. But he was clearly shaken and had Emma's body brought down and placed in a coffin at the foot of his bed. It remained there for three days. Even though they'd been on bad terms, he went into a deep mourning for her, writing poems and eulogising their love. His second wife, Florence, indignant, described the poems as *"a fiction in which their author has now come to believe"*. She couldn't accept there'd once been a relationship between Hardy and Emma different from the one she'd seen.'

'Sounds like,' I mentioned to Lionel, 'he made both women miserable because when he was with one he wanted the other, always wanting the one he didn't have.'

'Maybe if they'd had a child, they would have been happier. It would have given her something to do and something to share,' Mrs Finn said. 'It could have eased the tension between them.'

I was quite surprised that she even said anything but Meredith jumped right in without missing a beat, 'God, no. Children could have made it so much worse.'

Lionel said we should look in the garden where there was a druid stone and also where all the pets were buried. It made me think of my dogs – Polly and Milly and my little moggies – Mookie and Pud. I missed them and again wondered how Kiki was going, what she was up to. It felt strange not to know the small moments of her day, her comings and goings. I knew she'd take good care of my pets but Pud liked it when I rubbed his tummy – he'd roll on his back with his paws in the air – and Mookie liked it when you rubbed the top of her nose. I didn't tell Kiki those things because I didn't want them to like her more than me. Lots of people find Kiki easier than me, like Leigh-Anne does right now. I just need some things to be all for myself, for me occasionally to be the favourite.

I came to the big druid stone that Lionel had said was ancient. As I looked at it, I thought of the big rocks that made up the massive fish traps that Aunty Elaine used to talk about, boulders locked in place in the river so that floods wouldn't carry them off. They allowed fish to pass through and people only took what they needed to eat so the tribes down the river would have their share. There was one up where Aunty Elaine's people had come from that was older than the pyramids and Stonehenge, she'd said. Over forty thousand years old.

An old druid stone impresses people but most don't even know about the things Aboriginal people built. I once asked Aunty Elaine why people didn't know more about them and she said Europeans destroyed many of them when they arrived and didn't want to admit Aboriginal people had the skills it would've taken to build them. They'd rather think of us as backward with no connection to our country – just the way my father liked to see them. It made it easier to justify taking our land and our children.

It was like the second Mrs Hardy who wanted to write out the history of the first one. Like Lynn and Jenny writing me out of Jimmy's life at his funeral. Sometimes the truth matters and you shouldn't try to hide the facts.

Brett drove the minibus – just three miles northeast, he said – through narrow, leafy lanes. We stopped at a thatched cottage in a little village called Higher Bockhampton. Lionel said it was where Thomas Hardy had been born in 1840 and the small hamlet continued to draw him back almost to the day he died.

I thought of how we're connected to the place we're born. Some never leave, like Kiki, Jimmy and me, even though we'd had plenty of reasons to go over the years. Leigh-Anne only moved to the next town. And even though Jazzie never seemed to fit in and has made a point of not coming back, except for special things like funerals, Aunty Elaine always said she'd find her way home one day and I hope she's right about that.

The cottage had a large garden out back. Brett handed out little boxes with sandwiches, fruit and water in them for lunch. It's nice to travel with everything thought about for you. It's nice, full stop.

It was pleasant sitting in the garden in the sun, watching the things that had been planted and were now growing. Aunty Elaine said that before white people came, our people had cleared the places where the soil was best and kept those places where it was poorer for forests. You could still see it, she'd say, in places where no fertilisers had been used and no cattle or sheep had grazed. She knew how to spot the signs. I felt that punch in the guts of sadness that all those things that were in Aunty Elaine's head were now lost to us.

After lunch, Lionel walked us through the cottage and showed us the bread oven that was the same one used by the Hardy family. Aunty Elaine said that in the wetter areas our people grew yams; in the drier ones, grains. Seeds, covered in grass or stored in skin bags, were traded and grindstones have been found that were used more than thirty thousand years ago.

After looking through the cottage, we walked into the woods behind it. I told Lionel that even though I'd enjoyed what we'd seen the only story I'd heard of the ones he'd mentioned was *Tess of the D'Urbervilles* though I'd never read the book or seen it on the telly. As we walked, he told me the story of how Tess is mistreated and then the man who says he loves her won't forgive her for what happened to her until it was too late – even though it wasn't her fault. In the end, Tess is arrested, sent to jail and eventually executed.

'I like a happy ending better,' I said to Lionel. 'You get enough of the other stuff in real life. And I reckon that if she couldn't tell her man her greatest secret then he didn't really love her. It's kind of stupid to think that someone has made no mistakes. He only loved his own idea of her.'

'Proust said that the lover creates an image of the beloved in his mind that may bear little relationship to the real person,' agreed Lionel.

I don't know anything about this Proust but he wasn't that clever if someone like me could work the same thing out for myself.

If you thought Jimmy was going to be the villain of this story, you're wrong. He saved my life once and that's a fact.

I was fifteen years old when I ran away from home with my schoolbag and a small case packed with all I was taking with me. I came across Jimmy coming back from the river.

'You leaving?' he asked, as though it was no surprise that a fifteen-year-old would be fleeing town.

'Can't stay here,' I told him.

'Train's not till late tonight. You shouldn't stay at the station if you don't want to be found.'

I was pretty sure I wouldn't be missed but I followed Jimmy when he suggested lying low at his house.

This might seem like a strange thing to do but I'd known Jimmy all the years we'd been at school. He was a year older than me but taller than the other boys his own age, and he was the kind of person who you just knew straight away you could trust.

As we waited through the afternoon for the evening train, we lay on blankets on the floor of the shed at the back of his house. He held my hand. I moved closer to him, my head nestled into the warm crevice of his neck and took deep breaths to capture the comforting scent of him. The time to go to the station came and went. I knew then, amongst the boxes of old clothes, cobwebs and car parts that I'd found my place in the world. I knew from that day that he could know all the bad parts of what had happened to me and he could separate that from who I was and really see just me. Even with all that passed, and at the worst moments, he was always on my side.

I hid in the shed at the back of his house for three days, until his mother, Nancy, discovered I was there. She wasn't mad but said I'd have to go home. I can tell you that I wasn't at all sad that she'd found us because I couldn't go on living in that shed forever. 'But I'm not going back there,' I told her.

'We'll see what your parents have to say about that,' she said with certainty.

My mother drove over but didn't get out of the car, just honked the horn, expecting me to come out, get in and go with her.

I refused to budge from the house so Nancy went out and spoke to her through the car window. 'Call the police, then,' she'd called over her shoulder as she walked back to the house. Mum drove away.

I don't know what they said but when Nancy stormed back into the house she declared, 'Stuff that. You can stay here till we get you sorted.'

I found out I was pregnant not long after that and I've lived at Frog Hollow ever since. It might have been just on the other side of town but it was a world away from where I'd grown up. After a while I started calling Nancy 'Mum', or 'Mum Nancy'.

Lionel said that when Hardy died in 1928 it was decided he'd be buried in Poets' Corner in Westminster Abbey but it was also felt that he belonged in Dorset. The local butcher removed Hardy's heart, wrapped it in a cloth and put it in a biscuit tin. Lionel said it was said that Hardy's cat, attracted by the smell, got to the heart before it could be buried.

Hardy's ashes were sent to London and what remained of the heart was buried with his first wife. Then his second wife was buried with them when she died. All the bitterness they shared in life couldn't keep on festering when they were all buried in the ground together, turning to dust, mingling in the dirt.

'Well he had the last laugh,' said Cliff, amused.

'Well, that's because he didn't have a heart,' replied Meredith in a tone that I thought sounded a little cross.

Jimmy's sisters were pushy with my girls when they organised his funeral, until Leigh-Anne pushed back. Lynn even sent a message to me through Kylie saying that it'd be best if I didn't attend. But I wanted to say goodbye with everyone else and wanted to be there with my daughters – our daughters – and it was just meanness to try to keep me out. That's what I told Kiki and she said Jazzie and Leigh-Anne would want me there and I took a comfort from that. I won't share what she said about Lynn.

There were a lot of people. They stood around the walls and crowded out the doors. Leigh-Anne read a poem and Jazzie gave a speech about her times with her Dad and how clever he was. Lynn made another that was all about her and as though the two had got on. If it was me, I would have also talked about what a good father he was and how I'd never heard anyone sing better, how he was good with his hands and could fix anything and how his face would go all soft when he looked at his girls. And I would have told everyone how he taught me that when someone really loves you, they'll never hold a mistake against you. If you truly love somebody, you love them for everything about them, faults and all.

At the end of the service we passed by Jimmy's coffin to say a last goodbye, lay a hand of farewell, or nod respect. His favourite football jumper was laid out on top. He would have liked that.

I waited my place in the queue with everyone else and finally came close to him. Looking down at the coffin, thinking about him lying in there, I realised how far away from me he'd always be now. I looked at the jumper he'd worn so often and thought that if I held it close to my face, I'd be able to smell him again, that scent of his skin when he held me.

It was only when the jumper was pulled from my hands that I came back to the here and now. My instinct was to keep holding it, to not let this piece of Jimmy go, so it took me a moment to understand that Lynn was yelling at me although I could barely understand the words she was saying. It was just the excuse she needed to say she'd been right about not having me there at the funeral and now she was the victim and I'd spoilt it all.

Leigh-Anne was mad at me for what happened. I'd had a few drinks before I went because I knew I would find it so hard to say goodbye to Jimmy and that Lynn would not be happy I was there. I've pretended like I don't know why she's angry and I just hope it will pass. Whatever Jimmy was to me – and he was in my bones and blood – he was her father and it was her day to mourn him, too. And if I knew how, I'd tell her I was sorry. I'd tell Leigh-Anne about that place beyond comfort that Jimmy could take me and how I longed to be there again, even if just for a moment, so I never meant to make her angry or upset. But, as I often say, we've never been the kind of family who talks about these things to one another.

'Even though it was a huge theme in Hardy's books,' Meredith reflected to Lionel and me in the minibus on the way to a place called Bath, 'we're very lucky that we've never had the same restrictive class structure in Australia. It's our great strength, to be so egalitarian.'

Well, I thought, you haven't lived where I live if you think that. My grandfather on my dad's side was a policeman in town. Aunty Elaine said that back when she was younger that what we called Frog Hollow used to be a place where all the Blacks would live. We called it a mission but it was a government reserve. Everyone who lived there had to follow government rules – people needed permission to come and go, to work, to marry. There was no manager on the reserve so all these rules were enforced by the local police, including removing the Aboriginal children from their families. So, there was lots of conflict when the police had all the power and the Aboriginal people had none.

Aunty Elaine's mother told her how, when the pubs closed and the white men were drunk, they'd come down to the mission to find women and take them, knowing that the police wouldn't act if a Black woman said she'd been raped by a white man.

She said that some of the things that happened when Brittany went missing wouldn't have happened if she had been a little white girl. The policeman, the one with the salmon pink face who wasn't so nice, asked whether we were sure she was ours because her skin looked so much lighter than mine. Even the nicer one – the skinny, one – asked if perhaps she'd just gone walkabout.

'What on this earth would you know about walkabout?' Aunty Elaine had growled, looking him up and down in a fury I rarely saw.

Kiki once said that if Brittany's body hadn't been found, they'd have kept on thinking it was one of us. She reckoned they'd have said that of course it was us. What did anyone expect? And she's not wrong because even when someone else was arrested and went to court for her murder, even with all the evidence they had, people still treated me and Jimmy like we'd somehow been involved, as if we wouldn't have given all that we had for it not to have happened, for Brittany to still be with us.

Five years after she went missing, a white boy, James Peterson, drowned in the curve of the river. The rapids would swell if there'd been rain inland and we all knew not to swim there. There was even a story Aunty Elaine used to tell about an evil spirit that lived there so we were all too frightened to go in at that spot. Little James, so adventurous, so young, had been swallowed up whole by the rising water.

A memorial was put near where his body was found, a large stone with his name and words from his family engraved on a steel plate. I told Kiki we should get something like that for Brittany, too. Aunty Elaine started a petition, walking the streets to get it signed. We went to our local member of parliament. We even tried to get the local newspaper to do something. But nothing ever did come of it. In the end we stopped talking about it because we didn't want to admit that one child in our town could matter more than another.

I didn't tell Meredith all of that. I wouldn't have known where to start. So I just nodded at her.

The hotel at Bath was the nicest yet with a bigger room than we'd had so far, and a lovely garden outside the window. On the telly in the bar area we saw Shona's parents give their appeal. Her father spoke, dark-haired with dark circles under his eyes, his skin sweaty like he was fighting a flu.

'If you have our little girl, please bring her back,' he said, as he wiped tears away from his cheeks with his palm.

'We just want her back,' he pleaded. When he looked at the camera, you could see the bloodshot whites of his eyes. He and Shona's mother held hands. She was thin as a skeleton with cropped blonde hair, she stood beside him ghost-like, her bony shoulders hunched and defeated, her body shaking with her sobs.

A police detective then stepped in, asking for people to come forward if they knew anything, and asked that if anyone had her, to return her to her family.

'We love you, Shona,' her father added desperately.

I decided to eat my dinner in our room. I thought Jasmine would argue but she didn't. She put the order in for me before she left to join the others.

I turned the sound off on the telly and opened my gardening book. I read about how to sow seeds and that before you put them in the ground you have to make sure the soil is right. You can't just put them in anywhere. You have to add compost because it has nutrients and the roots suck them up with the water. I didn't know whether the soil in my yard was good or not but, whichever it was, compost would make it better. It made sense that you would have to do all that work beforehand to make sure your plants would grow. It's one of those common-sense things that you just never think about but when it's said plainly, it seems pretty obvious.

The news was repeating the interview with Shona's parents. I turned the sound up and watched them again.

'We just want her back,' her father repeated, the same look on his face, holding the hands of Shona's mother as she shook with the weight of her tears. 'We love you, Shona.'

JASMINE

I WOKE UP early and had the first shower, giving Mum more time to sleep in.

'Feeling okay?' I asked her when I got out, but when she brushed off my question I knew to drop it and just get on with packing, like it was business as usual. That was the unwritten rule of our family. If Mum or Dad had too much to drink in the evening, the next morning it was as if nothing had happened. Even if Aunty Elaine or Aunt Kiki had to get us ready for school, no-one mentioned the night before. We just got on with it. Made it all normal with our silence. It was the way it had always been back then and still firmly the rule now.

Toni had boarded the bus wearing a halter-neck leopard-print dress. Her lips were bright red, her lashes long. She looked like a '60s pin-up, not someone about to embark on day five of a literary tour.

'I like your dress,' I told her.

'Leopard print is my favourite neutral,' she replied.

'How long does it take you to get ready?' I marvelled at her perfect make-up with thin black ticks of liquid black eyeliner above her eyes.

'Quicker than it takes Sam to pick a shirt,' she teased.

'Hey, my shirts are my thing,' Sam responded.

'It must confuse people, the way you dress, when they find out you're such a strong feminist,' I said.

'I have to wait for them to get past their confusion when they find out I'm a lesbian before we even get into that,' she laughed. She was one of those women made even more attractive by her confidence. I thought of Leigh-Anne and the way she always said what she wanted, not afraid of what others thought of her. I thought about the images on Facebook that I'd 'liked' in the past few days and how full of life they were. She was a good mum, happy with her kids, out with friends, surrounded by family. She had found her place, perhaps always knew where it was. I couldn't help but admire her for it. She was, I realised with bittersweetness, happier than me.

Our first stop had been in Southampton, where Jane Austen had lived after Bath and before she moved to Chawton. The house she lived in and the places she frequented had mostly disappeared. It felt like chasing a ghost.

Thomas Hardy designed Max Gate himself and supervised its construction by his father and one of his brothers. With two levels and an attic, the modest Victorian home was built with thrift and practicality. It must have suited his purposes because here he was prolific, writing novels including *The Mayor of Casterbridge*, *Tess of the D'Urbervilles*, *Jude the Obscure* as well as many short stories and a multitude of poems. As the years passed and Hardy's novels became popular, he expanded the house, including the renovation of the two attic rooms for his wife Emma.

'She aspired to write, too. She didn't just want it for him, she wanted it for herself as well,' Lionel told us.

'No wonder over the years she became resentful,' reflected Sam. 'I have to say from the excerpts of her diaries I've read, she didn't have his talent. But his own career wouldn't have existed without her.'

'How so?' prompted Professor Finn, his tone genuine.

'She encouraged him to concentrate on writing. When he became sick, she set up a routine of work so he could meet his commitments. He even dictated a novel to her from his bed and she copied manuscripts. She kept in touch with publishers and in those early days probably saw herself as his literary collaborator but he treated her as if she was no more than a typewriter.'

'Ah, but she didn't have the talent. You said so yourself. And she didn't have the ideas. You can see his point about that. I can understand why he became infuriated when she referred to his work as "ours" and talked about her role in his creative process. Now, I'm not saying that hearth and home and all that aren't important,' Professor Finn said as he held up his hand in a signal to stop, 'but enabling genius isn't the same as having it.'

'I guess I take your point that it's possible to be a genius and an ass at the same time,' Sam concluded.

'I'm not sure that was my point,' he said, with a slight smile.

We were in the study, standing between a fireplace and a bookcase, architectural drawings and photographs on the wall.

Lionel pointed out that Virginia Woolf's father, Leslie Stephen, was Hardy's editor. 'She came to visit once. He hadn't read her work—'

'Lucky for him!' interjected Professor Finn.

'… but she wasn't *vain enough*,' Lionel stressed as he continued, 'to be offended by that. Her husband, Leonard, held the view that Hardy didn't write well but when you looked back on one of his novels as a whole, you could see it was a great work of art.'

'Didn't we just say that about Jane Austen?' Cliff half muttered.

'What Hardy did have was discipline,' Professor Finn conceded. 'He once said, "*I never let a day go without using a pen. Just holding it sets me off …*"' Professor Finn, sensing his audience, waved his hand with a flourish. '"*… in fact, I can't think without it. It's important not to wait for the right mood. If you do it will come less and less.*"'

'God,' said Toni, as we hung back from the group. 'I can't believe that I agree with that old windbag. I say that to my students. Train for writing like you're training for a marathon. Do it every day. Writing takes discipline.'

'Well, even a stopped clock is right twice a day,' Sam reassured her. 'Besides, you're not agreeing with the Professor. You're agreeing with Thomas Hardy, if that's any consolation.'

I found Mum walking in the garden.

'What did you think?' I asked her as we got back onto the bus.

'This garden is a nice place to bury your pets,' she observed.

Whatever cynicism Hardy had about marriage at the end of his life, he'd loved deeply when he first met Emma. They shared a common passion for literature and ambitions to become writers. With classic class snobbery, Emma's family thought Hardy beneath her, and they never changed their opinion about him no matter how great his fame and success. For their part, Hardy's family didn't like Emma. She was well born but penniless and just too old. Neither family was happy about the union. It was a bit like my family. I never met my mother's parents who both died when I was in school. Dad's mum died shortly after the trial for Brittany's murder and Dad's sisters hate my mum. So, no big Christmas dinners in my family, even though we all live in the same town.

Emma hardly saw her own family and was suspicious of her husband's. Hardy, for his part, felt torn between her and them. He took her side against his family but she could never forgive him for no longer including her in his work and for failing to find her an agent when he found them for his other female friends. Into middle age, she no longer wore her hair over her shoulders in curls and her features became heavy. Her conversation meandered and she became more difficult, often reminding him she was superior to him in background and education.

Hardy withdrew to his study, preferring silence to quarrels, holding his rage and depression inwards. Despite the disappointments in their marriage, they shared a bed for twenty-five years before Emma headed to the attic rooms.

Fanny Robin in *Far From the Madding Crowd* and Tess D'Urberville are romantic sufferers who'd fallen prey to men of higher social standing, driven to unhappiness and death. Hardy, I imagine, may have had some sympathy for Leigh-Anne, who found herself pregnant when she was barely seventeen. Leigh-Anne had her first child, Zane, to her high school boyfriend, Vince, the one every other girl dreamt of being seduced by. She moved him on when he couldn't stop seducing every one of those other girls. Leigh-Anne then became pregnant to Jack, the husband of her hairdresser, having her twins Teaghan and Tamara with him. Jack left his wife and moved with Leigh-Anne and the brood to the next town.

Unlike Hardy's defeated heroines, Leigh-Anne was no victim. She scandalised the town and enjoyed the notoriety. 'What are you looking at?' she'd call back if anyone stared too long or with disapproval. I imagine she would have worn a scarlet letter with haughty pride.

We ate lunch in the summer breeze in the back garden of the cottage where Thomas Hardy was born. The Boston sisters looked horrified at the prospect of a picnic on the grass, even with blankets, but Brett managed to find some chairs for them and they sat regally. Professor Finn reclined at their feet like a portrait by Manet, a pose that seemed more by design than accident.

'I'll concede,' he told them, 'that Hardy knew how to write landscape.'

In this gentle environment, a peace mingled around us, like we were all on the same side, and somehow it was like the awkwardness of Mum's performance at dinner last night had never happened.

White-winged butterflies circled in clusters against the sunlit summer haze. The ancient Greeks believed that after death a soul fluttered away from the body in the form of a butterfly. The Greek symbol for the soul was a butterfly-winged girl, Psyche. Aphrodite, the goddess of love, became so jealous of her beauty that she ordered her son, Eros, to make Psyche fall in love with him. Instead, he fell in love with her.

I looked over at Mum. She sat on the blanket, legs folded underneath her and eyes closed, head tilted to the sun as if her skin could drink it in. She looked serene, relaxed.

I shut my eyes, too. The soft wind felt like the day was breathing on me. There's a scene in *Jude the Obscure* where Jude, born to a class where access to higher education was impossible, could see the lights of the university town of Christminster that he dreamt of attending. As a teenager, sitting on Aunty Elaine's back porch after reading that passage, I too had turned my head towards the direction of Sydney – hundreds of kilometres away. I inhaled the air from that direction. 'I'll be there too,' I promised myself.

Not surprisingly, Bathsheba in *Far From the Madding Crowd* didn't like her name. Try being born with Jazzmine. Jazzie for short. 'Jazzie' always felt like a misnomer, that my personality should have been sequined and showy instead of bookish and shy. I hated the crassness of it – the hillbilly spelling, the yokel way it looked on the page. It seemed to sum up all the reasons people would look down on my family and me. 'I'm not being snobby,' I told Aunty Elaine. 'It's a real barrier.'

Aunty Elaine used to say that we're all made of the same stuff. No person, once you look past the colour of their skin or the place they were born, is better or worse than any other. And wherever we end up after the spirits call us home, our bodies all turn back to the earth. But that's how life should be, not how it is.

'But your mother loved that name,' Aunty Elaine told me. 'She said it was special – one of a kind – just like you. She thought the name sounded like a precious jewel.'

I told her about an experiment that showed how job applicants with African American names, like Lakisha and Jamal, had to send out fifteen resumes to get one call-back, while those with the names Emily and Greg only had to send ten.

'I don't know how those facts mean more than what's in your mother's heart?' she asked, puzzled.

Growing up, I had been hurt by Joshua Payne and Felicity Fletcher but there was a part of me that understood why their parents recoiled from us. When I was a kid, I thought it was natural that we'd all pile into one house and sleep on couches or on the floor one night and the next sleep in someone else's house. It wasn't like we didn't know where everyone was. We'd always been taught that older kids had to look after younger ones. We shared our toys and no-one took much mind about keeping their yards tidy – except Aunty Elaine with her carefully clipped roses. After Brittany went missing, people did start locking their houses for a while and were extra watchful of each other but after the trial we went back to living that way.

I can see how it looked from outside, how it might appear that we weren't looked after. Our parents would do their drinking and partying outside instead of inside so we looked rowdy and wild, openly displaying the behaviour white people kept from public view. I can see why we were judged harshly and I wanted to shed it, to say I wasn't like that. None of us were but I badly wanted to escape the stain. I've put an end to all that now. No more 'Jazzie'. I changed my name by deed poll while I was at university so I could graduate with the name Jasmine.

Leigh-Anne rang me one day when I was in my last year of university. 'Guess which loser just moved into this town?'

When she mentioned Joshua's name, I still felt a stab of anxiety. He'd gone to university to be a dentist and was home to work in the local practice.

'Imagine looking into someone's gob all day?' she laughed.

'It's not a competition,' I told her, even though for me it was.

It is a curse of its own, the attempt to reach the point of being acceptable to the people who think you are inherently unacceptable, to show them you're an 'exception', as if it will prove all their underlying prejudices are wrong.

I wasn't like Leigh-Anne. I was the quiet one. That's the story I tell myself. But if I'm honest, it's more 'the bad one' and 'the good one'. I didn't want to be the loud troublemaker, the disruptive one. She didn't care what people thought; I wanted to make a good impression, craved approval and acceptance. That's the truth of it.

Annie had once mentioned a phenomenon called 'stereotype threat' when she was writing an assignment on it. It describes the anxiety people feel when they fear being stereotyped about their social group. This anxiety affects their performance. For example, stereotype threat can lower the performance of African Americans taking the SAT test used for college entrance in the United States, if they are aware of a racist stereotype that African Americans are less intelligent than other groups. Importantly, a person doesn't need to believe in the stereotype for the threat to be activated; they just need to be aware that other people are holding those negative views.

What stereotype threat highlights is how hard it is to move away from the impacts of entrenched racist and sexist views that surround us. We can't shed that burden at the door.

And I carried it. I hadn't wanted to be like Leigh-Anne, I feared being seen as the negative things she was – wild, uncontrollable, unteachable, untameable. A mouthy Aboriginal woman who stands up for herself was something to be feared and derided. I'd tried to be the one who defied expectations and went to university. And for what? How had the entrenched racism in my home town changed in one single way because of my meekness and trying to prove a point? Leigh-Anne never felt the need to prove anything to anybody and, from somewhere inside, I felt a sudden twinge of jealousy.

We headed into Bath that evening, where Jane Austen had been a happy visitor but a reluctant, unhappy resident. Her father retired there after he'd handed his rectory over to one of his sons and Jane, as an unmarried, dependent daughter, had no choice but to follow. She lived in Bath until her father's death in 1805, then moved to Southampton with her sister and mother to live with her brother Frank, by then an Admiral, and his wife. From one male protector to another.

Mum decided to stay in our room for dinner. I didn't argue with her after her behaviour at dinner the night before. I ordered her a meal and joined Sam and Toni outside. It felt like we were skipping school. We found a pizza restaurant up the road that they joked was 'carnivore friendly' for me.

Sam topped up our glasses of wine while Toni asked me if I had any brothers or sisters.

'I have a sister but we're not close,' I said. Leigh-Anne had slipped into my thoughts all day but my immediate reaction was to distance myself from her, especially to two people who didn't even know her. And why didn't I say anything about Brittany? I had a sister but she died. It was too important to say lightly even though you couldn't understand the rest of us if you didn't know that.

'I like your Mum,' Toni said, almost to change the subject.

'That's because you don't have to live with her,' I said.

As we walked back to the hotel, I thought of Fiona McCoy. After being removed at the age of two from her mother, Fiona had turned out to be too much trouble, too much hard work, for everyone who took her into their care, and somehow the child protection department eventually made the decision to return Fiona to her mother. By then, Fiona was eleven years old. One can assume that Fiona would not have stabbed John Andrews if she'd not been on remand for attempting to kill her mother.

When I got back to the hotel I found the room empty, although the television was on and the room service tray had been plundered. I put the tray outside the hotel room door and went to find Mum. It wasn't hard. I headed straight for the bar and found her talking to the barman. A glass – of gin? vodka? – sat in front of her. Her head tilted back as she looked up to speak to the man in the white shirt and black vest that barely buttoned over his middle-aged spread. I could see Leigh-Anne in her. No wonder those two fought all the time. Two peas in a pod. Sure, Leigh-Anne is feisty like Kiki, but like Mum she knows who she is and is unapologetic about it. Neither saw any reason to change.

I could always see my family in each other but I never saw them in myself. The thought hurt a little, which didn't make any sense since I was trying so hard to be as little like them as I could.

'Time for bed, Mum,' I said. 'We've got an early start.'

DAY 6

DELLA

IT WAS NICE to just stay in one place and not have to pack our bags. It's only been a few days and I'm not complaining but I have to say I'm happy for the change.

We met up in the hotel lobby after breakfast, all except the Boston sisters who seem to always run their own race. Lionel rang their room and when they didn't answer we decided, like a mutiny on a pirate ship, that we'd leave without them. Even the Professor joined in. But just as we were about to set off, they emerged through the hotel doors. We were all a little disappointed that we couldn't make our point.

'Now ladies, you kept us waiting,' the Professor said in the voice I reckon he used when talking to a room full of students. They responded with a look that said they had no idea what he was talking about. I know plenty of people like that back home. It doesn't matter what you tell them, they refuse to see what they don't want to see.

This morning was a walking tour and it was lucky I packed those comfy shoes because we were going all over town again. I did like the places we walked with their wide streets and neat houses with white pillars, all like mansions. Compared to Frog Hollow, it was chalk and cheese.

We walked across a bridge that had little shops built into it and although Lionel said there were lots like that once – even London Bridge once had them – I can tell you I'd never seen anything like it before. You can't imagine building shops on any of the bridges back home.

I went to write *Bridge with shops* in my book and was surprised to see the words *Shona. Shona. Shona.* I didn't remember writing it but there it was in black and white in my own messy handwriting. It must have been from yesterday when I could've sworn I'd written no notes at all. Life's always full of mysteries.

We came to a place where there'd been a haberdasher's shop and I imagined hats with ribbons and lace. You don't hear the word 'haberdasher' very much these days but I guess you also don't see as many hats and lace as you once did. It's funny how a word can take you back in time. When Lionel started to talk about Jane Austen's aunt, Jane Leigh-Perrot, and what happened to her, well that made me sit up and take notice.

She spelt her name the same way as we spell Leigh-Anne. Jimmy's sister Lynn said the spelling was pretentious and I didn't know at first that she was meaning it as an insult, but if there was a connection between this Mrs Leigh-Perrot and my Leigh-Anne it was that both were people you'd soon be sorry you took on.

I was always interested in anything that had to do with the courts and law so the second thing that got my attention was that this Mrs Leigh-Perrot was arrested and accused of stealing some lace from this shop. It was a time when you could get yourself hanged for just stealing a loaf of bread so this was no small thing. Mrs Leigh-Perrot had her principles so she insisted on proving her innocence and spent eight months in custody living in the jailer's house waiting for her trial. She was acquitted and it turned out the whole thing had been an attempt to blackmail her by the shopkeeper that backfired because he'd picked the wrong person.

He'd think twice before trying that one again. I'm glad for her that a trial cleared her because I can tell you that if you think it's always going to put an end to things, you don't know as much about it as I do.

We stopped outside a restaurant that was all white and glass with napkins on the inside. Once it had been a place to be seen and was certainly nicer than anything at home. That wasn't the most remarkable thing about this Pump Room though. Underneath was a Roman bath. Lionel said you could try the water but it smells like sulphur and has a bitter taste. Helen Finn had a go at it. The look on her face meant the rest of us didn't feel much inclined to.

Lionel said that the Romans had settled here because of the hot springs. When he said we were going to see the baths I thought it would be like a bathtub but that wasn't the case at all. It was more like swimming pools and the word I thought of was 'labyrinth'. That's a word you don't use much in Frog Hollow but in these baths, each time you walked down a set of stairs there was another and there were several different pools with the water and pipes all interconnecting and a small-scale replica that showed you how everything would have looked – so grand and white, although the stones are now all dark and underground.

As I took each step, I thought about how many Roman feet must have walked across these same stones all those centuries ago. It was pretty impressive, what the Romans did with all their roads and buildings and what an impact it all had because you could still see so much of what they had done and even by today's standards, they did pretty well.

That must be what my father would compare Aboriginal people to – that we didn't build bathhouses and roads and the like. It was true that Aboriginal people didn't have pottery but is that the only thing you should judge by? The Romans had crucifixions and watched people kill each other for sport and had slaves. Aboriginal people didn't have any of that and they also didn't go around invading other countries and conquering people. Aunty Elaine used to say my father was ignorant. 'He has a heart the size of a pea,' she said once, and she didn't know the half of it. My father had no idea that Aboriginal people had places where they harvested and built weirs and lines and fishing nets and I'm not sure he would have cared to know if you tried to tell him. He was one of those people who don't want to hear it if they're wrong.

There must be evidence of all these things, too, if people knew how to find it like Aunty Elaine could. What might look like a marking in a tree was where a shield or a canoe had once been carved. What looked like rocks by a river bank was an old midden where people prepared and cooked their meals. We lasted generation after generation so we must have been doing something right. And we're still going – unlike the Romans who made it here, where everything now is buried ruins – which I wanted to point out to someone but there was no-one to tell.

I thought about all that as we went through the cool underground rooms and the place that was once the courtyard. We learnt about the Roman gods and how the Romans would throw objects into one of the pools for good luck and I thought of all the little trinkets that had been left for the children in the Foundling Museum that were like offerings in a different way, and how we give gifts as a kind of ritual or ceremony and hope good luck will come to us or pass on to someone else.

You sort of think of things as always moving forward but it seemed like there was as much to like about Roman times with their buildings and plumbing as there was to despair about the London that Charles Dickens wrote about with the poor houses and so many unwanted babies. So, sometimes the world goes forward but it's important to remember that sometimes it can move backwards too.

'It is so much more impressive than Stonehenge,' Meredith observed. 'I thought that was a bit like the *Mona Lisa*, you just think it's going to be bigger.'

I thought of Pat at the salon who could also talk about all the different places she'd been and for the first time I thought maybe those were things that I'd like to see, too, and maybe I could come back with Kiki one day. We might have to get separate rooms, Kiki and me, or there'd be blues. It would be the same with Leigh-Anne. We live close to each other every day but that's not what it's like when you're travelling.

In fact, I think Jazzie is the only person I could share such close spaces with. I smiled at the funny fact that the daughter I lived closest to was the one I couldn't be in a closed space with for too long, but the one who lived furthest away was less likely to get on my nerves. I don't love one daughter more than another, they're just different and so your relationship with each is different, too. There's no point in ranking them.

After all that up and down the stairs I needed a break and I was glad we were having lunch back in the Pump Room and I could rest up. I could tell that morning when I put on my trousers that they were a bit looser and I don't think there was much I'd done over the past years that had been as successful at taking off a little weight, though I often thought maybe I should try. But things just creep up on you. Life just passes by and the next thing you know it's Christmas all over again.

The afternoon had more walking and I said to Jazzie that she was right to come at this time of year to a place where it was such nice weather when the frosts were coming at home. I've never liked the cold. People who prefer the cold say you can always put more clothes on but when it's hot you can't take them off. Maybe they have a point but once the cold seeps into my bones I find that not much can take that chill out again.

We walked through a park and at the top of the hill there were houses all in a curve. Lionel said it was a crescent and I guess that's like the moon. Because it was a hill, there were views out over the countryside. Lionel said the houses were Georgian style with Ionic columns. I asked Lionel what an Ionic column was because I'd not heard of such a thing before.

'I'll show you,' he said, and looked through his folder for a piece of paper.

I handed him my notebook, which I opened to a blank page in the middle. I wouldn't have wanted other people to write in my notebook because they were my thoughts but I didn't mind him doing it. He drew three columns that would be on buildings. One had little scrolls across the top and these were Ionic, then there was one that had flat slabs on the top and these were Doric and then the Corinthian ones had fancy leaves on the top. I'd never thought about them before but now I was going to check out which was which. It felt good to know something about buildings that I'd never known before. Lionel was close when he drew in my notebook and his aftershave, spicy and musky, seemed to still hang between us after he moved away. I closed my book, holding onto it and the treasures it contained.

There were some benches that looked across the town and the fields. I sat on one with Meredith and Cliff and watched the view as Jasmine and her friends walked around the crescent looking at the houses up close. The Professor and his wife and the two sisters were off together, their own little group again, and he was pointing things out to them as they all listened intently.

'I was interested,' Meredith said to me, 'and I hope you don't mind me asking, but is it true that Dreamtime stories are like laws?'

I'd never have thought of myself as knowing all that much about it, especially not if you knew Aunty Elaine and compared yourself to her, but I guess others know even less than me.

'I like to call them cultural stories because they're still at the heart of our culture today,' I told her, saying exactly what I'd heard Aunty Elaine say about the matter.

So, I told Meredith about my favourite story, about a tribe where the women would gather food and the men would go and hunt but they would bring everything back to share. All the while, the grandmothers would look after the children. Among the tribe was a Cleverman who could change into different animals. He was a bad man and didn't like children, especially when they were happy.

'One day,' I told them, 'when the parents were away, he saw a whirlwind coming. The children became scared and ran to the camp but one little boy couldn't keep up and he was swept away, carried off. So, when the parents returned to the camp everyone was crying.'

Lionel had joined us and was standing nearby and listening. I tried to tell the story the way that Aunty Elaine had.

'The parents thought something was wrong and became suspicious about the old Cleverman. But they were cautious because they knew of his powers. Then men from another tribe came and said that they were going to the fish traps. They noticed that there was sadness in the camp and when they heard the story of what had happened to the little boy they said they'd ask their own Cleverman about it. When a man from the other tribe returned, he had two balls of red gum from one of the trees and said that these would help to catch the old man.

'The tribe knew that their Cleverman had a sore back and liked to have it rubbed by the fire. When they next rubbed his back with emu fat and goanna oil, the old man couldn't see the balls of tree gum. So, when he turned over with his eyes closed, they put the gum on his eyes. He screamed in pain and jumped into the air. Everyone expected him to land back on the ground but he kept jumping and screaming until he disappeared. Then the tribe heard a strange sound in the darkness that they'd never heard before. When they looked to see where the sound came from, they saw an owl with big red eyes looking down on them.

'So,' I said to my little audience, 'that's how the night owl came to be, a long time ago, back when the world was young.'

I usually feel like I don't know much that will help anyone and when those quiz shows on the television ask lots of questions, I don't know many answers except if it's about country music. I'd never had the feeling that what I knew was something other people were interested in. But for a moment I was just like the Professor except with a different audience. I was glad that Lionel had been there to listen even though I felt a little sad that Jazzie had missed it, because it was one of those things that when you tell someone about it afterwards it's not the same as being there.

Lionel took us back into town to what was called the Assembly Rooms that had been another place where people came in Jane Austen's time – to be seen, to dance and to play cards. It was now a fashion museum and I liked looking at all the clothes from all the different eras. There was even a black dress that Queen Victoria wore and I guess it was like that thing with Stonehenge and *Mona Lisa* where you'd think it was going to be bigger. She must have been a very small person, almost as wide as she was tall, which you don't pick up when you see her played by actresses on the telly.

Lionel said she'd gone into mourning when her husband died and he and Meredith both looked at me in a way that showed they were thinking of me and my recent loss. I turned to check where Jasmine was and she was with her friends looking at the dresses from the 1960s, like the ones my mother used to wear. Whatever else you can say about my mother, she always dressed nice. For her, it was what's on the outside that mattered.

There is a lot of work in the dresses, all the stitching that is done by hand. I don't want to sound like one of those 'back in the day' people but it wasn't that long ago that you mostly made your own clothes. Aunty Elaine would whip them up from those patterns that you could buy one of and it would help you make several different styles. All that has disappeared since you can just buy things cheaply in the shops.

Lionel said that everyone should do their own thing that night. I think he knew we'd need a bit of a break from each other and he probably needed one from us, too, which can make a person feel sad but it's not personal, it's just a fact.

I was right, too, because when we got back to our hotel I heard Lionel say to those Boston sisters when they asked him to dinner that he didn't have meals with people on the tour because of the rules. So I'm glad I didn't ask.

Meredith and Cliff suggested a pre-dinner drink in the garden and that sounded very pleasant and I was pleased Jasmine agreed to come along, too. Cliff ordered the drinks and was attentive in a way that brought to mind the word 'gentleman'. He's a lawyer – or he'd been one before he retired – and he spoke with Jasmine about a case she was working on that had been in the news.

Meredith was trying to talk to me to learn more about the Aboriginal things, which was nice in a way but also hard in another because I didn't know all the answers to her questions even though she seemed to expect that I would. But when people are well-meaning like Meredith, you have to meet kindness with kindness.

We talked about the cultural story I'd told earlier in the day. I'd always thought of it as being about how the owl came along and why it had red eyes but it's really about how to punish the old man for not looking after the children and letting one get taken. It also told you that you could use emu fat and goanna oil to treat pain and that the fish traps were a place where people would meet. It showed that the women would collect yams, echidnas and lizards and collect fruit and berries and that everyone had to share their food and carry the load. So, the more you think about it, perhaps it was like laws, not like in the books a judge might use, but in a community to tell you what you should and shouldn't do. The more you thought about it, the more you could unpick it all.

As I was trying to explain things to Meredith, I caught snippets of what Jasmine was saying to Cliff. Things like, 'cold-blooded killer' and 'release date'. She didn't talk about her work much, at least not to me, and strangely I hadn't thought before now about how much it might interest me. I had a lot of questions for Jazzie that I wanted to ask her when we were back in our room.

I was always proud of her with her studies and getting good marks and things but when we talk on the phone it's mostly about what's happening with me, Kiki, Leigh-Anne and my grandchildren or what's happening with her and her friends. All you want most for your children really is that they'll be happy and in that way she's a hard one to please. I often think she's got her work cut out for her in finding her way through some parts of life, even though she finds it easy in others.

As we walked through the bar to the restaurant, the telly was on and I looked at the screen to see yellow police tape and men in white protective suits like space men looking through what I recognised from the other news reports to be Hampstead Heath. In the text underneath the images I saw the words: *Shona's body found.* And you know that feeling you get when your stomach tightens because you know something bad is going to happen and you can't stop it? Well, I had that.

A body of a young child had been discovered in the park, not far from where Shona and her family had been having their picnic. It had been buried in bushes, wrapped in a blanket so it took some searching before it was uncovered. A policeman said that the matter was now being treated as a homicide.

I know that feeling too, of having your insides pulled out, of having hope turn to a cold acceptance and it's not the opposite of hope because it's so much darker than that. And despite the facts, you keep believing, against all the evidence, that there's been a mistake and somehow your daughter will come home again. I guess that's natural. 'Instinct' is the word that comes to mind.

I thought about the Romans and the ruins and all of the things that lie under the ground we walk on, about Shona's buried body and all the bones of people that have never been found, of the artefacts from people's lives that are long gone – the fishing hooks, earrings, spearheads, urns. All these things lie in the soil as forests and cities grow over them and as life moves on.

Jazzie and I were the only ones from the tour in the hotel restaurant that night. Lionel came in while I was eating my roast chicken. He was still in his suit from the day and I thought then how he would never get to relax because he is always working when he's on the tour. Jazzie asked him to join us but I remembered what he'd said to the Boston sisters.

'He's not allowed to. It's against company rules,' I said, so he wouldn't have to say no himself, to avoid him having to feel awkward or rude.

'Surely that's not true,' my daughter said, and I was annoyed because why would I make up something like that when I would have liked Lionel to have had a meal with just us?

Lionel nodded. 'I have some brushing up to do for tomorrow,' he said, waving the book under his arm. He went and sat at a table in the corner and I was sorry that he was on his own. It seemed a pity to me.

Afterwards, Jazzie set her computer up so we could call Kiki. I could see her on the screen with her kitchen behind her.

'It's all going well without you,' she told me.

'That's good,' I said, but I was also miffed as I wanted to be missed a little.

Kiki held up Mookie, my black cat with the white eye-patch and Polly, my little dog that was part Scottish terrier. Kiki's image would sometimes freeze on the screen and there was a delay in her words but I got to see them and that's better than just hearing them. Kiki said she was going over to see Leigh-Anne tomorrow and that gave me a little pang, too.

'I miss you all,' I told her, but the connection between us had gone and she was just frozen in time.

As I laid in bed later that night waiting for sleep I thought about the cultural story I'd told earlier in the day and how it taught messages about looking after children and sharing. I thought about Shona, her little life taken.

Then I wondered about what would have happened if they'd never found Brittany's body – if the whole thing had been left as a question mark, a void filled with nothing but shapeless rumours. Eight months after she went missing, a man walking in the bush on the other side of town came across a child's body. It was just a skeleton and they ended up identifying Brittany from the clothing, her blue heart pyjamas.

Jimmy saw the remains and he told me I shouldn't look at them. After I saw the effect it had on him, I took his word for it. Something broke in him when he had to see our little girl that way – one of those things you see and then can never unsee. And of course, he had the most proof that she was never coming back so hope was killed in him that way as well. If you didn't think your heart could break over and over again, I'm here to tell you that it can.

The police did show me her pyjama top with mud on it and the holes where there hadn't been any and the pink hairclip.

They also found some other things nearby – a man's T-shirt and a cigarette. They told me that the discovery meant two things: the bones, clothing and surrounding area might yield up more clues to help them solve the mystery, to find who had done this; and the discovery meant Brittany hadn't run away and they could now treat it as a homicide.

I can tell you that I was surprised and it would be an understatement to say that I was more than a bit angry when the police told me that because Brittany had only been seven and I knew all along that she hadn't run away. I'd told the police that from the get-go – over and over again. She was a child that stayed close, always looked after her sisters and was really doted on by Jimmy. She always loved her dad.

Finding her body gave me a chance to bury her. We had a coffin the size her body should have been but it was just fragments, so I added a few of her favourite things – a rainbow jumper and her unicorn that she'd once carried around everywhere. We'd had to make choices – about flowers, words and music. I left the songs to Jimmy. He didn't want to speak at the funeral, so picking a song was his way of having words that said what he felt.

Jimmy's sister Lynn said I shouldn't speak at all. Her attitude hurt me even though I didn't want to say anything. Kiki said it for me and I was grateful to her for that. She read a poem I'd heard in a movie that I liked, about the stars not being wanted anymore and packing up the moon.

Lynn and Kiki got into it afterwards and it was Jimmy who told them to stop. I won't repeat what they said to each other or what he said to them, but I remember because he so rarely said anything back at that time. He was never one to lose his temper so it always made an impact when he did.

Country town funerals are always large because everyone knows everyone else. So many people was overwhelming. The only thing that was any comfort was Aunty Elaine. She took me aside and we went for a walk down the road and onto her favourite bush path. She took my hand in hers. 'The earth has taken her back now,' she told me. 'The old people will look after her. She'll be safe with them.'

I often think about what Aunty Elaine said. I also remember that feeling I had that night when I saw the mist marching down the road. Now I like to think that however all that stuff works, Jimmy has joined Brittany again – and that would soothe some of his deepest wounds.

JASMINE

JANE AUSTEN HAD loved life in the rectory at Steventon where she'd grown up and it's said she fainted when told that, upon her father's retirement, she was to move with her parents and sister to Bath.

Bath is still a Georgian city. It became a great health and pleasure resort for the wealthy after Queen Anne visited in 1702. By the eighteenth century it was as famous for its shops, balls, concerts and the theatre where people could be seen, as it was for its waters where they could rest and relax. But by the beginning of the nineteenth century it had become a retreat for retirees like the elderly Reverend Austen. Jane wrote two novels largely based there. In *Persuasion*, written twenty years after *Northanger Abbey*, Bath is noticeably less fashionable. When Dickens wrote of it in *The Pickwick Papers* nearly twenty years on, the decline had clearly continued.

Unlike Southampton yesterday morning, Jane Austen could be found all over Bath. As we walked the boulevards, I felt I'd fallen into the pages of *Persuasion* that I knew by heart. Lady Dalrymple had lived in style at Laura Place; Sir Walter Elliot made his home in Camden Crescent. Milsom Street was where Anne Elliot encountered Admiral Croft to learn that Louisa Musgrove had married Benwick and Captain Frederick Wentworth was still unattached. In that same street is Mollands, the pastry shop where Captain Wentworth offers Anne his umbrella. The Westgate Buildings were where Anne Elliot visited her old school friend and learnt of her cousin's manipulations. The White Hart, once a coaching inn, was where the Musgroves stayed as they prepared for the wedding and where Captain Wentworth wrote his letter to Anne confessing he still loved her.

While all this made Jane Austen feel present in the pavements, her time living here was one of creative desolation. She produced nothing in the nine-year break between drafting her first three novels and her last three, a long silence by anyone's measure.

'What do you think it was about this place that meant she was so unproductive?' asked Toni, as she looked around the carefully planned arcades. 'It looks nice enough.'

'I guess it's like Virginia Woolf said, you need the right conditions to write. She had them in Steventon and Chawton,' observed Sam as she waved her arms around, 'but couldn't find them here.'

'Where you live doesn't always feel like home,' I added. I remembered how excited I was to move to the city, away from Frog Hollow, but how it wasn't as easy to build a new life as I'd thought it would be. I was the bookworm in the family and I had learnt to study with lots of noise in the background. From Kylie always watching television over at our place to Leigh-Anne's voice thundering through the house and all the other kids from Frog Hollow yelling outside as they played up and down the street, noise was a constant companion. At university, I needed the television or radio on with the sound down low or the murmurings of a coffee shop to be able to study, going directly against what Virginia Woolf thought to be the natural order of things.

Jane Austen mocked people who wallowed in their own afflictions but in *Sense and Sensibility*, when she describes Marianne Dashwood's inability to combat her misery at having her heart broken by Willoughby, willing herself into serious illness, she showed she understood the nature of depression. If she suffered from it during her time in Bath, it would undoubtedly have interfered with her ability to write; and not writing, an activity that gave joy, structure and discipline to her day, could have compounded her blackened mood. A vicious cycle.

In 1802, while living in Bath, Jane and Cassandra went back to Steventon and stayed at Manydown Park with their old friends, the Bigg sisters. While there, Jane received an offer of marriage from their brother – and heir to the estate – Harris Bigg-Wither. Said to be pleasant though awkward in manner, he was twenty-one years old to Jane's twenty-six. He was not a Mr Darcy or a Mr Knightley but nor was he a Mr Collins or a Mr Rushworth. Marriage would have allowed Jane to be mistress of a large Hampshire estate only a few miles from her childhood home and to ensure the comfort of her parents and sister.

Jane accepted the offer in the evening but by the following morning had changed her mind. Jane and Cassandra fled to the Steventon rectory, both distressed, and begged their brother to take them back to Bath. In a time when marriage was about practicalities, perhaps it mattered to Jane that she didn't love Harris and that he wasn't her intellectual equal. For all that the union would have given her, she didn't want to sacrifice herself for it even at a time when society expected women to do that all the time for financial comfort. A feminist before the word was first used in the English language.

'I think she knew that it wasn't the easy way,' Sam concluded, 'you've got to admire her for that. Even today, that would be a tempting offer. In her day, people would have thought she was certifiably crazy. You can't deny that for her time she had a world view that isn't out of place today.'

Harris Bigg-Withers for his part didn't pine for long. Two years later he married a woman from the Isle of Wight who did love him and they had ten children.

'There's no evidence Jane Austen ever regretted her decision to turn down the marriage proposal even when she found her life in Bath and Southampton trying,' observed Toni.

'She was no Anne Elliot, living unhappily with her decision to reject the offer,' Sam said, taking her hand. I watched their fingers entwine.

There's always been much speculation about Cassandra's role in the broken engagement. Did she have her own agenda in not wanting to lose her sister and closest companion, not wanting to see her marry when she herself hadn't? Or did she believe in Jane's talent and sense of independence and not want to see either compromised?

We walked back into town, to the Assembly Rooms where Jane Austen danced under the glittering light of its five chandeliers in the 'Upper Rooms' and where, in the Concert Room, Anne realises that Captain Wentworth is jealous of her cousin's attentions towards her. On the lower level there is now a fashion museum.

Toni, who today had a black wiggle dress with a print of red lipsticks on it and a glossy red belt, fawned over the Dior dress, pointed out the intricate needlework in the corsets and sighed at the grey Mary Quant dress with white blouse and its epitomising of the free-spirited style of the 1960s.

'Look at the structure in this dress,' she said, standing in front of a Vivienne Westwood in pale green silk that wrapped around the chest and flounced in a skirt. 'Or the structure in that,' she pointed to a Roland Mouret frock.

I wanted to say they were just clothes. Then, as if reading my mind – or perhaps my body language gave me away – Toni launched an offensive. 'Look at the fuss we all made of the architecture this morning. Clothes are also designs and we live in them every day. They reflect our personality, our style. Every time we choose clothing from a rack, we make a statement about who we are.

Clothes reveal things about our values, our taste. Look at the art in the needlework and beading, in the structure and the cut. Fashion is seen as frivolous, rather than as a skill or an art, because it is so much in the domain of women.'

'Fashion as a feminist statement,' quipped Sam. Toni withdrew her hand from Sam's, sensitive to the remark.

I quietly wandered away, leaving them to their own small tensions and wondered where Mum was.

When I found her she was with Meredith and Cliff.

'What did you think of all the clothes?'

'They were like works of art,' she said. 'You don't think about it but you look at the details and all the work that goes into it and it's a lot more effort than people think.'

'Quite right,' I replied with a smile, thinking of how Toni would have appreciated the comment.

I walked with Mum to the final stop on this part of our tour – the Jane Austen Centre where a Mr Darcy dressed in a blue jacket and cream pants of the era greeted us.

'It doesn't look very practical for mowing the lawn,' Mum told him.

'I suspect I had a lot of servants to do that for me,' the young Mr Darcy replied.

Inside, Mum looked around. 'I wonder if they have anything about that Parrot woman,' she asked.

I looked at her trying to recall what she could possibly have been talking about.

'You know,' she continued, 'the one who was accused of stealing the lace but didn't.'

I studied Mum surreptitiously as we meandered through the museum. She looked at the bonnets with their feathers and trimmings, the jackets with their tailoring and buttons, and the petticoats of delicate handmade lace.

With her father's death, Jane Austen lost someone who had encouraged and supported her talent and her financial situation became more precarious. Austen's heroines often see the faults of their parents and have to navigate them. Elizabeth Bennet has her foolish, indiscreet mother; Eleanor is almost parent to Mrs Dashwood; Emma has to indulge her hypochondriac father; Fanny Price's mother has made bad life choices; and Anne Elliot has her vain, irresponsible father.

My mother is no caricature. It was easy to draw the link between Brittany going missing and all that happened afterwards and now. Mental health issues are intrinsically selfish, and the struggle to be normal is complicated, made harder by the struggle to pay attention to the needs and cares of others.

'Are you joining us for dinner?' Toni asked, interrupting my jumbled thoughts of family and home.

'I'll stay with Mum,' I answered reflexively.

'She's welcome, too,' urged Sam.

'No, I think she might need to rest up.'

I agreed to drinks in the garden with Mum, Meredith and Cliff. One wouldn't hurt her, I always told myself – as if she ever only drank one. And I felt like I could sure use a glass of wine myself.

While my mother and Meredith were engrossed in their own discussions, Cliff spoke of his work in his local legal practice and the strain of a job where people only came to you when they were in trouble. In sympathy, I mentioned my work in the prisons, almost relieved to find someone who would understand the draining effect that casework can have on you.

Cliff exuded a kindness in the way he spoke, which stood in stark contrast to the jaded colleagues I'd come across, those who had become cynical and lacked empathy with the people they worked with. 'Have a tissue, it's tax deductible,' was the kind of thing they would say.

'It takes its toll, that kind of work,' Cliff smiled gently. 'You need to make sure it doesn't harden you up because that's not a good life for you. Certainly not at home. Don't learn that the hard way like I did.'

'My last case was the reason I needed this break. If you saw the news, you'd think my client was a cold-blooded killer. What she did was awful – to an innocent man, a family man with a wife and children. But then, when you look into it, the things she went through in her own childhood were horrific.'

'Were you working on that case where the girl – what was her name – killed the man working in the juvenile detention centre?'

I nodded sheepishly at my indiscretion.

'The media love a bad guy,' Cliff continued. 'A good soundbite or a headline that will sell a paper or make you click on it. When you work in the law, you know it's always a lot more complicated than that. But it must have been brutal. She went away for a long time, if I remember.'

'My real concern now is that there is no place within the prison system to really deal with someone with her complex issues. She has a release date and, sure, it's a long time off, but one day she'll be eligible for parole and there's nowhere that can cater for her, for the level of care she'll need to ensure she doesn't hurt herself or anyone else. That link between justice and fairness you think is going to be there never is.'

'That's why they call it a justice system, not a fairness system. And I've never been much convinced by the justice part either. Which is the cynicism you get when you have done as many ugly family law cases as I have.'

I nodded distractedly at Cliff because my attention had been drawn by the strange occurrence of overhearing Meredith asking my mother about one of Aunty Elaine's stories – something I had never heard Mum talk about before. I made a mental note to ask her about it later.

Walking through the bar on the way up to our room, the television was on with the sound down but Mum and I both saw the news banner: *Shona's body found*. We watched as the known facts were covered and started to repeat. Found on the heath. By council workers clearing an area near a pond. Wrapped in a blanket. Body identified as Shona's. Cause of death not known as yet. Autopsy being done.

The man who murdered my sister, Tom Hadley, was not suffering from a mental illness when he killed her even though what he did was not something that any sane person would do. He'd come into our room in the early hours of the morning and carried Brittany out while my mother, Leigh-Anne and I were sleeping. If I'd been the one sleeping closest to the door rather than nearest the window, it could have been me.

I'd come across his file a year ago. I shouldn't have looked but I did, requesting it to assist with the preparation of another case, and saw his psychological report. No psychiatric disorders but a history of criminal sexual behaviour with women that had escalated over time. His pattern was to drug women and sexually assault them while they were unconscious. He knew in these circumstances his victims would make bad witnesses in a 'he said, she said,' scenario, increasing the chances of getting away with his crimes. He chose his victims accordingly – young and easily manipulated, often with addictions, and he often targeted Aboriginal women, knowing that they were less likely to go to the police and less likely to be believed if they did.

Hadley was being considered for a reduction in his security rating because he was coming close to seven years before he would be eligible for parole. I had seen that Aunt Kiki was listed on the victim's register, so the time would come soon enough when we'd be notified and have to face the fact that Hadley would eventually be released. I dreaded that day.

Mum seemed cheered by the call with Kiki, distracted by her pets and talk of what was happening at home. She readied for bed and I sent an email to work asking if all was going well with my cases, if any issues had arisen, fishing for news about Fiona.

I waited until Mum finally turned her light off before I put my earphones on and started listening to an audio book of *Sense and Sensibility*. I fell asleep thinking about sisters and how Leigh-Anne used to bail up the kids in the playground whenever they were bullying others, especially me.

DAY 7

DELLA

Jimmy visits me in my dreams and I think he's back with me and that it is all these days, these long drawn-out hours without him, that have been the barren dream. For a flash second upon waking, we're as we've always been. But as my eyes start to see the real world, the truth reappears. He's not here and I've lost him once more. That feeling of disappointment, that sink in my stomach, is always like it's new. My head was sluggish with it. Even the hotel shower, which was either too hot or too cold, no matter how you moved the tap, couldn't wake me out of that aching tiredness.

I had the telly on while we packed even though it was only the same news as the night before – Shona's little body had been found and the police were increasing their efforts to find the man in the hoodie who'd been seen in the white van. They wanted to catch him before he hurt someone else. The drawing was repeatedly shown. The police were following several leads. That's what they always say.

When Brett had got us and all our bags in the van, Lionel told us about Oxford because that's where we were heading next.

'In a place so steeped in history we will be structuring our time by focusing on Lewis Carroll's most iconic work, *Alice's Adventures in Wonderland*, so you'll see the city through a unique lens.'

I remembered what I knew – that Alice chases the rabbit down a hole and there's a tea party with a Mad Hatter and a Queen of Hearts or tarts, or something. These didn't seem like real people or events so I thought this Oxford must be interesting if it could be the basis for all these strange critters and goings-on.

One thing about travelling in England that I liked was that it wasn't far to get to places. It took four hours to get to Sydney from Frog Hollow and that was after all the freeways had been built to speed things up. Once upon a time it took much longer than that. Aunty Elaine had family who had to drive eight hours from their town just to get to ours. But here we could go from one historic place to another in just an hour or two, so that seems its own kind of miracle.

Oxford was full of bell towers and church steeples, narrow lanes and gardens, markets and rivers. Lionel said that it's still a university town, so I wrote that in my notebook. We went for a walk through some colleges on the way to the museum. Trees lined the pathways and the fields were green, like back home after the rains have come.

As soon as you arrived here to study you must have felt you were special and in your own little world and I wondered what it would have been like for Jazzie when she first went to the city and became Jasmine. I looked at her as she walked ahead and I felt a little ashamed that until this moment I'd never thought much about what a big change and adjustment it must have been for her to go to such a new place like a university. It's the sort of thing I guess you don't think about if you haven't done it yourself. Of course, a part of me was happy for her to go away and study because that's what she wanted so badly – and it was good to be able to tell people I had a daughter at university because they wouldn't have thought that by looking at me. But I guess I was more focused on how much I missed her when she left, so I didn't think about it from any sides other than just mine.

The Professor seemed like he was in his element and the Boston sisters seemed to be impressed to be in Oxford with a real-life Professor though Meredith said, looking at them huddling around him, you'd think they'd have seen plenty in Boston. I guess Professors must be everywhere even though there are none in our town and I couldn't imagine one ever coming to Frog Hollow, at least not one like Professor Finn.

Lionel took us inside one of the buildings and although it looked all stone from the front like all the other museums, the large central court was light from the mix of wrought iron and glass, like a church opened up with windows. In this building, among the specimens of birds, butterflies and bones, we were looking for one critter.

'He's not very attractive, poor thing,' said Meredith, which was exactly what I thought when I saw the dodo. It was in *Alice in Wonderland*, though I hadn't remembered that bit of it and, if you'd asked me, I would have told you it was a made-up creature, like a dragon. From all the fuss you hear of it, you'd imagine some bird like a peacock or a rosella with bright colours or impressive feathers. Instead, it was a smallish brown bird, stuffed and displayed in some kind of bush scene, as if that was possible with a dead thing in a museum behind glass. That must be what the saying 'Dead as a Dodo' is about. I didn't realise that until now but people say something like that because everyone says it and you don't necessarily think about where the saying comes from. I wrote: *Dead as a Dodo – extinct* in my notebook.

'His mother probably thinks he's beautiful,' Cliff replied, pretending to be outraged on the bird's behalf. His point of view was probably right. Beauty is in the eye of the beholder and all that. A parent's love for their child is blind for the most part, or at least that's how it's supposed to be. As for Jimmy, there was never anyone who I thought was as handsome as he was and even though he wasn't like any of those movie star types, he was to my taste. There was something about his eyes and the curve of his lips that seemed to make his nose, which some might have thought too wide, and his teeth, which some might have thought too crooked, seem just perfect to me. I wouldn't have ever changed a single thing about him.

I'd never known Jimmy to go to a museum but I thought he'd maybe like this one. He always liked to know how things worked. He could take a car engine or any other machine apart and put it all back together again. He just had that kind of curious brain. Although this was all about natural things, with the skeletons of dinosaurs and all sorts of other animals, you could see how they could move and how their bodies worked together, so I think Jimmy would have liked all that.

There were also lots of rocks and that might sound pretty dull but they were crystals of all different colours and rocks with flecks of colour in them and opal and other stones that are not boring at all. I thought Jimmy would like these, too, as it was interesting to see all the things that could come from the earth. Now it seemed like another missed opportunity, another thing we never got to do.

Lionel said that there were millions of specimens of animals and insects in this museum and many were rare or extinct. That made me a little sad, to be honest, all those losses to grieve, a hard reminder that many times what's gone can never be brought back. We walked along the display cabinets and I thought about how much destruction we cause and how so many animals are innocent. Sure, they kill other animals because it's all a big food chain, but how many kill for fun or sport or pleasure? Some of it's just a natural evolution but there are other things where environments have changed. I thought of Aunty Elaine and what she had said about the way Europeans didn't know how we kept everything in balance.

Aunty Elaine was always suspicious of museums, at least the ones where she thought they might treat Aboriginal people as something under a microscope and our culture as a relic. 'I don't trust these head-measurers,' she'd say. She didn't even like doing surveys. Someone once rang her to see if she'd be a part of a customer study about what kind of products she used in the kitchen and she told them, 'Our people have been prodded and poked to death and I'm done answering any more questions.'

It's no fun being prodded and poked, I can tell you that much for free. When I was a witness in Brittany's trial, I was put under a microscope like a bug. You'd have thought I was the one who was on trial. Those questions haunt me even now and I sometimes answer them the way I wished I had back then. But you are in a seat looking out at the court and they're all looking at you, even him, that man whose name I don't like to speak because it's like a curse. A villain's name. When it creeps into my mind I try to drive it out but I fear, once I've thought of it, I've unleashed some kind of bad luck. I had invited him to the party that night and carry the shame of having been the one who asked him into our home.

At the trial, I tried to look at Jimmy because I thought that might make it easier but he wouldn't catch my eye. Why were we drinking that night? Why were the children at the party? How did you know the accused? Why had he been at the party? All these questions about things you don't think about at the time, that you don't think you'll ever have to explain or justify because you think it's going to be another night like any other, not the night where your whole life will change forever.

All my answers were turned back on me, and I can tell you, I almost thought he was going to get away with it. 'Don't fight battles you can't win,' was what my mother used to say. She was never one to give comfort and I only ever think of the cold things she'd say when life is really bleak. In this battle, I had no choice. When the jury went out to consider the verdict, I felt pinned down, motionless, like the critters and bugs stuck under the glass in a museum, unable to move.

When the lawyers rushed past us in the hallway of the court and waved for us to follow, I almost didn't go back in. I couldn't bear to find out that we'd lost – that he'd won. I stood with Kiki and she put an arm around me as the judge asked the jury to stand and deliver the verdict. Only when Kiki reached for me did I realise that she was as uncertain as I was. She'd been the one to be strong for all of us so I guess we forgot she might have her doubts, too.

I cried on the spot just from the sheer relief of hearing that one word. *Guilty.* I'm glad to the core of my bones that the accused went to prison but I can tell you now that nothing went back to the way it was. You do sometimes wonder what it's all for. Some things once they're done can never be undone. After all these years, everything still hurts.

Kiki would say we could never have known what evil he brought with him but that didn't mean I felt any better about it all. And one day he'll come out and be able to live his life, however small and insignificant that might be. But every smile, every bit of laughter, every enjoyment, every happy moment he has – that's more than Brittany will ever get. Those are the kinds of thoughts that can turn your insides bitter as they swirl around in your mind. I shook my head to push it all away and tried to focus on the here and now and the sunshine in the streets.

Lionel walked us over to a part of the town that seemed more 'mediaeval' and I was thinking that very word when he mentioned it and I can't tell you how pleased I was with myself. It might seem like a small thing to some people but it was a big thing to me.

Lionel talked about the martyrs who'd been killed in the square because they had different religious beliefs and I thought of our warriors again and how we were taught that they were enemies of progress when they stopped white people from advancing across the country. But those Aboriginal people were heroes really, when you think about it, because they fought for what they believed in. It's all about which side you're looking from and who's telling the story. I wished Aunty Elaine was still here so I could talk to her about it. There were lots of things she'd say and I'd love to have whole conversations with her about things she mentioned when we were still all together but no-one really wanted to follow up with her about. I guess we all just weren't ready to really listen then, and that's on us.

There was a tower that was part of St Michael at the North Gate Church. Lionel said it was the oldest building in Oxford but there were too many stairs for me even though I was feeling fitter than I did when all this touring started. So, I waited on a bench just outside, enjoying the sun and a smoke. I decided that I would write in my book. And for the first time, I didn't write of the dodo or *Alice's Adventures in Wonderland* or the martyrs but I started to write down the story I had told Meredith yesterday, the one about the owl who didn't look after the children. I started on a clean page, two after the one that Lionel had drawn the building columns on. Even though it wasn't something I saw on the trip, it was something I thought about. I was well into it, too, before everyone came back down from the tower, so I put my book away, determined to finish it later.

When everyone was back together Lionel took us to a street where a sign said 'Alice's Shop' and then across the road to Christ Church College where Lionel pointed out the window that was Lewis Carroll's room.

Lionel told us this Lewis Carroll arrived in Oxford in 1851 and stayed there his whole life. I guess he was like me in that he didn't feel the need to travel very far – though I'm beginning to understand why you might now I've done it, and can see how much you learn.

Lionel said his real name was Charles Lutwidge Dodgson. It was a mouthful and I guess you could see why he changed it. He never married but wrote some books on mathematics. With all that, this Lewis Carroll sounded a bit sad and lonely but surely writing a book like *Alice's Adventures in Wonderland* that so many children read and loved would be its own kind of reward. Lionel said that his stutter had disappeared when he was with children. I told Lionel that I thought that showed that he was relaxed with them and that perhaps the adults made him nervous.

We walked past another building that Lionel said was the Deanery because the Dean of the College lived there. Alice from the Wonderland book was based on his daughter, so we looked at their garden. It occurred to me that the Dean in the garden at Winchester was probably like a university Dean, not a man named Dean.

'There was a story,' Lionel continued, 'that Queen Victoria was so enamoured with *Alice's Adventures in Wonderland* that she requested Lewis Carroll's next book be sent to her – it was titled *An Elementary Treatise on Determinants*. A copy is said to have arrived at the palace but Carroll denied ever sending it.'

'That's an old wives' tale,' I heard Professor Finn say to the Boston sisters.

How do you know? I wanted to ask him. Were you there? That's what Kiki would have said.

We had a proper afternoon tea with teacups, teapots, scones, sandwiches and sweet biscuits, and I have to tell you I never eat this well at home. I'm not much of a cook and I'm lucky that my girls never minded doing it. Now that it's just me I often go to Kiki's and when I'm on my own I just eat what I can find even if it's not much of a meal. I suppose I should make more of an effort but I find it easier to have a bigger lunch and then not worry as much for dinner.

Later, while driving around the outskirts of Oxford, Lionel read out a passage from *Alice's Adventures in Wonderland*. It was about a Dormouse who is at the Mad Hatter's tea party and he talks about three sisters who lived at the bottom of the well and Alice wants to know what they live on and the Dormouse says that they live on treacle, even though it made them very ill. Alice then asked why they lived at the bottom of the well and the Dormouse told her that it was a treacle well. Alice cries that there is no such thing.

You could see why it was good to have someone who was an actor on the tour because Lionel made the story all come alive with the way he read and the voices he gave the characters. I clapped when he finished so everyone else did too, and I think that made him happy.

'I can tell you,' said Lionel, 'there *is* such a thing as a treacle well and we are going to see it.'

You can imagine what I thought – that it was a well filled with treacle like you buy at the supermarket and Kiki puts in the baking and I looked forward to some miraculous thing. When Brett drove down a narrow country lane we pulled up outside what Lionel said was Binsey Church. It was small and quiet, lit by candles, and it seemed like it was almost intrusive to be walking around in it but I guess they are used to people coming and going. Lionel said it had been a place of pilgrimage for hundreds of years. Outside was the well, which was just a small concrete square filled with water. You might have felt a bit ripped off if you travelled very far just to find it. It didn't have treacle in it either.

Then Lionel told us a story about a princess who became a nun and restored the sight of a king who fell in love with her. The healing waters from the well were called treacle, so it was a treacle well after all. As Lionel talked I thought about the owl story I'd been writing down. The story Lionel told was a different kind, but it was not unlike home where the mountains and rivers and rocks, even the trees, had stories attached to them and they tell you something.

Every place has a story, its own little history, even a little well which you might not think about it if you were just walking past it.

We got back on the bus and drove to another field on the outskirts of Oxford, called Godstow. It was in the fields here that Lewis Carroll had come on a picnic in 1862 and where he first told the story that became *Alice's Adventures in Wonderland*.

As the others walked towards the ruins where the nunnery once was, I stayed by the minibus to have another smoke with Brett.

'We're a dying breed,' he said, and I smiled at him even though it took me a moment to work out that what he said had two meanings. He didn't make small talk, which I appreciated. In friendly silence, we watched the sun lower a little in the sky and the figures of our party walk in and out of the blondish-grey stone ruins in the paddock. I could see Jasmine with her new friends and it was nice to see her so happy. She looked over and gave me a wave and I nodded back.

Butterflies played around the fields and I thought about what Aunty Elaine had said once about moths coming in large numbers at different times and how they would be collected from the crevices in rocks, swept into nets or kangaroo skins. They would be cooked in hot ashes for a short time until the wings and legs singed away and then they'd be put on bark to cool and then sifted so the heads fell off. You could eat them after that or they would be made into a dough and cooked. It seemed like a lot of work even if it was a source of protein. And I know I haven't tried them but I just can't imagine them tasting all that good. Still, you can't judge what you don't know.

I closed my eyes to look like I was napping as we headed back to the hotel. I was pleased for Meredith's interest in things about my culture but to be honest it was also a bit exhausting and I needed a break from her and her questions. Also, answering them had stirred up lots of thoughts of my own.

Alice's Adventures in Wonderland is based on a story where a girl has a dream. I can see why Aunty Elaine didn't like the word 'Dreamtime' for our stories as though it was something that was make-believe. These 'cultural stories' as she would call them, always had a little message, a meaning, that explained the world around you, what values you should live by. It's not just a thing for the past but describes the world today.

Aunty Elaine had said that in none of the hundreds of Aboriginal languages that existed was there a word for time. That sure impressed her but when you think about it, even the word 'dreaming' is an English word so it's only a translation from the Aboriginal idea into the closest thing, and that doesn't mean it's accurate.

Often there's no word to describe what you feel either. 'Grief' always seems too poor a word to capture so many layers of what it means to lose someone, 'hope' is too poor for the strength of our dreams, 'tragedy' too poor to describe the worst things that can happen in your life. These words put you on the right track but they don't really get to the heart of anything. All in all, English is a pretty poor language, especially when it comes to feelings. The word that comes to mind is 'impoverished'.

I was glad to get to the hotel, which Lionel called 'Tudor' in its design. It was dark with wooden beams and poky corners. I dawdled around after he gave out the keys, telling Jasmine I'd go for a smoke and join her upstairs shortly. But I wanted to talk to Lionel. Something had been on my mind and I needed to put it right.

'I hope you didn't think I was rude last night. Jasmine thought I was rude. But I heard you say to the Boston women that you couldn't join them, and I just didn't want to put you in an awkward position of having to say, "no".'

'Of course. I understand. And I appreciate it. It's just, can I be honest? I only said that to them because I didn't want to offend them. I didn't mean for anyone else to hear. The joke is on me because now I've missed out on dinner with more delightful company.'

I didn't know what to say to that. I felt sad, like I'd missed something that I couldn't get back. But happy that, if there hadn't been some confusion, Lionel would have liked my company and not that of Celia and Nessa who had better schooling than me and knew all about the ins and outs of manners and the like.

When I got up to our room after dinner, I turned the telly on to see if there was any news. I wanted to finish writing the owl story and maybe the things I remembered about the moths but for some reason, I felt funny writing in front of Jasmine, like I wanted to get my ideas together before writing them down and not wanting her to ask what I was doing. Why I felt this way, I couldn't tell you.

So instead, I picked up my gardening book, which also reminded her that I was right to buy it because I was reading it. I read all about how to water plants – that it's best with a can and you do it evenly. You can put your finger in the ground to see if it's moist enough and if not, you need to water more. Reading about it made me want to do it and I wrote a note in my notebook, *Watering can*. I didn't have one and I'd need one if I was going to start a garden. I didn't know you should water around a plant and not on its leaves because it can go mouldy or get what they said was leaf scorch. And then there was a tip about putting containers outside to catch rain water as this is best for the garden – though if it's been raining, you'd assume that's gone on the garden, too. I wrote *Bucket* on my list. Now it's a bucket list, I thought to myself. Jimmy would have liked that joke. Though my list had only four things on it so it wasn't much of a list.

Just as I was closing my book, Jasmine turned the sound up on the telly. The headline said Shona had been beaten to death. I told her I was going downstairs for a smoke. When I got outside, the air was still warm and it was still light even though it was past nine o'clock. *Beaten to death*. It's a phrase that was even worse when you think about what it really means. Brittany was hit with such force on the back of her head that her skull was crushed in. He'd used a hammer, one of Jimmy's that had been left in the house. It was lucky that there was other evidence – the saliva on the cigarette found near her body and on her T-shirt had come from him, the accused – or the finger would have been pointed straight at Jimmy. People speculated about him being to blame with much less evidence than that.

The thought I hate the most is how scared Brittany must have been as she was carried out of our bedroom while we were all sleeping. You can only hope that she didn't suffer – and that's the most awful kind of terrible to have to hope, that it was quick. It's the hardest thing when you love someone to know that you weren't there when they needed you most, when you could have stopped their pain, you could have protected them.

You wouldn't believe how people say to me that I should move on. Even if I could ever forget my little girl and what happened to her, even if I could ever unimaginably forget that, how do you get over the fact that you couldn't save your own child? I'll carry that burden forever – and I know in my heart of hearts that Jimmy took that same feeling with him to his grave.

As I was thinking about Jimmy and these things that bound us together like peas in a pod, a rabbit came past. It stopped and looked at me. Not scared. Just curious. 'Hello little fellow,' I said to him, and that was enough for him to be satisfied and he went on his way. It wasn't a dream but I knew it was the kind of thing that if I told anyone about it, especially about the rabbit saying hello, well, they just wouldn't believe me.

JASMINE

THERE IS AN exchange in *Alice's Adventures in Wonderland* when the Caterpillar, all fat and squishy, asks Alice, '*Who are you?*'

She replies, '*I-I hardly know, Sir, just at present – at least I know who I was when I got up in the morning but I think I must have been changed several times since then.*'

A butterfly is the *Cinderella* story and 'The Ugly Duckling' story rolled into one – the seductive idea that you can grow into something different, something beautiful, something that no-one else can see but you know is hidden deep inside, ready to come out.

Walking through a place of learning and knowledge, with its expansive lawns, stone buildings and iron gates, reminded me of the first time I walked on to a university campus as a student and the mix of feelings that overwhelmed me. I had the chest-warming pride of being the first person in my family to come so far, getting to the place where I believed my real life would start, along with the irrational fear I'd be turned away despite my early entry acceptance and marks, because how could I possibly be worthy of this? But there I was, just as I'd imagined I always would be, all the way from Frog Hollow, transforming from Jazzie into Jasmine. Then with Bex, Annie and Margie, I finally found friends who I felt understood me.

Our tour group walked around the edges of the Botanic Garden (the first one to be founded in the UK in 1621), through the grounds of Magdalen College (founded in 1458), and came to the round stone building that displays the treasures of the Bodleian Library. It had one of its four Magna Cartas on display (the one issued in 1217 to King Henry III) alongside a tiny book – a sermon in shorthand with a silver chain attached to it to ensure that this smallest manuscript in the collection was not taken away by mice.

If there was another hint of the history and wealth of Oxford, it was in this trove, with manuscripts as impressive as those at the British Museum speaking to science, religion, law and love. Here, under glass, the beauty of the written language, something that can last through decades, centuries and even, in the rarest of circumstances, millennia, gives special weight, a kind of reverence, to the word on a page.

Looking at these manuscripts, where each word is a gilded treasure, it's easy to see why the law puts special weight in what is written, to letters immovable. It's definitive. Authoritative.

Books have been my lifeline, my escape. There's no doubt about that. But Aunty Elaine would remind me that there is more than one way to tell a story; there can sometimes be more than one truth. 'The silences are as important as the words,' she'd often say. There is what's not in the archive, not in the history books – those things that have been excluded, hidden, overlooked.

The law values the written word over oral traditions, trusting one more than the other, but scholars have found that Aboriginal stories across Australia record events from over seven thousand years ago when the sea levels rose, faithfully handing down the stories for over three hundred generations. These seismic climate shifts occurred around the world but only in Australia have they found the evidence of these ancient events reflected in cultural stories.

The main attraction at the Oxford University Museum of Natural History was supposed to be the dodo. Meredith and Cliff swept Mum away to see it, so I decided to follow Toni and Sam as they went to find the 'Red Lady' of Paviland. From South Wales, the bones of a partial skeleton found in 1823 were covered in red ochre and surrounded with beads and other ornaments. This led to conclusions that it was a woman buried during Roman times, about two thousand years ago. Subsequent technology dated the bones and trinkets to thirty-three thousand years ago, making it one of the oldest examples of ceremonial burial in Western Europe. And it turned out be male.

The Red Lady proved that Western science has its own false facts and its own preconceptions and biased conjectures. There's something about keeping and collecting not just objects but bodies that seems to be a part of the colonising process – the right to take, to rename, to catalogue, to hold in the name of the advancement of your own theories, knowledges and sciences. Museums are full of collectables from conquests.

I liked my new friends, Sam and Toni, who spoke a language I understood, but suddenly I found the museum stuffy. When Aunty Elaine would talk about it, our culture felt alive – the sewing of possum cloaks, the knots of weaving, the sweeping brush stroke of painting, the gift of telling stories. They were living and breathing, not relics of the past, frozen in time. Looking at the artefacts surrounding me, I couldn't help but feel I had missed an opportunity with Aunty Elaine to capture her knowledge. It was the kind of wisdom that wasn't within the walls of the university but had been right under my nose the whole time. Now it was like a treasure under glass I could no longer touch, I could only search in the gaps, in the silences.

I'd always rightly embraced education, treasured it, just as I had valued reading about the human condition from authors from other cultures, other times, other eras. While embracing all that, I'd taken Aunty Elaine and her knowledge for granted. It was slipping from me and I didn't have a museum to keep it in.

I walked around the glass and iron structure and found myself heading upstairs to the cases of butterflies. I looked at their soft, velvety wings pinned under the glass and all I felt was sadness. We take the life of a living thing, hold it to display, because we feel entitled to the knowledge, entitled to the owning, the possessing. Scientists estimate that every day between one hundred and fifty and two hundred species of mammals, insects, birds and plants become extinct. That's nearly a thousand times the natural rate. All gone between the time we wake up one day and the time we wake up the next. So what wisdom has all this knowledge given us?

In our own ways, Bex, Annie, Margie and I were learning the tools so we could change the way history was told and how the law treated us. Even Margie, who was studying business with a major in finance, made the point that Aboriginal people need accountants and financial advice, and it's better to be doing that through an Aboriginal business than to be giving our money away to white people.

Sure, when I first went to study there was inclusion of Aboriginal content in the curriculum – native title, deaths in custody, international law and the Declaration on the Rights of Indigenous Peoples, even an Indigenous Peoples and the Law elective – but in Aunty Elaine's stories there was already a legal system in place. We already had a set of rules, codes of conduct, morals and values, and they shouldn't just be carved up and slotted into Western concepts and knowledge systems.

Within the walls of the university, I'd left the wisdom of Aunty Elaine at the door, content to accept the way Western knowledge works as the only thing that mattered. Getting into institutions that my parents hadn't had access to was its own act of decolonisation.

But shouldn't there have been an assertion of sovereignty, too? If I was studying now, I realised, I'd take a different approach and ask a different set of questions.

As I made my way back to the Museum Shop, always the sure place to find people on our little tour, Meredith told me that Mum had gone outside to have a cigarette. By the time I found her we were ready to walk to our next stop, to Saint Michael at the North Gate Church. Toni, Sam and I climbed the ninety-seven steps of its Saxon tower, one of the oldest in Oxford, to see the view across the city and into the nearby fields. On the walk up and then down, we saw the church's own treasures, including Sheela Na Gig, a small rotund sculpture of a woman, a symbol of fertility.

'It looks so—' began Toni.

'Fecund,' Sam concluded. 'Like she could so easily get pregnant.'

'A reminder of the power of women,' I added, thinking of Aunty Elaine and her view of men's business and women's business – which was just one reason why she viewed the concept of unisex toilets with suspicion. She'd explain that men's business and women's business in our culture didn't mean one was superior or inferior to the other. Each had different roles and different strengths. Women collected around eighty per cent of the food so they had their own economic power. But then, when viewed through Western eyes, through male anthropologists' eyes, they were seen as inferior, their sites not protected. Aunty Elaine had been the most senior woman in the town. No man would have challenged her authority and she didn't need a robe, an office or a title – other than 'Aunty'.

While Lewis Carroll's family had been poor, they were intelligent and well read. He had ten siblings and entertained them with magic tricks, puppet shows, card games and creating a family newspaper full of news, puzzles and riddles. I imagine he'd have appreciated the world of Frog Hollow with kids everywhere, creating their own fun. At Oxford in 1854, he attained a first-class Honours degree in mathematics and was appointed as a tutor, a condition of which was that he had to remain unmarried and celibate. He stayed at Christ Church college under those conditions until he died in 1898. The older he got, and as he took on more responsibility for his family, he moved into the role of pious old man and he was known for his letters of complaint when rules or regulations were breached – the way his food was cooked, the amount of milk he was allocated and the time of postal collections.

That wouldn't have endeared him to adults but children were always drawn to him. He seemed comfortable with them after his childhood in a large family where he had a leading role and loved to entertain. Much has been speculated about his relationship with Alice Liddell, the daughter of the Dean of Christ Church, because of the wide appeal of the story she inspired.

'Older men taking young girls down the river,' said Sam. 'You'd never get away with it now.'

'Times sure have changed,' I added.

'Thank God,' concluded Toni.

'I say Dodgson was dodgy,' declared Sam.

Toni nodded agreement.

By the time *Alice's Adventures in Wonderland* was published in 1865, the real Alice was in her teens and never admitted to being the muse until later in her life when she wished to sell the manuscript Charles had given her as a gift. There's little evidence of obsession or immoral infatuation. In his own diaries at the time, Charles makes more comments about Alice's older brother, Harry, of whom he was fonder. On 4 July 1862, the day he first began 'Alice's Adventures Underground', his diary didn't mention the story at all.

Later that day, after the trip to Binsey Church and a drive to Godstow to see the field of the famous picnic, I thought about how Toni and Sam had reacted with suspicion about Charles' motives with Alice and her sisters. Naturally, we look at Dodgson's relationship through our modern eyes. At the time, the eyebrows weren't raised about Charles' attention to Alice, but about his perceived infatuation with their governess. Alice herself, who provides the most proof of what the dynamic was like, always spoke kindly of him.

His family, protective of him, never saw anything wrong in his relationships with children but went to great lengths to hide his interactions with older women in order to protect his reputation.

Ironically, their attempt to erase evidence of relationships with women created an impression that there was something shameful to hide and perhaps caused him more harm. His diaries go missing from 1858 and only resume in 1862. In those later years, Charles speaks of his own failings and transgressions, leading to speculation they contained events that caused him to have regret and remorse. Charles often expressed concerns about his feelings for women and felt he was away from temptation if he spent his time with children. He was never anxious about inappropriate feelings with them. He lived in pre-Freudian times, in which sexual repression was an aspiration, a time when mastering one's body and living in a pure way was seen as a virtue. In Victorian society, children were sexless and therefore did not represent a moral danger.

As I watched Mum sleeping beside me on the bus, I thought about the fruitlessness of family secrets. I lived in a town where gossip was like oxygen and where, whatever the truth of our family, others made their own judgements – 'your mother's a murderer', 'a bad influence'.

Things we wouldn't talk about with our family, like my mother's drinking, were known by everyone living around us. There's no hiding some things. If there's a silence, baseless speculation and self-righteous judgement rush in to fill the void.

At dinner I sat between Mum and Cliff.

'Jasmine, I've been thinking about what you said about your case,' Cliff said. 'You mentioned the girl, your client, had been returned to her mother.'

'Yes. At the age of eleven. And almost immediately her mother started prostituting her out.'

'But when she went into care as a toddler there was already a history of sexual abuse, wasn't there? Didn't you say she already had a venereal disease?'

I nodded.

'Have you thought of suing?'

'I'm pretty sure her mother – and all the men who paid to have sex with her – won't get called to account for it.'

'I was thinking about the Department. They knew and made the decision to place her back there. They've breached a duty of care.'

I pondered the idea. It might give Fiona some resources for her care when she was eventually released from prison. She'd need constant psychiatric support for the rest of her life. Without the option of an institution that could handle her, more innocent victims were a highly likely outcome.

Maybe Cliff was right with his idea to hold the department responsible for their mistakes in sending Fiona back to her mother. They'd contributed to the chain of events but they weren't the main villains in the story, the ones who betrayed the greatest trust, who'd raped and abused a young girl until she turned into a monster.

Back in the room, while Mum read her book, I checked my emails to see if there was any news from work. All I had was a reminder that I needed to do the new on-line modules for Occupational Health and Safety and Bullying in the Workplace. I contemplated Cliff's suggestion and how I might take this up with work when I got home. Would they allow me to run such a case at Legal Aid or would I need to see if a law firm would pick it up?

I checked in on Bex and liked her posts and saw a direct message from Leigh-Anne. She asked how things were going with Mum and I found myself feeling defensive. I should have gone to see the dodo with her. Why didn't I take her to see the butterflies with me? Toni and Sam were nice but I'd never see them again. What was I doing?

The news came on that Shona's autopsy had found she was beaten to death.

Mum said she was going down for a smoke. I told her not to be too long but she'd already closed the door. The news story of Shona played again and I got up to turn the television off before getting into bed. I'm the last person to go easy on sexual predators. One killed my sister, destroyed my family. He had drugged my mother at a party – his usual predatory behaviour – and he came back to our house later when all the other adults had left and took my sister. There's no physical evidence of what he did to her other than a fractured skull – but there is a lot of horror in the silence of what we know.

The man who killed my sister didn't break in during the night. He was invited to a party after he had cultivated a friendship with my mother, given her drugs, played up to her. I know from my work that child abusers often aren't strangers lurking in parks; they're much more likely to be family members or people who have sought positions of trust – at scouts, in the church, at schools – so they have access to children. Virginia Woolf is just one reminder that sexual abuse of children happens more in the family than anywhere else. Abusers are manipulative and urbane, able to convince parents their children are safe with them. After convincing parents to trust them and victims not to tell each other, they seem to have no trouble manipulating the psychologists. 'Model prisoner', their reports would say, and it filled me with scepticism. We didn't really understand what made them tick so I have little confidence we're able to treat them or trust they wouldn't reoffend the first chance they get. How about that for a thought about the monsters that might be lurking around you? I could only imagine what Shona's family were going through.

Freud at first thought that sexual abuse was rife. He'd seen it in all his patients and was disturbed by its prevalence among women from affluent, respectable families, who described sexual abuse at the hands of fathers, uncles, family friends or male relatives. He made initial efforts to publicise the trauma of incest. But he moved from that and developed his 'seduction theory', insisting women fantasised about it and so setting the stage for disbelieving victims of sexual abuse for the next hundred years.

Lesser known is the remarkable work of Freud's daughter, Anna, on the idea of repression and what happens if we let things fester. She developed the concept of defence mechanisms – repression, denial, projection, rationalisation, intellectualisation, reaction formation and regression. All of the things we repress to stop them coming out. And if that wasn't enough, she recognised that symptoms in children differed from those in adults, and she effectively created the field of child psychoanalysis. I'd come across her work during my research while preparing Fiona's case, who had signs of multiple personality disorder, a result of survival mechanisms to suppress experiences and memories. The more intelligent a child is, the easier it is for them to trick their mind and disassociate and find mechanisms to survive. Such a person is likely to be a good student, masking everything that they're going through. On the outside, no-one would be able to tell there was trauma rotting the insides.

I was relieved when I heard the door click, indicating that Mum had come back in. I was too tired to run down to the bar to find her tonight. I kept my eyes closed and took some deep breaths to imitate sleep. My mind filled with images of butterflies pinned down, of the scratches on Fiona's arms and of the small details of people's lives buried in files.

DAY 8

DELLA

I WAS SURPRISED when the Boston sisters were already on the bus, but it turned out Lionel had deliberately told them the wrong time. The Professor had been in on it and also played along. I was pleased to see the Professor working with Lionel rather than against him so that was one less black spot against his name.

Brett was driving us to Stratford-upon-Avon, which was where Shakespeare had lived and was a large part of the reason the Professor didn't want to be late. As we pulled into town I saw thatched cottages and buildings with white walls and dark brown timber that I recognised as Tudor from our other travels, and I was pleased with myself for knowing such a thing.

There were tourist buses everywhere. In all the famous writers' places we'd visited so far on this trip, our group was often the largest. Today, we were the smallest, compared to the organised crowds from the big buses.

There were lots of people squeezing into the bedrooms that were already small enough, so it was better when we got outside and there was a garden with herbs and flowers, including roses that made me think of Aunty Elaine.

Professor Finn was disappointed the town was so full of tourists. Lionel and I nodded sympathetically as he tried to look on the bright side. 'I suppose it's good to see so much interest in The Bard.'

I decided not to point out that many were probably just like me and had read some at school but had pretty much forgotten most of it, and I'm hardly likely to pick it up any time soon. Lionel said that Shakespeare made up lots of words – 'lonely', 'critic', 'lacklustre' – all words that you would have thought were known before but if you said them the first time no-one would know what they meant. And he liked putting an 'un' on words to make other ones – 'undress', 'unearthly', 'uncomfortable'.

It's all very clever but when I get a word wrong or say a phrase I think means the right thing and its different, it's seen as a mistake, not a new thing. Maybe that's the difference between when you write something down and lots of people read it and when you just say it and it goes into the air.

Lionel also mentioned some of the phrases we use every day that are in Shakespeare – 'As luck would have it', 'green-eyed monster', 'good riddance', 'love is blind', 'heart of gold' and 'you can have too much of a good thing'. I wrote some of the words and phrases in my book and I had a little smile about all those times I was quoting Shakespeare and never knew it.

Outside of Nash's House, where Lionel said Shakespeare's last direct descendants lived, was a garden. A large part of it was a knot garden with carefully trimmed bushes in a pattern and flowers of yellows, pinks and reds. Lionel said a knot garden is when there is a square with a design in it and the plants are all aromatic so it smells nice. I hoped there was something about knot gardens in my book and if there wasn't maybe I could buy another one about it or look it up on the internet. At least my book might have a list of flowers that smell nice because that's a good idea, to make a garden that has lots of nice smells in it. I wrote down, *knot garden, not 'not garden'*, as my own little joke.

While we were looking around I told Professor Finn that I was very pleased to have learnt more about it all to keep his spirits up. It just goes to show that, even when someone rankles you most of the time, it doesn't take much effort to show a kindness and it can make a big difference all round.

We all walked up the road for a short while to a place that was called Anne Hathaway's Cottage, like the actress, but it was where Shakespeare's wife lived before they were married. The garden was wilder, not so ordered and designed as the knot one – with yellows and whites and a few trimmed hedges. There was also an orchard and sculptures. This time, the person I asked about moving Aunty Elaine's roses from one spot to another really was a gardener. I told him that I was going to start a garden when I got home and he was very kind and wished me good luck with it.

Jasmine was off with Sam and Toni and I couldn't see Meredith and Cliff so I was stuck with Professor Finn and his wife and the Boston sisters, who I wouldn't have chosen but Lionel was with us and that made it alright. He said there were several spellings to the name Shakespeare and Professor Finn added that there was also no known picture of his likeness.

'It's strange that Shakespeare is so famous but we really know so little about him, not even his proper name or what he looked like,' I said.

Everyone nodded in agreement, which was a nice change.

Brett arrived with the minibus and we all got on board. While we were waiting for the others, Lionel said that there was a period of seven years when Shakespeare went missing and no-one knows what happened. 'There are several speculative theories – butcher, glove maker like his father, a romance. What explanation do you think most likely, Professor?' he asked.

The Boston sisters looked at Professor Finn, expecting something wise as he took the stage and I thought about how kind Lionel was to try to make Professor Finn feel better.

'There were of course two periods of absence, the first after his schooling finished in 1578 until his marriage in 1582,' he said, sounding once more like he was giving a lecture in a classroom. 'But the more mysterious is when he disappears in 1585. At this time, he has a wife and three children and we don't see him again until 1592, when he's working in a London theatre company. I believed the most likely explanation to be that he worked as a teacher and then perhaps worked in a travelling theatre company – but it's nothing more than an educated guess.'

'So, you don't subscribe to the theory that he was avoiding punishment for poaching?' asked Lionel.

'I find that most unlikely. Similarly, with the speculation that he was living with a Catholic family for the period. The idea he was a soldier? Perhaps. But he was a gifted man of letters. Teaching and then a move to the theatre sounds the most logical, if not the most romantic answer.'

Lionel gave Professor Finn a nod, which showed respect and was, I thought, very polite.

My Jasmine bounded over with Sam and Toni and took her seat next to me. We had to wait for Meredith and Cliff but they weren't late yet. Talk started about Shakespeare's wife and a will and a bed, but I couldn't stop thinking of the mystery of seven years missing and then returning. That's a long time to be in the wilderness. I can sometimes wake up and forget what happened the night before but to disappear for such a time, it would seem impossible today with the internet and everyone putting the details of their life where all can see. Before all that, it was easier for there to be silences in a life.

Meredith and Cliff got on the bus so we were back together and on our way to a town called Eastwood, like Clint. Everyone was still arguing about the bed, the will and the wife but one thing Professor Finn said pricked my ears up.

He said: 'No other culture produced a Shakespeare.' And I thought, well, no other culture produced an Aunty Elaine. And I wondered why it was that people had to make those comparisons the way that my father used to. He would go on about how Aborigines were stone-aged and never invented the wheel but I remember seeing on a show once all the things that the Chinese invented, including paper, silk, printing, gunpowder and a wheelbarrow. They were all things my father's ancestors hadn't invented, unless there's a Chinese one somewhere in there.

And if a civilisation can sustain itself for over sixty-five thousand years like my mother's, why do you assume that you have nothing to learn from it about how it keeps the peace and keeps on going? The whole ranking one over another seems like a nonsense. Look for the best in everyone, Aunty Elaine used to say, and I think that goes a long way.

I'd thought a lot about Aunty Elaine on this trip when you would have thought it was Jimmy who was most in my thoughts. You might wonder why he and I didn't stay together but that's a whole other can of worms and I could no more account for it than I could explain why the tides followed the moon.

If I hadn't met Jimmy when I did, I'd never have thought that any kind of love was possible. His family showed me a different way of being. Not everything got fixed but it's better than what would have happened if I hadn't run into Jimmy that day when I was going to take the train to the city, barely fifteen and with no money. It's a fair bet things would have turned out badly for me if I'd travelled all the way down that road, if Jimmy had never crossed my path.

We'd lived in his mother, Nancy's house, but when we had Brittany and then Leigh-Anne on the way, she made sure we put our names on the waiting list for our own place with the Aboriginal Housing. It might seem lucky that we ended up with the house two down from hers but not many people wanted to live in Frog Hollow. For us though, it couldn't have been more perfect.

Things got tough between Jimmy and me after Jasmine came along and we had a huge fight – he didn't like my drinking and I didn't like his. We were young, stubborn and had the pressures of three girls, and never enough money. Brittany had woven us together so I suppose it was inevitable that when she was taken from us, everything would start to unravel.

We stopped in front of a large red-brick building with white decorations. Lionel said it had been the offices of the mine that had been the central business of Eastwood back in the day. I didn't know much about this D.H. fellow other than his books were supposed to be shocking at the time and now I also know that his father was a miner and that he'd lived in this town for the first twenty-three years of his life.

Brett dropped us off at the house where D.H. was born that was now a museum. They had a kitchen and laundry all set up like it would have been when he lived there so you could see how things would have been like day to day. You can quickly forget how people lived before. Like the washing was done on a Monday because it was the day that there was less soot in the air because the mines were shut on Sunday. All these little things you never think about and take for granted now. Kiki would have found this interesting, how things had changed over time and I thought maybe I'd ask Jasmine if we could get her on the computer again so I could tell her about all I was seeing.

Next was a walk through the main street and Lionel gave us all a map with a blue line around the town that we could follow in a kind of a loop and meet back up. No-one was paying me any notice so I was able to go into a shop to buy some smokes. I walked around the store and got some supplies. Lucky, my bag was big and had enough room.

I was tired of walking and thought I would skip ahead to the end of the trail and wait for the others. There was a bus stop there so I sat on the bench and I thought about Jimmy. I'll admit that we both drank back in those days. I liked the way it would make me forget and feel happy. Even when I felt sick and sluggish the next day, I was always drawn back to that giddy, floating feeling. And it was true that I'd started taking more than alcohol. At the party, Jimmy knew that people were coming who were dealing drugs and he didn't want the girls near it and he was right.

I took them to his house and he said I had to keep them, making a point, and so I did although I was mad at him. I told everyone no drugs at the party and I didn't do any that night. My girls came first. There were lots of kids there with their parents and it was mostly drinking and just smoking cigarettes. But, then of course, someone did come in, did drug me, so the police eventually thought. When they found Brittany's body, they could link the evidence to the accused, who I'd invited to the party because he'd bring me drugs when the girls weren't around.

So, you can see how someone could hold that against themselves. I worried for a long time that Jimmy couldn't forgive me for all that had happened. It ate me up. Mum Nancy was kind to me, and that was a relief. But Jimmy's sisters, especially Lynn, always said it was all my fault. One morning, when Kiki was nursing me back to health, she said that it wasn't me Jimmy couldn't forgive; he just couldn't forgive himself. I was always truly grateful she'd said that to me, I can tell you, and I took a lot of comfort in her words. After Brittany's death, Jimmy and I just fell into a pattern where we tended to each other as if we each had broken wings.

My thoughts were interrupted as Professor Finn walked past. He saw me and then, to my surprise, asked if I minded if he joined me, though he was already sitting down. I smiled. 'Enjoying it?' I asked, because it's the kind of broad thing you can say that's easy for people to answer the way they want.

'Well, I hoped it would give me a fresh perspective, you know? That I could bring more life into my lectures if I saw some things that I could then relate to the students. They get younger and younger every year and I get older and older. I need to bridge the gap. I felt a little like old Lewis Carroll, unable to connect. They're very challenging, students these days. They think we need to adopt their views and ways of seeing the world rather than believing that there might be something that someone like me might have to teach them.'

I nodded sympathetically. I knew what it was like when people assumed they couldn't learn from you, were never interested in what you had to say. Nessa and Celia came into view. The Professor and I watched them approach. Celia spoke first, 'Professor, we were just talking about the merits of Mr Lawrence's writing and I wonder if we could get your thoughts.'

'Thank you for the conversation,' the Professor said to me as he stood. It's like that thing where you say nothing but at the end of it the other person tells you what a good time they had.

Celia linked the Professor's arm as they set off towards the minibus. Nessa told them she was going to stay and catch her breath but they seemed not to hear her. She sat down next to me with a groan of relief and watched her sister walk off. It was the first time I'd seen the two apart.

'She paid for the trip and I know that's very generous but there's a difference between being a companion and being a slave. She's always bossed me around.'

I was about to tell her about Kiki and how she's the same with me. I know it's just her way of trying to look after me, even when it gets my goat.

'I can't tell you how miserable that woman has made me, especially trying to upstage me in front of the Professor,' she stood to go, and added, 'But I think he likes me best. Don't you think?'

I nodded and smiled.

Just as she left, the Professor's wife came into sight. As she approached, I noticed how we seemed to think of her as 'the Professor's wife' because he was the kind of person who took up so much attention that it was harder to see those around him. I made a note to myself not to think of her just as 'Mrs'.

'Hello, Helen,' I said as she approached. 'You just missed your husband,' I told her, as she sat down next to me.

'Yes, I assume Celia and Nessa were with him?'

I nodded, expecting her to be annoyed or upset about it.

'The attention has been good for him, to be honest. He's had such a difficult time at work with all the changes they expect. It's hard to keep up with the trends and it was once so easy for old white men like him and now, well, they want women and other diversity people and he feels the pressure of it all. Women students want to learn about women writers and I think that's fair, don't you? Certainly, I don't blame them but it's been very hard for Oscar to adjust. Change is very hard at his age.'

I nodded and thought about how much love there was for her to be so generous about her husband's needs. She was the kind of person whose good qualities were overlooked. 'Well, I better go catch him up,' she said, by way of farewell.

Meredith, Cliff and Lionel came along next. Cliff and Lionel were deep in conversation and barely noticed as Meredith sat down next to me.

'I love him but when he gets into his legal mode, well, I can only hold my attention for so long.'

'But it's so nice to see you so happy after all of these years.'

'Married three years this October.' She must have noticed my surprise. 'We're in the throes of young love, not old,' she said. 'After my last husband died, heart attack, Cliff was doing the probate. Two years later, he'd left his wife and we were married. It's never too late for a new romance.' She smiled at me as she stood.

As I watched her go, I thought about how when you look at people, you think you know things but you can't really tell anything that way. It's that thing about never knowing how deep the still waters are.

I was about to get up and head towards the minibus where Brett would be waiting, when I saw Toni, Sam and Jasmine coming along. Funny that the youngest were the slowest. They were also deep in conversation and it was Toni who saw me first. Jasmine offered her hand to help me stand up but was soon back talking with Sam.

'I always like how you dress,' I told Toni. Someone who goes to such effort to express themselves probably appreciates getting noticed. Today it was a black dress with a flared skirt that had little pineapples all over it.

'I thought of being a fashion designer but I really love my poetry. And Sam is really encouraging. She's having her own time of it. She was hoping to get promoted in the last round but was passed over again – a male expert on Philip Roth will always get the jump on the feminist literary scholar.' She rolled her eyes as she spoke.

I smiled as though I understood everything she was saying but I think it was enough to know that it was a bad thing for Sam and Toni was upset for her. That was the heart of what was important to understand.

Back on the minibus, I thought of how Aunty Elaine said people would always confide in her, would come and confess to her all the time. 'I'm a Black woman. Who am I going to tell?' she'd laugh. Or maybe it was just that she looked friendly.

As I heard the bits and pieces of everyone's life, all the while I had a swirl of thoughts about Jimmy. Mum Nancy had died not long after Brittany's trial, and she'd been such a glue for us all – as much as Aunty Elaine had. And she could keep Lynn and Jenny in line. I often wonder, if she'd still been with us, whether maybe it would have been easier for Jimmy.

When we checked into the hotel in Leeds I went straight up to our room and put the telly on. There was a newsflash. Shona's parents had been taken into custody and were expected to be charged with her murder. There had been no man in a hoodie. No white van. That was all a lie to cover up their crime. My heart felt heavy for the little girl.

That night we were supposed to have dinner in the hotel restaurant but I wasn't in the mood. Shona was troubling my mind. Her disappearance and then her murder had made me remember all we went through with Brittany, bringing back what she suffered and our agony after it. But now it turned out it wasn't like that at all. It wasn't about the failure to protect a little girl; it was about abusing one. A shocking thing, a parent harming a child. Most people can barely believe it. I can tell you, what happens inside a home can be more dangerous for a child than what's outside it.

It started on my thirteenth birthday. I thought when my father came into my room he had an extra present for me in that way you think things when you're waking up and trying to understand what doesn't make sense. He stood for a while near the door and I started to feel uneasy. I also knew, after only ever knowing the strict rules of the house, that you couldn't argue with my father, couldn't talk back to him. We'd lived our whole lives trying to avoid making him angry.

The pain of it all is something that I try not to remember. And I try not to think about how, when he'd finished, he warned me not to tell my mother.

The next morning, I went downstairs and got ready for school, as though it was as normal a day as any other. My father sat down, reading a newspaper at the table just like he always did. Had I imagined it? I asked myself. I'd thought foolishly in that moment that it must be some strange, one-off thing.

But, of course, it wasn't. Each time after, I hated the sticky mess of it and his stench. His sickly aftershave would smother me. I'd feel like I was choking. If I ever smelt it on someone – a stranger in the street, a man at a bar – it would trigger the same reaction: the gasping for air to stop drowning, a churn in my stomach like I'd eaten bad food.

One night, several months after it started, my father had left my room and I had the urge to slip into Kiki's bed for comfort. And I remembered how, many years earlier, I'd been found with her and we'd both been punished and it made me wonder whether what was happening to me now could have been happening to her and that's why I wasn't allowed to visit her room.

Even after I thought that, it took me a long time, over a year after it started because I'd had another birthday, to get the nerve up to ask Kiki about it. You have to understand the shame of it all to know why it's so hard to say a word about it to anyone, to say it out loud, even to someone you love and trust like I did Kiki. I worried she'd think less of me, that she'd see it as my fault.

Then, one afternoon, Kiki and I were walking home from school and from somewhere within finally came the courage to speak. 'Does Dad come into your room in the night?' I asked her.

She stopped in her tracks and turned and looked at me. She didn't say a word at first but I could tell from her eyes and the curve of her lip what her answer was. 'I thought it was just me,' she finally said.

I had a panicked feeling of being trapped. Kiki, as always, kept us strong.

'I'm going to finish school and get a job and then we can get away. I've got eighteen months to go. Can you hang in that long?' she asked.

I nodded.

Kiki did a lot to protect me. She made sure that breakfast was prepared, that our uniforms were clean, that we got to school. I'd get these terrible gut aches and crippling headaches that felt like my skull was caving in; always I felt nervous and fidgety.

So, it went on for more than another year until I couldn't take it anymore. I planned to take the train and get a job in a shop in the city. It was a bad plan but I thought that whatever was out there couldn't be worse than being around my father.

When I left the house, so did Kiki. There was no need to protect me anymore so she turned up at Jimmy's place a week after it became clear I wasn't coming back. Mum Nancy barely blinked and took her in even though we were all squeezed into just three rooms. It was its own kind of chaos and Kiki didn't get the marks at school she'd hoped for. We could have moved away but I had Jimmy and Kiki wouldn't leave me and my girls. She had trouble having children so it was lucky she was always there to look after mine.

This might sound strange but Kiki and I never spoke about what happened since that day walking home from school. I think we always thought that if we didn't mention it, it could stay in the past. Even when I had to go and talk to the doctors about what happened with Brittany, I never mentioned my father and what he did to me for fear of the floodgate. But it's as raw now as it was then and I think maybe it was a mistake to keep it all bottled up inside.

When I had Jimmy, it was easier. He was the only other person I ever told. And now he's gone. You can see why I loved him right through my bones, though 'love' seems like a poor word for it; it was so much deeper than that.

I think back on it all and the world feels like a scream in my head as if I'm falling down into a dark rabbit hole. So, the drink and then the drugs and then Brittany and then more drink and no Jimmy and more pain and more need to escape it. Fracturing us. Cracking until everything splits apart. All of it a scream with no sound coming out, one that would vibrate through my whole body.

In the blinding pain of it all, I swear I can hear a voice saying, 'Mum, it's me, Jazzie.'

JASMINE

WE'D ARRIVED IN Leeds that night. Mum had skipped dinner and I knew I shouldn't have left her alone after the news report. She'd been following the story of the little girl. We both had. In a way, the arrest of Shona's parents had solved many questions but I should have known it's never as simple as that. Trauma runs its own path.

When I went upstairs after nightcaps with Sam and Toni, our hotel room was empty. I hadn't seen Mum in the bar and thought it most likely she'd gone for a smoke. I put the television on but when the news repeated, anxiety seeped in.

I went downstairs, checked outside and then in the dining room, which was now empty, and took another look in the bar. I went back to our room, my skin tightening as I wondered what I should do next. Surely, she'd turn up? Breathe – *one, two, three*.

I watched the news again and tried to distract myself by scrolling through Bex's social media to give her a dose of 'likes.' Then I thought to check if Mum had her purse with her. Glancing over at her bed, I noticed her notebook on the side table.

I looked at the open page and saw large letters in her scrawling hand:

You know not to tell your mother.
Does Dad come into your room in the night?
Kiki – I thought it was just me.

I could feel a cold stab through my chest as I re-read the words. I flicked through the pages.

Plague, 1603. One in five people died.
Great Fire. 1666. Few lives lost.
Ye Olde Cheshire Cheese Public House

I flicked some more pages:

Calendar House – 365 rooms, 12 staircases, 7 courtyards – 1456
Winchester – very old. Cathedral. 900 years like yew tree
Shona. Shona. Shona.

Then to the back of the notebook:

Aunty Elaine's flowers?
Easy to grow?
Watering can
Bucket

On another page was a story about an old man who turns into an owl, a story Aunty Elaine had told me. On another day, it would have given me comfort but I turned back to the original page:

You know not to tell your mother.
Does Dad come into your room in the night?
Kiki – I thought it was just me.

I'd heard enough confessions in my work to know one when I saw one. Then I noticed the empty bottle of vodka in the bin near the television. No sign of Mum's handbag. I headed swiftly downstairs.

I stood at the front of the hotel and looked in each direction trying to guess which way might have tempted her. I thought back over the day. Mum had seemed happy enough walking through Stratford-upon-Avon with Lionel, whose company she seemed to always enjoy. So, I might have paid less attention to her as I shared my interest in Virginia Woolf with Sam and Toni, who were familiar with *A Room of One's Own*.

Against the backdrop of white walls and thatched roofs with its colourful gardens, among the throng of the crowds, we had been caught up with Virginia Woolf's answer to men who had decried that there were no Elizabethan women poets. She speculated about what would have happened if Shakespeare had a sister who was as talented as he was. Such a woman wouldn't have been encouraged to write or learn the classics; she'd have been kept at home to learn domestic duties and skills. She wouldn't have been given the freedom or time to travel and grow her craft; she'd have been married off in her early teens, valued by how many children she had, with a high chance of dying giving birth to one of them.

As we wandered from the heart of the village up to Anne Hathaway's house, we reflected on the rates of women dying as a result of domestic violence, the higher percentage of women living in poverty, wage inequality and the lack of women in high positions and other metrics. However far we'd come, there was still so much further to go. It felt like in no time we were back on the minibus, and Mum had been there smiling at me as I took my seat next to her. Nothing seemed amiss.

After the rest of the party arrived, we headed off to Eastwood and the talk was no less lively. Lionel had mentioned the controversial clause in Shakespeare's will that left his 'second best bed' to his wife.

Celia was rightly outraged. 'What cold treatment of a wife of thirty-four years,' she exclaimed.

Sam jumped in: 'At the time, a wife automatically got a third of the estate and a life interest in the family home so it was not as if that was all she was left with.'

'I quite agree,' Professor Finn began in words that surprised Sam. 'Remember, ladies, beds were expensive items in those days. The best bed was usually placed in the guest room so visitors could see how well you were doing.'

'The second-best bed would have been the one where they slept, where the children were born, and in that way, it seems like it could have been a gift from the heart,' Sam concluded.

'But for the man who wrote the sonnets,' Celia offered, 'it seems so – indifferent, so lacking in passion.'

'I concede the verse is sparse. The note about the bed was added in his own hand just a month before he died. It seemed to me almost like an affectionate in-joke.'

And just as he and Sam seemed to have found some middle ground, he added, 'As the most important writer of the English language, he certainly left a large enough portfolio of his works for us not to speculate too much about one codicil. I'm sure you'll agree that no other culture has produced a Shakespeare.' He turned to look at Sam playfully. They now seemed to enjoy the roles they'd crafted as adversaries.

Sam replied in the same spirit: '*The very stone one kicks with one's boot will outlast Shakespeare* – Virginia Woolf, *To the Lighthouse*.'

Mum had been quiet through all of this but it wasn't the kind of conversation that would draw her in.

At Eastwood our attention had been given over to D.H. Lawrence. Mum asked lots of questions at the Birthplace Museum about how the washing was done and how things were cooked. She'd asked about talking with Kiki later that night and I sensed she was missing home. I'd stayed close by her for most of our time in the museum but as we were getting ready to start a walk around the village, I resumed my conversations with Sam and Toni.

'I confess I was first drawn to D.H. Lawrence because I thought there was something of a repressed homosexual about him,' Sam said. 'He never minded writing about male beauty or men giving each other a good rub down. There's that scene in *Women in Love* where Rupert and Gerald wrestle naked and even though he ends up with a woman, Rupert feels empty without Gerald and says, "*I wanted eternal union with a man too: another kind of love.*" But I think I was just projecting.'

'It's hard to find a greater ode to heterosexuality than *Lady Chatterley's Lover*,' I replied.

By this time, we'd begun the walking trail around Eastwood with a view over the very fields that Lawrence himself had walked and had so vividly written about.

'Complicated relationship with his mum though,' Toni added. 'Typical.'

'She brought the cultural element to the house and encouraged his writing, yet he also finds her manipulative and demanding. He loves her and despises her at the same time,' laughed Sam.

'It always seemed to me,' I added, 'that her ambition helped him escape the drudgery of his working-class life – she believed in him. He can be unhappy with her faults but at some stage you have to take responsibility for your own life and your own choices.'

'That's very black and white,' Toni said, not unkindly.

'Maybe it's the lawyer in me. You hear too often people blaming others for their actions as a way of not facing up to what they've done themselves. Sentencing can account for some of it but the fact of the matter is that our prisons don't focus on rehabilitating offenders. They often come out worse than when they go in.'

It was then, as we were almost towards the end of our walk, that I saw Mum sitting at the bus stop, resting. When we reached her, I offered her my hands and helped her up. Was she unsteady on her feet? Usually I can smell the alcohol. Had I missed anything?

The hotel at Leeds had less charm than any we'd stayed at so far and would not have looked out of place beside an international airport. The rooms were large and clean, functional but impersonal. As was our habit, we turned the television on and were greeted with the breaking news that Shona's parents had been arrested for her murder. As Mum watched the story I'd wondered how it might affect her, but she'd seemed genuine when she'd said she was tired and wanted to go to bed. I'd been caught up in conversation with Sam and Toni at dinner and hadn't thought about Mum again until faced with an empty hotel room. Now she was gone and she'd left behind the words in her diary:

You know not to tell your mother.
Does Dad come into your room in the night?
Kiki – I thought it was just me.

I always accepted that Mum's father wasn't part of our lives. Our family was full of so many other people that there were no gaps that needed filling, particularly not with a man who everyone around me had thought so little of. I hadn't thought more deeply about it because I never needed to. The loss of Brittany washed over everything; I knew Mum was damaged by it so it was hard to see other hurts, other scars she might be carrying.

I remember the day Aunty Elaine had first told us the owl story. She'd taken Kylie and me out into the bush and when we got to a particular rocky outcrop, she stopped for a rest. Before she started she told us that the story was very important. At the time I was around twelve or thirteen. I didn't see it as more than a strange story, surreal and as mysterious as it was mythic. Kylie loved it and wanted another one. 'You can only hear them when you are ready to hear them,' Aunty Elaine replied.

'But I am ready,' Kylie insisted, sitting up straight as though she was in class.

Aunty Elaine smiled. 'You have to be ready to listen. Don't worry, when that time comes, I'll tell you.' She patted Kylie's hand and indicated it was time to keep walking.

My first instinct was to argue with Aunty Elaine – I can't hear what you don't say. It's hard to listen when you're speaking in riddles. Then, I heard Aunty Elaine saying the word 'winanga-li', a fragment of the old language that means 'to hear or listen'.

Maybe it was frustration. Maybe it was fear, but as I looked up and down the empty street, no trace of Mum, no idea where to look, I let out a deep guttural scream, the kind that's a purge, that empties out all the air inside you but is also a release. The kind that leaves you with tears in your eyes though you're not crying.

Winanga-li. You have to be ready to listen.

Annie had given a presentation when we were at university. Bex, Margie and I went along to be the friendly brown faces in the crowd. The presentation was about the ethics of collecting and keeping oral histories. In explaining her methodologies, she spoke about the concept of 'deep listening'. It was the idea of listening with respect – hear, think, don't hurry, listen to the story – and consider what's in the spaces. Don't interrupt with questions. Wait to hear what the speaker wants to tell you. You can't guide what you want to know. You prepare the space and listen, to take in the wisdom you are about to receive and contemplate it, understanding that you might not fully comprehend what you are being told straight away. You need to think, to grow into the knowledge.

As Annie was presenting her ideas, I remembered Aunty Elaine's wisdom – 'the silences are as powerful as the words'. Annie's academic polemic had its roots – the idea of listening and of being ready to hear – in our ancient cultural ways. Winanga-li.

I don't know how long I stood outside the hotel, mentally going over the events of the day, looking to the left and to the right, wondering which way Mum had gone, which way to follow her, paralysed by indecision and uncertainty.

To the left, the street looked more deserted, more office workers heading home late. To the right, a couple of restaurants and a convenience store. Back to the left, at the end of the street, I saw what looked like a pub.

I found Mum seated at one end of the bar, a glass in front of her, her head falling forward as if she was asleep or praying. I should have been angry but I was just awash with relief.

I walked up behind her but she didn't move.

'Mum,' I said. And still no response. I put my arm around her shoulder and shook her gently, 'It's me, Jazzie.'

DAY 9

JASMINE

The night passed in a restless jumble of thoughts and sleep was elusive. It wasn't long before the sun started to filter through the window in the young hours of the morning.

I remembered overhearing Grandma Nancy saying to Aunty Elaine that Mum's father was a brutal man. He had his presence on the local council, at one of the local pubs and with his business, a car dealership. That our paths could so rarely cross was testament to how segregated our town was and he remained a dark looming presence in the background. But I did wonder why we never saw our other grandmother and I once asked Aunty Elaine about it. Her reply: 'Whatever happened in that house, it broke your grandmother's spirit. Anyone who knew her before she married would hardly recognise her now. Lucky your mother and Kiki found a life here. That's the blessing of it all.'

Somehow, I'd left it at that, satisfied with a snippet. Mum and Aunt Kiki clearly wanted to leave behind whatever had happened in their past. The words in Mum's notebook were pieces. The clues. The breadcrumbs. Even if I missed the signs as a child, I knew from my legal work how rife abuse was in families. There were classic patterns: silence, threats not to tell, isolating victims. I had known from studies I'd read at law school and even knew it from disclosures from friends, articles in magazines, the biographies of the women I admired. Through cases like Fiona's I'd understood more deeply the consequences of abuse and the coping mechanisms victims used to survive. But in my own family, I hadn't, couldn't – wouldn't? – join the dots.

We trust what we see with our own eyes. We often demand that level of proof to be convinced by something. In criminal trials, the most persuasive evidence apart from a confession are eye-witness accounts. Seeing is believing. Yet our reliance on what we see – what we take on oath and swear we've seen – has been challenged over and over again. The Innocence Project in the United States found that seventy-one per cent of the first three hundred and fifty-eight people they exonerated using DNA evidence had been wrongly convicted by eye-witness testimony. Of those, forty-one per cent involved misidentification across racial lines. But the eyewitnesses were absolutely honest in their belief of what they saw with their very own eyes. Those wrongly convicted served an average of fourteen years, a harsh penalty for someone else's mind playing tricks.

It's not that I thought Mum had a duty to tell me, I just felt that with all my education and training, I should have figured it out.

When the hour came to get up, I was tired and prickly from lack of sleep. I knew what to do when Mum had a night like this, so I went down to the buffet and got her some coffee and two slices of toast with a bit of sweet jam. By the time I got back to our room she was in the shower. When she came out, I asked her how she was feeling.

'I've got a slight headache,' she said.

When we arrived at the Brontë Parsonage Museum at Haworth it had none of the romantic moodiness I'd dreamed of – three sisters writing by lamplight in a crowded room, wind and rain lashing the windows. When the Reverend Patrick Brontë came to oversee the parish in 1820, he brought his wife, Maria, five daughters and one son. Soon after they were joined by their aunt, Elizabeth Branwell. Even in the soft brightness of summer, the Parsonage seemed compact and cramped. In Charlotte's room, dresses were laid out as a reminder of how petite the literary giant was. 'Less than five feet tall,' Lionel was telling Toni and Sam.

A year after the Brontës came to live in the house, Maria died. Her last words – *'Oh God, my poor children'* – were a prophecy of what was to follow, even though Aunt Elizabeth became a permanent fixture in the family, taking over the role of looking after everyone. The eldest, Maria, would die at the age of eleven after being mistreated at the Clergy Daughters' School and sent home with tuberculosis. A month after she was buried, the second eldest, Elizabeth, was sent home with the same ailment. She died at the age of ten. Reverend Brontë quickly removed Charlotte and Emily from the school. Charlotte was next eldest, then a son, Branwell. He died in 1848 of tuberculosis, complicated by his addictions to alcohol and opium, aged thirty-one. Emily, the next in age, died four months after him, aged thirty, from complications from a cold she caught at her brother's funeral. The youngest, Anne, died in 1849, aged only twenty-nine.

Charlotte was the one who travelled the most – spending time overseas in Brussels – and had the most contact with the outside world, including with her publisher, George Smith, and author Elizabeth Gaskell. She was also the only one to marry. When Arthur Bell Nicholls, her father's curate, first asked for her hand Reverend Brontë hadn't approved the match; Nicholls was successful when he asked again two years later, in 1854. Charlotte died nine months after they were married, from complications arising from pregnancy, just weeks before her thirty-ninth birthday.

Moving through the exhibition, I passed the Boston sisters with Professor Finn and his wife. Celia sighed as she looked around the room, 'You'd know everyone's business, so many people living in a house this size.'

'Spare a thought for poor Mr Brontë, alone in the house, his wife and children all gone,' Meredith said.

'"What's God's plan?" he must have asked himself many a time,' Cliff added.

We lived on top of each other back in Frog Hollow and it was hard to keep a secret for the most part, but there were larger ones that could remain buried under everyone's nose.

Unlike the Reverend Austen who actively encouraged his daughter, Reverend Brontë had placed most of his hopes in his son and hadn't known his daughters were writing books. The sisters had been groomed as governesses but repeatedly failed at this thankless, unrewarding task. All back at home, they wrote poems and then novels, published secretly under pseudonyms. When they finally revealed their success to their father, he seemed to take a restrained delight in what they'd achieved. It was quite a legacy, with Emily's *Wuthering Heights* and Charlotte's *Jane Eyre* enduring classics.

Mum and I joined Sam and Toni as we walked down Church Street, past the Old School Room towards the Old White Lion Hotel where we were to have lunch.

'It's very pretty,' Mum said to them, 'I like how it feels like you've gone back in time.'

Sam agreed.

'No television or streaming services meant more time to write letters,' Toni replied.

At the pub, Mum looked at the menu but wasn't hungry so I suggested takeaway coffees out on the moors.

We walked back along the road to the parsonage, passing

Meredith, Cliff and Lionel, and set a designated time to meet back where Brett had parked the minibus.

As Mum and I strolled through hedged and leafy lanes that soon gave way to the moors, I imagined Catherine and Heathcliff walking them, or Jane Eyre taking refuge after she discovers Mr Rochester is already married. In the world I'd conjured, the moors were moody and untamed. In the sun, the heath looked peaceful and I could imagine it gave the people who loved them – Charlotte, Emily and Anne – a similar sense of belonging that walking through the bushland near our town gave Aunty Elaine, my mother and me.

I looked behind me as Mum followed along the path.

'I've been working on this case, one that has really bothered me,' I started.

'Is this the one you've been talking to Cliff about?'

'That's the one. My client killed a man when she was on remand. She'd been arrested for trying to kill her mother.'

'That's awful. Why would she try to kill her mother?'

'That's the thing, isn't it? It didn't come out of nowhere. Fiona's mother had abused her and she'd been put in state care but somehow, the state gave Fiona back when she was eleven – foster parents and children's homes found her very difficult because she was already so damaged – and her mother prostituted her out.'

'That's terrible,' Mum said, shaking her head sadly.

'I've struggled with it because she killed an innocent man, so she's a murderer, but I often think of how much damage was done to her – by her mother, by the men who paid for sex with her – and the fact that, although she's guilty, there were things that happened to her as a child that were themselves crimes. No-one helped her with the trauma of that and so all there was in her was rage. And now she's caused more tragedy.'

I had lost my way a bit in making my point so thought I should try to refocus.

'I guess it made me realise that things happen in families and trauma impacts on one generation to the next. And even if it's not spoken, it's still there and it has repercussions. I'm just saying people don't need to talk about it unless they're ready. I just mean, we shouldn't be ashamed. There's strength in saying things.'

Mum stopped walking. 'I'm glad you shared that with me,' she said. She looked out over the moors, contemplating, and a part of my heart felt light for having reached out to her this way.

Back on the bus, we drove to a small farmhouse, Ponden Hall, with its ageing dark brick and white framed windows. It was said to be the inspiration for Thrushcross Grange, the home of the Lintons in *Wuthering Heights*. Brett stopped the bus and we walked to the Brontë Waterfall.

Lionel came up and started talking to Mum so I lingered with Sam and Toni.

'I loved the book as a child,' Toni said. 'I re-read it recently. Those relationships. So dysfunctional. No wonder women put up with so much if they think that's a love story.'

'Emotionally abusive, we'd call it today,' I said.

'I think you can teach it for its writing and then critique how we would see what it tells us now,' Sam reflected. 'It doesn't advocate that those relationships are healthy and should be the norm. In fact, I think there is a reading where the message is clear that those toxic relationships can spill into other areas, to ruin other people's lives.'

Back on the bus, I thought about how, even in her own lifetime, Charlotte Brontë changed her perspective. Her first novel, *The Professor*, was based on her own experiences teaching at a school in Brussels and an attraction to a teacher there. It was written from the perspective of the male headmaster. It wasn't published until after her death so it seems like it came after her novel, *Villette*, which had been published four years earlier in 1853. This later novel reimagined the same story but from the perspective of the female character. Charlotte shifted her perspective and gaze, saw the relationship through a world view much closer to her own, deeper in her own truth.

It's not just the dominant male gaze that's been challenged over time. Jane Eyre's is the main perspective of her eponymous book and we see her relationship with Mr Rochester through her eyes. His wife is a secret until Jane uncovers her existence on her own wedding day. Mrs Rochester, Bertha, is portrayed as a ghost-like figure before she is discovered and a mad woman until her death. In *Wide Sargasso Sea*, Jean Rhys imagined the life of Mrs Rochester in the Caribbean before she comes to be imprisoned in the attic of a large house. In shifting the gaze, Bertha's mental illness is given context and humanity.

It's compelling, the uncovering of the other side of the story, the story that has been suppressed, written out or wilfully misinterpreted. I remembered sitting in class at law school with people talking about crime statistics and I would think about Brittany and my mother, my father, then Aunty Elaine and Aunt Kiki, even Leigh-Anne and me – all the human stories that lay hidden under numbers and graphs, buried underneath, waiting to be found.

When we reached the edge of Wycoller – a little town with stone buildings, moss-covered bridges and a bird sanctuary – we stopped at a large country house, said to be the inspiration for Ferndean Manor in *Jane Eyre*. Walking among the ruins, with a floor of grass and a ceiling of sky, I thought of Jane Eyre, who seemed so drawn from Charlotte's own life – the terrible experiences in boarding school, including the death of a loved one, the exploitation of governesses, the challenge of being plain and overlooked in a world where you wanted your intellect challenged and you knew there was more beyond the village and circumstances you grew up in. It was the heart of these experiences, translated into the world of a story, that makes the novel ring so true.

I found Mum sitting on a wooden bench near one of the stone walls. 'It must have been a grand old place,' I said.

'I like it as a ruin, though,' she answered. 'It's like we're seeing the skeleton and it's even more interesting, otherwise it'd just be another big house. Now it's really something.'

That night, back in Leeds, I reminded Mum she hadn't really eaten much all day. When we joined the others for dinner, I was surprised to find Sam and Professor Finn discussing the merits of *Wuthering Heights* and *Jane Eyre*.

'The prose and sense of place stand up. Such a powerful example of gothic writing with the supernatural,' Professor Finn opined.

'Virginia Woolf would agree with you,' Sam quipped, and almost everyone laughed at what was now a running joke.

Sitting next to Mum, I could see she was less engaged, perhaps not knowing the books as well. Perhaps just tired.

'Funny how people can come together over a shared love of a story,' I said to her.

'I often think of Aunty Elaine's stories,' she said.

I remembered the snippet I'd seen in Mum's journal. 'I feel sad that we've lost them, now she's not with us,' I replied.

'Funny, sometimes I can hear her voice in my head. She tells me things, like what she'd say if she were here,' Mum added.

'I know. I guess while we think of her, and remember her, she's still with us,' I replied.

Like Dad. Like Brittany.

I put my hand on her arm. Amongst loss, you need to hold on to what you still have.

DELLA

Do you know what's harder than guilt to live with? Shame. When you wake up those mornings and your head is full of blank spaces, like those puzzles in the paper where they only give you some of the letters in order to work out the words.

My head throbbed but it felt like a punishment I deserved. I got in the shower with the usual problem of the water too cold and then too hot. No two systems in any of these hotels were alike and it's a mystery why they don't all do the same thing and then a person would know where they were. The burst of icy water kept my body in shock until I could get the warm water to come through. Then I stood, letting it wash over me.

By the time I was out, Jasmine had come back with coffee and toast. I felt a mixture of affection and embarrassment but I'm good with just getting on with it. I learnt that long ago. You put yourself on a kind of autopilot and go through the motions of what you need to do, shower, get dressed, comb your hair. If you can do that, you move forward and further away from what has just happened.

Lionel talked about the Brontë sisters on the minibus and usually I would pick up bits and pieces but my mind was still thick and I could only focus on the main things: the sisters were writers. I'd known of them having seen *Jane Eyre* and *Wuthering Heights* on the telly and the second one had the song about Cathy and Heathcliff coming home. It says something if you write a book back when they did and people still like it today.

It was nice to get out of the bus and be in the fresh air. Lionel said there were lots of deaths when the Brontës lived here and it would have been hard to believe in such a pretty place, except for all the headstones in the cemetery. I couldn't help but think of Brittany and her little coffin.

Lionel also said that one survey undertaken when the Brontës lived here showed that forty-one per cent of children died before reaching the age of six and the average life expectancy was twenty-five, equal to that in the worst parts of London. The poor health of the community was blamed on the over-crowded living arrangements, the lack of toilets and the open sewerage that ran through the streets, all exacerbated by poor water supply that was both inadequate and contaminated. I was glad of the dull ache in my head and for the way one pain can distract from another.

We went into the building which was the parsonage. The Brontë father was also a reverend and I asked Lionel about that because Jane Austen's was one, too. Was it a coincidence?

Lionel said that the men both believed in education for women though it was mostly so they could go on to be governesses and useful wives and good mothers. I often wonder when the moment was that men decided that women weren't as good at things, especially when they never stopped bringing up children and running homes and solving everyone's problems. No-one ever thought I'd amount to anything and I do sometimes feel a bit sorry I didn't finish high school and set a better example for Leigh-Anne. Jazzie did alright, that's for sure, and it would have felt nice to feel like I was more responsible for that than I am.

There were lots of interesting things in the house and Jasmine seemed to like the letters and little writing desks that the Brontë girls had. I liked the tall clock that stood like a guard in a nook. Lionel said Reverend Brontë would wind it every night. There was something reassuring about the idea that time would be kept and you had a ritual to keep it going. I don't know why it's strong ticking gave me comfort, but it did.

When Jasmine and I got to the lunch place, none of it seemed to be something I wanted and I was glad when she suggested we just grab coffee and keep walking. Lionel had given us a map so we could go on the moors and not get lost. 'You'll see heather just as it was in the time of the Brontës,' he said, 'but there are other plants taking over now so the ecosystem is more fragile.'

Even though I'd never been to the moors before and was unlikely to ever return, what Lionel said made me sad. Perhaps because it reminded me of all the ways we were losing animals and insects back home. Change is natural in the world, the cycles of the year, one thing dying and making way for the next. But there's no arguing that we are killing things off and not thinking about the consequences. That's just a fact.

We had been to lots of interesting places and towns, houses, castles and museums, but I really liked the moors and being out in nature in a different country with its own way of being. Two small birds came by and circled each other before flying off on their adventures, not realising how far we'd travelled to see them.

Jasmine started talking about the legal case she was working on. It was the same one she'd been speaking to Cliff about. She told me what was on her mind and how unfair it was for that woman she was representing. I could see how Jasmine would be torn about the fact that the mother and those others who did crimes against Fiona would get away with it, and not have to pay for what they did. And I thought, as she spoke, that I couldn't imagine any circumstances in the life of Brittany's killer that would make me feel sorry for him. An evil deed is an evil deed.

I thought again of poor Reverend Brontë, alone in his house, with the last of his six children gone. I looked at Jasmine as she walked in front of me. I ached so much for Brittany – a constant soft pounding in my head and heart, a bang for each heartbeat, and I now grieved for Jimmy in the same way. I will forever, as long as I breathe, as sure as night follows day, and all the stars coming out on a clear night. But the thing is, there's many blessings if you look for them – there's Jasmine, Leigh-Anne, Kiki, and Zane, Tamara and Teaghan – it's just the blessings don't cancel out the griefs. They circle each other in an ongoing dance, just like those two little birds had done.

I was pleased Jazzie confided in me about her work. I know she'd spoken to Cliff about legal things but it was still clearly on her mind and I liked that she wanted to talk to me about it, too, since I didn't have much to offer but a listening ear.

'I'm glad you shared that with me,' I said, because I'd hoped she'd talk with me more like that, about the things in her life, and also it's not often that I get a chance to comfort her.

When we were back on the bus, I pulled out my notebook and wrote: *Blessings don't counter griefs but they're still blessings.*

We stopped by to see a brown brick building that had been in *Wuthering Heights* and then Brett drove us to where we could walk to the Brontë Waterfall. I liked that we got to do more walking and I was certainly feeling better than first thing in the morning, especially before the shower and the toast.

Lionel and I found ourselves walking together and he asked me if I'd like it if he told me the story of *Jane Eyre*. I thought that was very kind of him because it was clear everyone else knew it – or were pretending to – and he asked when no-one would hear so I wouldn't be embarrassed. It seemed like such a kind way to be and I remembered Aunty Elaine once saying that it was important that a person be kind and curious. I remember that because I thought at the time, well, Jimmy is both those things.

Lionel said I would like Jane Eyre. 'She had a very independent spirit,' he said, 'And although quiet, could speak her mind. She had deep thoughts.'

'I'm not sure I'm like that but I like people who are,' I replied.

He looked through his notes. 'This is a quote,' he said. '*I am no bird; and no net ensnares me: I am a free human being with an independent will.*'

He looked at me as if to say he was proving his point and continued. 'And this: "*I do not think, sir, you have any right to command me, merely because you are older than I, or because you have seen more of the world than I have; your claim to superiority depends on the use you have made of your time and experience.*"'

He closed his folder. 'Don't you see a bit of yourself in that?'

I didn't know what to say. It sounded more like Kiki than me but I didn't see the use in pointing that out because he'd never met my sister. But I smiled, because it was nice of him to try and pay me a compliment, which is how I think it was all meant.

I'd liked the moors but I liked the waterfall even more – rocks on the hillsides, the way the river looked like it cut them, how green it was, and how damp and cool even on a summer's day. There was a stone bridge that looked like it was naturally there and I felt like this part of the country had even more personality than the moors we'd walked along – if that makes sense.

On the way back I thought about Kiki, maybe because of what Lionel had said about birds and independence and will. I thought I should ask him for the quotes so I could write them in my notebook.

Kiki had always protected me even though she was the first to tell me what to do and always liked to boss me around. She protected me in the house. She protected me when Brittany disappeared and through the many long years of living in the shadow of her death.

She's protected me from Jimmy's sister Lynn and always takes my side against everyone else and will say whatever she wants to say to my face. The words 'loyal' and 'honest' sprang to mind. And through the thudding pain that had been niggling all day, I felt a warm surge for her in my chest, the wave you get when you feel a dose of pure love for someone. I wanted to tell her that I was lucky to have her and how she'd saved my life. But we just weren't a family who spoke to each other like that, especially not about feelings.

That night, we had dinner with the others and I liked that Jasmine spoke to me most. We talked about Aunty Elaine and how much we missed her. I thought again about what Jasmine had said on the moors, about the strength in saying things and it's like a curtain being lifted.

Before falling asleep, I looked through my gardening book and I learnt all about air plants. They are like a strange magic that doesn't need soil, just air and water. They need the barest of things to be able to survive. In the wild, they attach to trees but you can keep them in a jar. You need to water them once a week and every two or three weeks give them a longer soak, putting them in water with the leaves down. You just need to dry them before putting them back in their jar or they will rot. They grow little shoots – the book called them 'pups', like they were little pets. When they are half the size of the mother, you can separate them and put them in their own jar.

I guess everything gets to the point when it separates from the thing that made them. I'd never thought of air plants but that's because I didn't know they existed. So much better than a plastic sunflower that dances to music.

DAY 10

JASMINE

WHEN I CAME out of the shower, Mum had the morning news on and there was a small item about Shona's parents and the murder charge. An image of Hampstead Heath came on but I decided against letting Mum know that we'd be passing near there later today. It felt like the storm had passed and I appreciated the peace that was now between us – and how quickly we found our equilibrium again with each other.

We had an early breakfast and were on the minibus by 7.30 am to make our way down to Cambridge.

'Rupert Brooke, John Maynard Keynes, Salman Rushdie and E.M. Forster all studied here,' Professor Finn declared as we walked through King's College.

'So, did Zadie Smith,' added Sam with a smile.

From King's College, we walked through Trinity to see the library designed by Christopher Wren and completed in 1695 with its stone pillars, arched windows and its own treasury of manuscripts.

'You'd feel so smart studying in a building like that, as if all the knowledge would seep into your pores,' Toni said.

'There's no shortcut to reading them. I remember how, back in the day, I used to feel I'd read a book if I'd photocopied it in the library,' Sam replied.

'Today's equivalent of downloading,' Toni said, giving Sam a playful nudge.

There was something in what Toni had said about how being in a place of learning puts you in the mindset of it. I'd liked school and university. I'd had my challenges but I'd enjoyed learning. Being here made me realise how much I missed it, and I wondered if maybe I hadn't finished with it. Annie was doing further study. Sam talked excitedly about hers. It wasn't an impossible thought.

Lionel and Professor Finn reeled off the famous graduates of Trinity College – Lord Byron, Alfred Tennyson, John Dryden, A.A. Milne, Vladmir Nabokov and then, as we approached it, those of St John's College – William Wordsworth, Douglas Adams, Cecil Beaton. I realised all of these great names, these great talents, were all white men.

There's a difference between the hard racism that sits beneath a town like the one I grew up in, where there is a legacy of historical marginalisation, and the racism in a place like a university or in the legal profession, where it's harder to pin down. People know you shouldn't be racist so they hide it but it seeps out. It gets labelled 'casual racism' and 'soft racism', as if racism can ever be either of those things.

Bex, Annie, Margie and I all had instances where it was assumed that, because we were Aboriginal, we'd been 'allowed in' as opposed to admitted. 'Even though other people complain in class that you got in under special admission, I think it's great to right an historical wrong,' was a good example from a well-meaning classmate. She placed herself amongst the 'good ones' by telling me she's not racist, no doubt making herself feel good, but left me with the knowledge of what had been said about me by anonymous classmates so from then on whenever I entered that classroom I didn't know who to trust. And all this from someone who it turns out got a lower entrance mark than me.

Bex, Annie, Margie and I would 'decolonise' – our term for Friday night meals where we discussed the week's events, a tradition that was as much fun as it was essential for our mental health. 'You're really pretty for an Aboriginal,' was Bex's favourite example of a backhanded compliment. Annie had to suffer the indignities of a tutor who every time she said the word 'Aboriginal' paused and nodded at her as a sign of acknowledgement that, although meant kindly, mortified Annie.

We came to St John's College for a view of the Bridge of Sighs. Opened in 1831 it is a beautiful stone and glass structure that copies its namesake in Venice. This one crosses the River Cam that runs through Cambridge, with ducks and boats purposefully drifting along.

'It couldn't be more scenic if you were making it up for a movie,' I heard Meredith say to Mum. 'Pity we can't walk over it.'

'But we can see it so much better from here,' Mum replied. 'If you stood on it, you'd only see this bridge we're on now.'

Meredith smiled in agreement.

Mum's way of looking at the world was easy to patronise, but there was a wisdom you couldn't find in books. Leigh-Anne had never read about 'stereotype threat' or 'white privilege' but she knew racism when she felt it and she called it out: 'Stop with your white shit.' In their own way, they were more like Aunty Elaine than I was, a thought that was both a revelation and painful at the same time. I may have wished for a different relationship with Leigh-Anne, one on my terms, but she always stood up for me when it mattered.

We walked further through the town, parallel to the river, to Magdalene College and the Pepys Library.

'He was, by far, their most famous graduate,' Professor Finn announced.

'The Professor is right, as usual,' was Lionel's conciliatory answer.

A quick rest stop – and a cigarette for Mum – and we were back on the bus.

Having woven in from the suburban outskirts to the high-fenced mansions of the wealthiest parts of London, we pulled up at The Wells Tavern for an early lunch. After we ordered our food, Lionel said he'd give us an overview of our next stop, Keats House.

'First,' he began, 'a few facts about Hampstead Heath, which is not far from here. It is 320 hectares of parkland of ancient heath only six kilometres from the centre of London with a zoo, athletics centre and three swimming ponds. Hampstead itself has some of the most expensive housing in London and has more millionaires than any other part of the United Kingdom.'

Mum excused herself to go to the bathroom as Lionel shared some facts about Keats House – built in 1815, and named Wentworth Place, Keats had been a lodger there in late 1818. The next year he wrote *The Eve of St. Agnes* and his famous poems including 'Ode to a Nightingale'.

Mum still hadn't returned as the food arrived. I encouraged everyone to start eating and went and looked for her. There was no-one in the bathroom and I couldn't see her outside in the street. I walked all the way up to the corner and still no sign. At the end of the street, Hampstead Heath was visible. It wasn't hard to guess where she'd gone.

I went back to the pub and told Lionel that Mum wasn't feeling well. He looked concerned but I reassured him that she'd be alright and I'd take her straight to the hotel. I didn't want to make everyone late and we'd see them for the end-of-tour dinner that night.

My instincts told me she'd go to the main street to buy alcohol – unless she already had a stash somewhere. Then she'd go to Hampstead Heath.

Three hundred and twenty hectares of parkland. That's what Lionel had said. As I stood at the edge of the park, I wondered which way Mum was most likely to walk. I looked right, then left, and eventually I spied her in the distance, sitting on the grass near a pond.

I stormed over to her. 'You could tell me before you run off. And if you don't care about me, what about Lionel, the inconvenience to him?'

'We can catch them up,' she said meekly.

'I told them we'd meet them at the hotel. I didn't know how long it would take me to find you.'

'Lionel said the house we're going to isn't far.'

Mum was right. We could catch them up. I'd taken us off the tour as a punishment, a gesture to highlight her thoughtlessness in running off, but she was clearly unfazed, which was all the more maddening.

I looked into her face. Was she drunk? She didn't seem to be, though her eyes were red.

'I'm fine,' she said, as if she'd guessed what I was thinking.

I realised then that she'd been crying.

'How do people do such terrible things to their own children?' she asked.

'I don't know,' I said, sitting down on the grass beside her, my frustration giving way to exhaustion. 'All this talk of beware of strangers and the worst of it's in your own home.'

We sat for a while and I thought about how Mum had been following the case of Shona Lindsay on the news and all the old hurts this would have surfaced.

'What happened to Brittany wasn't your fault,' I said, stating an obvious truth. 'I read the file and the sentencing remarks. He was a predator, lurking around Frog Hollow because he knew there were vulnerable people there. That's how people like him work.'

Mum had her body turned away from me so I couldn't see her face. And I was reminded of what I'd recently learnt from her notebook.

'Like I said yesterday, sometimes it helps to say things aloud,' I told her. 'If you can't say it but you need to get it out, put it on paper and write it down. You should try it.'

There was a pause as we watched the world around us move on, people exercising, going to where they needed to be, caught in their own worlds. A blue butterfly danced by, flirting with the grass. 'You loved butterflies as a little girl,' Mum said, as we watched it frolic.

'I'm not sure it's something you grow out of,' I replied.

'Remember the story Aunty Elaine used to tell about them.'

'Remind me,' I said, because even though I knew it by heart, I liked the idea of hearing it again. And I leant back on the grass and watched the wispy clouds change and transform as Mum took on the role of storyteller.

I got Mum back to the hotel by taxi. We still had a few hours until dinner and Mum wanted to have a cigarette before she came upstairs to our room.

'If you run off again, I'm not coming to find you,' I said as I stepped into the lobby, only half-joking.

When the door closed behind me, I checked the time difference between London and Sydney. I knew it would be late for Leigh-Anne but I felt an urgency to speak with her. I took a deep breath and dialled her number.

'Are you back?' Leigh-Anne asked, by way of a 'hello'.

'I'm still in London. One more day before we fly home.'

'What's wrong?'

'Nothing. But I wanted to share something with you. Something that's come out. About Mum – and Kiki.'

'What are you talking about?'

'Mum and Kiki were abused by their father growing up. Sexually.'

A short silence before Leigh-Anne said, 'Explains a lot.'

'That's what I thought. I know it doesn't excuse things, but I see Mum in a different light.'

'Then and now's two different things. You have to take responsibility for things.'

'Like I said, it's not an excuse, it's just something that helps to make sense of why things are like they are.'

'Not everything is a do-over.'

'I don't even know what that means,' I told her, exasperated.

'Really? The fancy university education doesn't help?'

'Why am I under attack all of a sudden?'

'Just because you thought you had it hard growing up – which you didn't by the way – doesn't mean you have the right to tell me how to treat Mum. You turned your back on your family when you left us, and just because you've decided to take this big trip with Mum doesn't mean you know her better than the rest of us. At least I'm not ashamed of who I am and where I come from.'

'You just can't accept me for who I am. Just because I'm trying to better myself,' I replied, 'doesn't mean I don't care about my family. You've got the kids. I'm in the city. No point in pretending we're closer than we are.'

'Is that what you think? I don't resent you, Jasmine, I feel sorry for you.'

'You pity *me*? For being free of you, the town?'

'I'm not talking about you and me. I'm talking about the way you treat Kylie.'

'*Kylie?*'

'She did nothing but love you. Followed you around like a puppy and you never thought she was good enough for you. You were a snob long before you left Frog Hollow. The way you've ignored her since you left, well, I don't think you deserve her.'

I hung up with the white fury of indignation burning. And it simmered just under my skin all through dinner.

Everyone made a fuss of Mum when she came down. Our excuse had been that she wasn't feeling well and we both played along. Meredith and Lionel paid her particular attention while I was able to exchange contacts with Sam and Toni. They were leaving early in the morning for Scotland. They promised to post pictures of the next part of their trip.

The Professor gave a nice little speech about what a great tour guide Lionel had been who seemed quite touched by it. There was a gift, a collected works of Shakespeare, that everyone had chipped in for. Meredith made sure Mum and I were included on the card. It was nice to see Mum the centre of attention in this odd gathering of souls.

The dinner ended with goodbyes and we headed up to our room. Over the past few days my thoughts had kept returning to the concept of deep listening so I emailed Annie, asking if she could recommend some reading. After sending her the request, I had a second thought and typed another note: *Why don't we apply for those scholarships to study overseas? I've been to both Oxford and Cambridge on this trip and I reckon I'd be happy at either.*

I'd barely formed the thought in my head – further study, abroad. Where all those impressive dead white guys had gone to learn. As I typed it on the page, saw the words across the screen, I thought, why not me, too? A project on looking at the responsibility of the State to children in out-of-home care. That's what I wanted to do. I pressed send before I could take it back, a wish to the universe.

My call with Leigh-Anne was still niggling me. It was just like her; I'd ring about one thing and she'd turn it around to make me feel bad about something else. God she was annoying. Breathe – *one, two, three.*

And why did she bring up Kylie? Sure, I might have neglected her since I moved to the city, but I had new friends and interests.

As if to defy Leigh-Anne, I sent a message to Kylie, asking how she was, telling her a bit about the trip.

To loosen my annoyance, I thought of the butterfly story Mum had told me on Hampstead Heath, the one that Aunty Elaine used to tell, until it lulled me to sleep.

DELLA

LIONEL STARTED TO tell us about Cambridge and how it was the second-oldest university in the English-speaking world; we'd already been to the oldest when we went to Oxford.

'Our guide is quite right to make the distinction,' Professor Finn told the Boston sisters. 'The University of al-Qarawiyyin in Morocco was founded in the ninth century so it is the oldest if you take a broader view about higher learning institutions. In Europe, the University of Bologna is older than Oxford; the University of Salamanca in Spain older than Cambridge.'

You had to admire the Professor, I guess, who did know lots of facts and figures off the top of his head that, although you might not need every day, no doubt had their uses. These universities and their big buildings and big thoughts aren't a world I know so I guess I'm not best to judge what would be important and what wouldn't be. There was still a lot that got my goat about him – and the word 'windbag' often came to mind when he carried on, but Aunty Elaine said you had to always look for the best in people.

Cambridge did make you wonder why the British didn't think they had everything they needed right here in their own country so had to go and claim someone else's. And if you take someone else's land, like they came and took ours, why do you feel such a need to replicate your own things on that country, trying to erase what was there before. I guess because you think one is superior to the other, but Aunty Elaine knew about plants and medicines and the stars that, if you were really smart, you'd value what she knew as its own kind of knowledge.

Lionel had a walk worked out through different buildings and the others prided themselves with saying the names of the people who'd gone to this one and that. I liked the green lawns and the sense of order in the large buildings, bigger than mansions, old but each with their own style like they were trying to have a different personality, though they still seemed the same to me.

As we walked, I kept turning over the news of Shona in my mind. While Jasmine had been in the shower that morning, I had turned on the telly. I knew what I was waiting for and it didn't take long. The reporter went over how Shona had been killed by her father – beaten to death because she wouldn't stop wetting the bed – and he and Shona's mother had covered it up with the story of the picnic and the man in the hoodie and the van. Shona's father was charged with murder; her mother with helping. I could hear Jasmine coming out of the bathroom so I went back to my packing as though I'd never stopped. It's not hard to guess that Shona's bedwetting came from stress.

On the bus, I didn't sleep but I pretended to so I wouldn't have to chat. I came back to Shona and the thing that had been on my mind. Her father had killed her. That was terrible but straightforward. But her mother was charged with helping. Being an accessory, they call it. She'd told lies to cover things up.

I'd not protected Brittany because I had invited the accused into our house. I live with the what-ifs of that every day. When I go over it, I think of what I'd do different – how I'd have stopped him, screamed for help, killed him if I'd woken up. How I'd have died protecting Brittany. What was Shona's mother doing now? I wondered.

As we got closer to where we were having lunch, Lionel said we were right near Hampstead Heath. He said it was so many hectares and so many kilometres or miles from London, yet in all the things he said, he never mentioned the most important thing about it – Shona.

After I'd ordered my lunch, I went outside for a smoke. I could see a glimpse of grass at the end of the road and walked towards it. I can't tell you what I thought I would find there but as I reached the park, I found people strolling here and there and cyclists on the paths. There were also clusters of people sitting – a couple here, a group of friends there. One mother was sitting, watching, as the father helped two children, a boy and a girl, around five and three, with a kite.

I sat down and watched as the man showed the children how to hold the kite and run with it to make it fly. The little girl, with her short legs, stumbled as she followed her older brother, but the delight on her face, well, it was something to see. All the while the mother sat, looking on.

I thought about the word 'accessory'. I thought of Shona and how she would have wanted her mother to love her, the way I wanted mine to love me.

My mother was always well groomed. Dark curly hair, brown eyes, nails always perfect. She was so thin that her bones would stick out but her clothes sat well on her. For someone who took so much pride in their appearance, did every little thing to look good, she rarely left the house.

There's no way she didn't know what was going on. She'd have headaches – migraines – take her medicines and go to her room, the heavy curtains always closed. As I got older, I realised she was either numbed by her medications or drunk. Perhaps both. We all pretended nothing was wrong and pushed things under the carpet.

One morning, we were eating breakfast and she fell off her chair. We all kept eating in silence as she picked herself up off the floor, straightened her dress and sat back down.

After a beating from my father she would always say when we were alone, when the storm had passed, 'I don't know why you choose to make him so mad.' Not angry, or tender, but like she was giving me a tip to survive in the bush. So that kind of sums up where she was coming from. I never told her what was happening at night. I just knew she wasn't going to be on my side.

I tried to never think of my father. 'Hate' is too simple a word for all I felt; 'rage' is, too. I don't know what the word is in English. But my mother, that was something I found even harder to think about. 'Pity' could be one word but 'betrayal' sure was another. Finally admitting that to myself was its own release.

At first, when Jasmine appeared, I thought it was something I had willed. Her face was cross, her forehead wrinkled the way it does when things don't go the way she wants. Never one to yell, the look in her eyes said it all.

'How do people do such terrible things to their own children?' I asked her.

She said something about it not being strangers who are the real worry and we spoke about Brittany, which was to be expected though not something we usually did. She said what happened wasn't my fault, something about us being victims, too.

Then she said she had gone and looked at the file for Brittany and I felt a sharp pain right through my heart thinking of Jasmine trying to find answers to her sister's death, looking at papers in a room somewhere, at this evidence I imagine was locked away. It haunts her like it haunts me, I realised. I looked away, as if something had caught my eye, so I could keep my tears to myself.

A tiny little butterfly danced around. I remembered how much Jasmine loved them when she was a little girl. And I thought of

281

Aunty Elaine and her story. Jazzie said she'd like to hear it again, so I told her the story of a time long ago before there had been any death until, one day Ghingee the cockatoo fell off his branch in the tree and broke his neck. The animals and the healers all tried to wake him but they couldn't. They'd never seen death before so they called a meeting to work this mystery out. Eaglehawk, the great leader of all the birds was asked to explain. He threw a pebble into the river and it hit the water and disappeared from sight. 'There,' he said, 'just as the pebble has gone into another existence, so has Cockatoo.' This didn't satisfy people so they asked Crow. Everyone knew he was a wicked bird, but he had a lot of knowledge. He took a spear and threw it far out into the river. It sank beneath the water and then gradually rose to the surface, where it floated. 'See,' he said, 'we go through another existence and then we return.'

Now the mystery was somewhat explained, Eaglehawk declared that someone had to go through this experience to see if they would indeed come back. Many animals offered to take the test. Eaglehawk told them they had to not be able to see, taste, smell, touch or hear, just like in death, to see if they would return in another form. Winter arrived and the animals that went into holes and hideaways during those months – goanna, possum, wombat and snake – went away. The next spring, the tribes gathered. Goanna, possum, wombat and snake returned, looking the same but half-starved, though snake had changed his skin. The insects – moths, water bugs and caterpillars – volunteered to try next. This was ridiculed at first, as the insects had always been looked upon as ignorant and inferior. But they persisted, so Eaglehawk gave them permission to try. The water bugs asked to be wrapped in fine tea-tree bark and thrown into the river. Some insects asked to be placed in the bark of trees; others asked to be buried under the ground. The different bugs and caterpillars promised to return in the springtime in another form and meet back in the mountains. Everyone went their separate ways. When springtime approached and the stars were in the right position, Eaglehawk sent out a message and all the creatures travelled across the land to the place in the mountains. That night, the dragonflies, gnats and fireflies flew from tribe to tribe and around their campfires, telling everyone what a wondrous sight it would be. The wattle put forth all of its wonderful yellow and green, the waratah its brilliant red, and all the shrubs and wildflowers blossomed. As the sun rose, the dragonflies came up through the entrance of the mountains, leading an array of the most beautiful butterflies. First the yellow butterflies came, then the red, the blue, the green, and so on, right through all the families of butterflies and moths. The birds were so pleased that, for the first time ever, they started singing, creating sounds unlike anything known before. When the last of the butterflies and moths arrived, they asked, 'Have we solved the mystery of death for you and returned in another form?' And all nature answered back, 'You have!'

We caught a taxi back to the hotel and I was sorry that Jazzie didn't get to see the rest of the tour. I told her we could come back tomorrow on our free day but she said there were other things she wanted to do. Being with my girl had made me feel a little better, like she'd wrapped a bandage around me. I was proud of her going to university but I guess, at the heart of it, I was proud that she found a way to be the person she wanted to be, and you can't wish more for your child than that.

I thought about the story of the butterfly and how it said what Aunty Elaine seemed to say and what I felt, that when people die, they don't leave us, they come back in another form, even if that is just in our memories, our dreams and the way we repeat the things we learn from them.

AT LEISURE

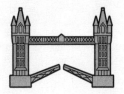

JASMINE

By MORNING, I had received a reply from Annie: *Yes, yes, yes. Will send links to applications – and scholarships!* She'd included Margie and Bex. Bex wrote: *Awesome! Can't wait to hear about the holiday since you haven't posted anything online! What's that about?* Margie added: *If you don't do this, I'm never speaking to you again (-:*

There was no reply from Kylie. I worked out I hadn't spoken to her since Dad's funeral. There's no reason why she'd drop everything to get back to me, just because she once followed me around, devoted, while I craved attention from the other kids at school.

I planned to take Mum to the Museum of London that morning as she'd seemed so interested in the history of the places we'd been visiting. On the way out of the hotel, we ran into Lionel, Meredith and Cliff. Mum exchanged details with Lionel and Meredith; I got Cliff's email to take him up on his offer to help if I decided to bring a civil case on Fiona's behalf.

The museum, with its exposed walls from the old Roman city, held panoramas that showed how the city had evolved over the ages, weathering war, plague and fire. Genocide, dispossession and colonisation can also test the resilience of a people. It's the most remarkable thing, the extent to which people can survive and stay strong, and are not destroyed by the worst that can happen.

I thought of everything Mum had survived. Of everything I had held against her and the way she handled her grief. I could see now I should have also celebrated that she still had the capacity to be a mother who loved, even if I always wanted more from her.

One history builds over another. Our truths are shaped by what is said and what isn't, formed by the beats chosen to tell a story. The books I read, the education and university training I received, all shaped who I was and how I saw the world. Even though I'd let that education bury Aunty Elaine's stories and knowledge, they were still here, in my memory and Mum's, waiting for us to unearth them.

When we'd finished our walk through the museum, I suggested we go to Harrods so Mum could do some shopping, and was surprised when she said she wanted to go back to the library instead. 'I didn't really get to see it,' she explained. 'I wasn't feeling well that day.'

It was a warm cloudless morning, so we decided to walk across the city. 'It was nice to hear the story of the butterfly yesterday,' I told her, as we walked along Holborn Street and turned into Grays Inn Road. 'I always feel like I'm closer to Aunty Elaine when I hear them. I worry one day we will forget them and they'll all be lost. Why don't we write it all down? The stories, the bits of wisdom, even her little sayings, everything we can remember.'

'Will you have the time?'

'I'll come home for a visit. We can do it then. Together. And we can ask Kiki, Leigh-Anne and Kylie. Capture the things we all remember, and keep them for the kids.'

After some lunch at the British Library cafeteria, Mum said she was happy to rest for a while and write down her thoughts. I left her to it and went back to the Treasures Gallery. I walked among the display cabinets and looked again at the gilded pages, their truths asserted with assurance in black and white.

Social psychologist Claude Steele had unpacked the idea of the 'stereotype threat'. His book, *Whistling Vivaldi*, was named after an anecdote from an African American who wrote for *The New York Times*. Brent Staples hated the way white people would cross the road when he was approaching them. He knew this was because of their negative stereotypes of him as a Black man, as violent, as criminal, so he began to whistle Vivaldi to counter their assumptions – the imagined Black person who scared them wouldn't know classical music. By challenging their stereotype, they'd lose their fear and not cross the road.

It wasn't just the way Staples – and anyone in his position – would feel, to be seen as a threat because of the colour of his skin. That seemed awful enough but what stayed with me was that he had to confront the negative stereotypes of the people around him to ensure that his life was not impacted by their underlying prejudices, their racism. Why did Staples have to be the one to change his behaviour to be perceived as less threatening? Why didn't the people who crossed the road challenge their own prejudices? And if Staples was found to be acceptable by the people whose stereotypes he had countered because he whistled Vivaldi, how long would it be until there was another stereotype imposed on him?

'It's not my job to educate you,' was one of Margie's usual replies to racist questions or comments. I respected the idea that the burden shouldn't fall on us: surely a large part had to be borne by the person with the prejudice? That was Leigh-Anne's attitude, too. I'd rejected too much of who I was in trying to prove others wrong. I always took my sister's barbs defensively, as criticism of my aspirations, but in her own way, I suddenly realised, she'd been telling me to just be myself. And I thought once again of her, sticking up for me in the playground when it really mattered.

We had dinner at a restaurant near the hotel, shared a bottle of wine and agreed to an early night before our flight the next morning.

Back at the hotel, there was still nothing from Kylie. I sent another message: *I'm back on Monday. Should we have a chat? It's been too long.* I looked at the words. They spoke of a separation, perhaps due to busy schedules rather than neglect. I checked her Facebook page and saw photos of her at an exhibition at the shire council gallery. Two of the paintings were hers and they were good. Her painting of an owl with glowing eyes had won second prize.

I sent a message to work to remind them I'd be back on Monday, and another to Cliff to make sure he had my number. I scrolled through Leigh-Anne's Facebook page and saw a picture of her with Kylie and the kids at the park. I 'liked' it and sent her a message: *Heading home tomorrow. I'm coming for a visit.*

She replied immediately: *I thought we weren't fancy enough for you?*

It's the new me. Besides, I have a project. Mum and I want to collect Aunty Elaine's stories and put them in a book. For all of us to keep. Kylie too, I added.

She replied: *I loved Aunty's stories. Sounds like you've had a good time over there.*

I wrote: *I'm thinking of coming back. I'm going to apply to Oxford and Cambridge. See which one might take me.*

I waited for the usual mocking of my ambition.

Instead: *Cool.*

It's still weird to be without Dad, I wrote. *I miss him every day.*

Me too.

When Mum went down for a smoke, I called Kylie.

'What do you want?' She wasn't being rude. Just surprised.

'I'm coming home for a visit soon. I thought we might catch up.'

'Okay.' She was non-committal, unexcited. What did I expect?

'I'll be doing a project on collecting stories about Aunty Elaine. Or ones she told. I thought you might like to join in.'

'Sure,' she said, like she was shrugging her shoulders.

'I saw your painting of the owl. It was really great.'

'Thanks,' she said, pleased but still guarded. The distance stung me. My own fault, valuing her so little, she who had also always loved me for who I was. Aunty Elaine always said you had to work for the things that really mattered and I had some making up to do.

When Mum came back into the room, we called Aunt Kiki on Skype.

I started with sharing the news that I'd be visiting shortly because of the project we were starting, to compile Aunty Elaine's stories.

'She always said you'd be back one day,' Aunt Kiki said.

'I remember,' I replied, '"It's all very well to run, but you need to know what you are running to," she used to tell me.'

'That sounds like her,' Aunt Kiki smiled. I left her to talk with Mum while I finished packing. As I listened to them banter, I was reminded of all those times I'd sneak into a room and hide so I could listen to them. Their chatting was soothing, just like it had been when I was a child. I could hear Aunty Elaine's voice – *This is what you were looking for. This, right here.*

As I lay in bed, I thought of something Virginia Woolf wrote: *The great revelation perhaps never did come. Instead, there were little daily miracles, illuminations, matches struck unexpectedly in the dark.* I realised that at that moment on Hampstead Heath when Mum had told me the story of the butterfly, I'd gotten all I'd wanted from the trip. Aunty Elaine's story had woven Mum and I closer and would keep weaving us all together – Mum, Aunt Kiki, Leigh-Anne, Kylie and me. She had said I would come home and

I now realised that she didn't mean back to town but back to my family and the stories we held.

DELLA

IT WAS SAD to say goodbye to Lionel on our way out. He gave me his email but I told him that it wasn't really my thing. He looked a bit glum when I said that but I told him that if he had a postal address, I could write him a letter and he smiled. Meredith asked for my address, too, so she could write as well.

Jasmine had decided that we'd go to a museum where there were little models of the city at different times so you could see how it grew. Even before the Romans came, people lived here because of the river. That was what it was like when colonists came to Australia. Aunty Elaine would talk about how they took the best bits. And along the rivers, too, because everyone needs water.

There was more in the museum about the fire that swept through in 1666 that Lionel had spoken about on the first day. That fire was an angry one – violent, hot and intense. Back home, fire was used to keep the land healthy – a cool fire could help clear the undergrowth. I thought again about how Aunty Elaine said fire helped some plants regenerate but it also helped clear the country so it could be used as hunting grounds or for planting yams and grains. I tried to remember all I could about it. There were complex rules about where fire burning should take place that considered the time of year, the conditions of the bush, the weather and the growth cycle of the plants. Aunty Elaine said that if Aboriginal people couldn't do their traditional fire practices, the country became sick. This time, I took a minute to write everything I could remember into my notebook.

When Jasmine caught me up in the gift shop I was buying some presents for my grandchildren. She seemed surprised when I suggested we go back to the library. There was a part of me that felt bad that I'd cut her time there short. I didn't tell her that I had something on my mind and sometimes you just need to go to where it's the best place to do the thing you need to do.

We walked all the way over from the museum to the library and Jasmine talked about how much she had liked Aunty Elaine's stories and that we should write them down. It was that thing when you have already been doing something but until someone puts it into words, you don't quite realise that it's what you've been thinking. Over the last few days, I thought of all those bits and pieces I'd been noting down and now it seemed like somehow the spirits had brought it all together and planted this idea that we should record it. And, as Jazzie said, if we both remember things, others might too and we could capture all of that before we all forget it and it's not passed on. It would be something not just for us but for Zane, Tamara and Teaghan and whoever comes along next. I can't tell you how much I liked the idea and how much I wished I could tell Jimmy all about it.

When we got to the library, we had some lunch and I told Jasmine I wanted to write in my notebook, which also made her pleased. She wanted to run and see the books and things she'd rushed through the last time and said she'd be back in a little while.

With Jasmine gone, I opened my notebook and saw the pamphlet about looking up things online. This was the place that held precious letters, like the ones Mrs Dickens had.

Once I started writing, all the thoughts in my head tumbled out on the page.

Dear Jasmine,
Thank you so much for bringing me on this tour. I never could have imagined all the things I saw. They will be memories I will have for the rest of my life. Of all the wonderful things that I saw, the best part was having time with you. I know I gave you a panic on a few occasions and I'm sorry for that and thank you for looking after me. It was also a time to reflect on how much you miss your dad and I can only tell you that he was always so proud of you and loved you so much. You made him very happy. You know I've always been proud of you, too, and love you very much.
Your Mum

I looked at it when I finished and marvelled at the words on paper that I never would have said out loud. I tried another. But after *Dear Kiki*, I got stuck. So, I went to another clean page and started a different way.

Dear Leigh-Anne,
You will be surprised to get this letter from me. I am writing this because you aren't speaking to me and I need to say this to you – that I am sorry for what I did at your dad's funeral. I know my sadness at his dying shouldn't have meant I did what I did.
It is hard for me to say this but I also know that I shouldn't have drunk what I did beforehand. It made my judgement bad. I never meant to embarrass you. I know you are mad at me and I hope in time that you can forgive me. I do love you.
Your Mum

It's true you don't know what someone is going to do when they get your letter but what I realised was that just writing the words down can make you feel better, especially when it's something you need to say. I owed Leigh-Anne an apology and whether she forgives me or not, well, we're halfway there now.

You'd think the letter to Kiki would be easiest because she and I aren't blueing but it was the hardest because of there being so much between us and so much unsaid. I went back to the page I started.

Dear Kiki,
I have had a lovely trip but while I have been here I have realised some things. I know that I have to apologise to Leigh-Anne for the funeral so she will forgive me. But there was another thing that has come to my mind a lot lately. Maybe it was after losing Jimmy and all we've been through with Brittany. I know you might say that we shouldn't turn these stones over and we don't have to say anything if you don't want to. I'll never speak of it again if you don't, but it might make a difference to you for me to say this – it did happen, we survived it, our mother should have protected us and didn't. It doesn't mean being sorry for yourself – it's just what happened. And I need you to know that I would not have gotten through it without you. I don't think I'd be here without you. I'm so lucky to have you as my sister. I love you.
Della

On the way back to the hotel I asked if we could stop off at the post office and I sent my three letters to their homes. Even though Jazzie was right beside me and I could have handed her letter to her, I liked the idea of it being sent to her across the sea.

It was early evening when we walked back towards the hotel and had dinner. As we ate, we spoke about the things we liked the best on the tour. I'd liked the dodo and the treacle well church, the walk on the moors and to the waterfall, and driving to different villages. Jasmine had liked the Austen and Brontë parts, and Oxford and Cambridge. It was like picking stars in the sky because everything was good in its own way, but it was a nice way to go over the many things we'd seen as we walked along the London streets and driven through the country.

'In the end, I didn't even mind Professor Finn all that much,' Jasmine said. I had to admit that he grew on me, too.

Back in the room, we started to pack using the trick to roll up the clothes to get them all in the suitcase. I'd gotten better at it, so it just goes to show that you can improve at most things if you do them often enough. Practice makes perfect, Aunty Elaine would have said. It did seem a small miracle to get everything into the bags, including all my gifts for the kids, but we did.

When I went for a final smoke, the man in the lobby in the green hat and coat who opened the doors said there was something for me at reception.

'You're mistaken,' I told him. 'I don't know anyone in London.'

But he was adamant. A small package had been left with my name on it.

When I unwrapped it, I found a copy of *Jane Eyre*. Lionel had put the quote I liked in the front – about birds and independence – and wished me well on my travels. It was really thoughtful and I put it in my handbag so Jasmine wouldn't see it. I just wanted to keep my feelings about it to myself.

When I got back upstairs, Jazzie got Kiki on the computer. She said she would drop my pets off so they'd be there when I got home and I could already imagine them all welcoming me.

'I've liked the trip,' I told her. 'I wouldn't mind another one.'

'I always wanted to go to the Barrier Reef – where the rainforest meets the sea.'

'I'd be in that,' I told her.

'We would need to get the right deals.' Which is her way of saying 'yes' even though it sounds like a 'no'.

'I also want to start a garden.'

'This sounds like another thing you'll start and not finish.'

'No. I've been reading about it and I think it would be a good thing to do.'

'Well, if you're serious, we could make a start next Sunday.'

I knew exactly how it would go. She would boss me around as if she had always gardened but, in the end, I'd have some nice plants. And if anyone could make sure the people who now live in Aunty Elaine's house will give us some of her roses, it's Kiki. I imagined my yard, with flowers, herbs and vegetables, and how much Jimmy would have liked such a thing.

Just as we were saying our goodbyes, Kiki added, as though it were nothing at all, 'Oh, Leigh-Anne rang just before. She told me to remind you that the twins' birthday party is Saturday week.'

I thought of my letters, already on their long travels to my daughters and sister.

In bed, I read some of my gardening book. I read about cut-and-come-again plants. Like a lettuce, you cut them and you eat them and more leaves grow back in their place. I read about how you can protect plants from slugs and snails. And about how some flowers are edible.

But the thing that really got my attention was the bit in the book about companion plants. When they grow, they keep other plants around them healthy. They might keep pests away or attract garden-friendly bugs. So, chives keep aphids away from tomatoes, while sunflowers, with their happy faces, can deter slugs and snails. Marigolds next to salad plants and vegetables keep away aphids and attract helpful bugs. Dill attracts garden-friendly bugs including ladybugs and pest-eating wasps. Mint is good for tomatoes. So, it's all interrelated, like a little town.

I thought of Aunty Elaine and the way she also made everyone around her better, like a companion plant. I got out my notebook. There was one more thing to write, even though I didn't know where to send it.

Dearest Brittany,
I know we talk almost every day and in my dreams but I need to say this. I love you. And I am sorry. I'm sorry I couldn't protect you. I'm sorry I never got to see you grow up. I'm sorry you never got to experience love, never got married, had children, fought with your sisters and probably with me. I'm sorry the world never got to see what a special person you are. You will always live in my heart and be a part of me. I know your father will be with you now. He never stopped loving you either. None of us did.
Your Mum

JASMINE'S TOUR READING LIST

SHAKESPEARE
Romeo and Juliet (1594–96)
Shakespeare: The World as Stage (2007) by Bill Bryson
Shakespeare's Wife (2007) by Germaine Greer

SAMUEL PEPYS
The Diary of Samuel Pepys (1825)
Samuel Pepys: The Unequalled Self (2002) by Claire Tomalin

CHARLES DICKENS
Oliver Twist (1838)
Nicholas Nickleby (1839)
David Copperfield (1849)
Bleak House (1852)
Great Expectations (1860)
The Invisible Woman: The Story of Nelly Ternan and Charles Dickens (1990) by Claire Tomalin

VIRGINIA WOOLF
Mrs Dalloway (1925)
To the Lighthouse (1927)

Orlando: A Biography (1928)

A Room of One's Own (1929)

Virginia Woolf (1996) by Hermione Lee

Virginia Woolf (2011) by Alexandra Harris

Living in Squares, Loving in Triangles: The Lives and Loves of Virginia Woolf and the Bloomsbury Group (2015) by Amy Licence

VITA SACKVILLE-WEST

The Edwardians (1930)

All Passion Spent (1931)

Portrait of a Marriage: Vita Sackville-West and Harold Nicolson (1973) by Nigel Nicolson

Inheritance: The Story of Knole and the Sackvilles (2010) by Robert Sackville-West

JANE AUSTEN

Sense and Sensibility (1811)

Pride and Prejudice (1813)

Mansfield Park (1814)

Emma (1815)

Northanger Abbey (1817)

Persuasion (1818)

Jane Austen: A Life (1997) by Claire Tomalin

THOMAS HARDY

Far From the Madding Crowd (1874)

Tess of the D'Urbervilles (1891)

Jude the Obscure (1895)

Thomas Hardy: The Time-Torn Man (2006) by Claire Tomalin

LEWIS CARROLL

Alice's Adventures in Wonderland (1865)

Through the Looking-Glass (1871)

Jabberwocky and Other Poems (1871)

Lewis Carroll: A biography (1995) by Morton N. Cohen

The Mystery of Lewis Carroll: Discovering the Whimsical, Thoughtful, and Sometimes Lonely Man Who Created Alice in Wonderland (2010) by Jenny Woolf

D.H. LAWRENCE

The White Peacock (1911)

Sons and Lovers (1913)

Women in Love (1920)

D.H. Lawrence: The Story of a Marriage (1994) by Brenda Maddox

The Life of D.H. Lawrence: A Critical Biography (2016) by Andrew Harrison

THE BRONTËS

Wuthering Heights (1847) by Emily Brontë

Agnes Grey (1847) by Anne Brontë

The Tenant of Wildfell Hall (1848) by Anne Brontë

Jane Eyre (1847) by Charlotte Brontë

Villette (1853) by Charlotte Brontë

The Professor (1857) by Charlotte Brontë

The Brontës: Life and Letters (1908) by Clement King Shorter

The Brontë Sisters: The Brief Lives of Charlotte, Emily, and Anne (2012) by Catherine Reef

JOHN KEATS

The Complete Poems (1817)

NOTES ON THE LITERARY TOUR

Della and Jasmine's literary tour can be done as a self-directed trip and includes the following destinations. Be careful to note the opening times with the National Trust: www.nationaltrust.org.uk.

- The Sherlock Holmes Museum, Baker Street, London
- Shakespeare Walking Tour, London
- Dickens Walking Tour, London
- Foundling Museum, Brunswick Square, London
- The British Library, Euston Road, London
- The British Museum, Great Russell Street, London
- Bloomsbury Walking Tour, London
- Knole House, Knole Lane, Sevenoaks
- Sissinghurst Castle, Biddenden Road, Cranbrook
- Monk's House, Rodmell, Lewes, East Sussex
- Lewes Walking Tour
- Jane Austen's House Museum, Winchester Road, Chawton, Hampshire
- Winchester Walking Tour
- Southampton Walking Tour
- Max Gate, Alington Avenue, Dorchester
- Hardy's Cottage, Higher Bockhampton, near Dorchester

- St Michael's Church, Church Lane, Stinsford, Dorchester
- Bath Walking Tour
- Lewis Carroll Walking Tour, Oxford
- D.H. Lawrence Walking Tour, Eastwood
- Oxford University Museum of Natural History, Parks Road, Oxford
- Brontë Parsonage Museum, Church Street, Haworth, Keighley
- Cambridge Walking Tour
- Keats House, Keats Grove, London
- The Museum of London, London Wall, London

Additional places you can visit along the way:
- Chartwell, Winston Churchill's country retreat, Westerham
- Blenheim Palace, Winston Churchill's ancestral home, Woodstock
- Hastings battlefield and Battle Abbey, Battle, East Sussex
- Lamb House, Henry James' home, West Street, Rye
- Charles Dickens' Birthplace Museum, Old Commercial Road, Portsmouth
- Hever Castle, Ann Boleyn's childhood home, Hever Road, Edenbridge
- Charleston Farmhouse, Vanessa Bell's country home, Firle, Lewes
- Freud Museum, Maresfield Gardens, London

ACKNOWLEDGEMENTS

I DID THE literary tour with Michael Lavarch. He proposed at the end of the trip. He's been unwavering in supporting my talents. This book would not have been possible without him.

I would like to thank my publisher, Madonna Duffy, who always believed in this book. Also thanks to my editor, Jacqueline Blanchard, and the rest of the team at UQP.

While this is a book about a difficult relationship between a mother and daughter, I've been blessed with mine – Raena Behrendt. She encouraged me in every way, particularly with reading and writing.

Thanks to my brother, Jason Behrendt, and to Kate Grenville, Rachel Griffiths, Tony Birch and my colleagues at the Jumbunna Institute at the University of Technology Sydney.